The Theory of Flight

Siphiwe Gloria Ndlovu

CATALYST PRESS
Pacifica, California

For further information, write Catalyst Press at
info@catalystpress.org

In North America, this book is distributed by
Consortium Book Sales & Distribution, a division of Ingram.
Phone: 612/746-2600
cbsdinfo@ingramcontent.com
www.cbsd.com

Originally published by Penguin Books,
an imprint of Penguin Random House South Africa,
in South Africa in 2018.

FIRST EDITION
10 9 8 7 6 5 4 3 2 1

Library of Congress Control Number: 2020933732

ISBN 9781946395412

Cover design by Karen Vermeulen, Cape Town, South Africa

Printed in India by Imprint Press

For the beloved memory of

Sibongile Frieda Ndhlovu

Characters

Dingani Masuku: *Thandi's husband; Marcus and Krystle's father; Genie's adoptive father*

Krystle "Chris" Masuku: *Thandi and Dingani's daughter and Genie's adoptive sister*

Eunice Masuku: *Dingani's mother*

Bhekithemba Nyathi: *journalist working for The Chronicle newspaper*

Cosmos Nyathi: *Bhekithemba's grandfather*

The Man Himself: *current head of The Organization*

Valentine Tanaka: *Chief Registrar of The Organization*

Vida de Villiers (also known as Jesus): *a street dweller and later Genie's partner*

David: *an educated street dweller*

Goliath: *a street kid and gang leader of The Survivors*

The Survivors: *a gang of street kids*

Matilda: *housekeeper of The House That Jack Built*

Stefanos: *gardener at The House That Jack Built*

Dr. Prisca Mambo: *Genie's doctor*

Esme Masuku: *Marcus' wife*

Xander Dangerfield: *vet who works at an animal rescue shelter*

The War Veterans: *current occupiers of the Beauford Farm and Estate*

Mr. Mendelsohn: *undertaker*

Prologue

On the third of September, not so long ago, something truly wondrous happened on the Beauford Farm and Estate. At the moment of her death, Imogen Zula Nyoni—Genie—was seen to fly away on a giant pair of silver wings, and, at the very same moment, her heart calcified into the most precious and beautiful something the onlookers had ever seen.

A few had already been chosen to witness this event. However, most of you have eyes that are not for beauty to see, and because of this you will not believe that such a truly amazing phenomenon did take place. It is because some of you will have doubt, and those of you who do not have doubt will be curious, that this story is choosing to be told.

Like any event, what happened to Genie did not happen in a vacuum: it was the result of a culmination of genealogies, histories, teleologies, epistemologies and epidemiologies—of ways of living, remembering, seeing, knowing and dying.

In other words, the story of what happened to Genie on the Beauford Farm and Estate on the third of September is also the story of how Baines Tikiti, in a bid to quench his wanderlust, walked into the Indian Ocean; of how Prudence Ngoma learned how to build character; of how Golide Gumede shot down an airplane and in doing so created a race of angels; of how Elizabeth Nyoni sealed her fate with the turn of her ankle; of how Dingani Masuku came to be haunted by the blue-violet flowers on his mother's dress; of how Thandi Hadebe looked into the distance as though it held a future in which she was not particularly interested; of how Krystle Masuku, at puberty, welcomed guilt as her constant companion; of how, for Marcus Masuku, love happened under a jacaranda tree while he was listening to a story about swimming elephants; of how Valentine Tanaka became a hunchback with a heart of gold; of how Jesus came to be saved; and of how the Beauford Farm and Estate knew exactly what to do with its sacrificed darlings.

BOOK ONE

PART I

Genealogy

Genesis

Genie's beginning was like all our beginnings—beautiful and golden. After spending the night with Golide Gumede, Elizabeth Nyoni felt something give way in the space that he had come to occupy in her heart—it traveled through her body and found its way onto her mattress. When Elizabeth picked it up and placed it delicately in the palm of her right hand, she discovered that it was a shiny golden egg. It was at that moment she realized that her fate was sealed: she was bound to Golide Gumede for an eternity.

Golide Gumede had been born Livingstone Stanley Tikiti. But before he could be born, his parents had to meet. And before his parents could meet, their circumstances had to be such that when they did meet they could actually do something about it.

His father had been born on the Ezulwini Estate and christened Bafana Ndlelaphi. Bafana had had the great fortune of being born within the sphere of Mr. Chalmers' benevolence. Mr. Chalmers was a gentleman farmer, and, as such, had had the time to teach the young Bafana how to read and write. He taught him these things not necessarily because he believed that the boy would be able to use the skills when he grew up, but because those were the skills he could teach the boy when he was at his leisure.

As a result, Bafana grew up to be an enterprising young man who was a rare thing for his time: a moderately educated black man. Without much effort he got a job as the assistant of a Greek traveling salesman. Because of this he became an even rarer thing—a black man who had the opportunity to travel the length and breadth of the country. Bafana found that he loved to travel. He marveled at the often incongruous nature of his country: a raging waterfall, rocks that balanced precariously on top of one another, and a flower that looked like a roaring flame that had once upon a time caught its breath and never exhaled. He often wished he had a way to capture the many sights he saw, but all he had was his memory. In Mr. Chalmers' library, in leather-bound, somber-looking books, were the journals of great men: David Livingstone, Thomas Baines, Henry Morton Stanley, men who had been able to record what they discovered on their travels. Bafana felt an affinity to these men, these explorers. He felt that he too was an explorer, or would have been had he not had the misfortune of being born in the wrong century. He felt that the name that he had been born with, Bafana Ndlelaphi —which literally meant, "boys, which is the way"—was not fit for an explorer such as himself and so he changed it to Baines Tikiti. Tikiti—a ticket, something one purchased in order to go on a journey. Something that gave one purpose.

The Greek traveling salesman felt his fortune in having Baines as his assistant. Baines was a natural-born charmer who, even with the limits of language, was able to get the most miserly and frugal woman to reach into that space underneath her left breast that held the grimy handkerchief that held the even grimier sixpence that stood between the woman and absolute poverty. There often was hesitation once the handkerchief had been brought out into the light of day, but after Baines said a few words in the seductive and universal language of commerce, the woman would smile and then nod resolutely before untying the tightest and truest knot, using her teeth and calloused, blunt fingers to pry the handkerchief open and reveal the thing that she had treasured most until that very moment: a sixpence that a husband or son had labored for in the mines, on farms or in the cities. The once frugal woman would walk away with her new treasures—an oil lamp whose leak she had not yet discovered, a smooth blanket that she did not yet know might pill after its first wash, a dress she did not yet know was either several sizes too small or too big because she had not been allowed to try it on, a mirror whose silver edge would inevitably tarnish, then corrode and rust.

Women, young and old, single and married, abandoned and widowed, loved Baines, and Baines tried to love them in return, but he loved his travel more, and, as a result, he broke quite a lot of hearts. This, however, did not stop him from selling cheap European trinkets to unsuspecting African women throughout the colony.

Then one day Baines and the Greek traveling salesman arrived at Guqhuka—a village that was soon to be turned into the Beauford Farm and Estate—and something very surprising happened: for the first time Baines was not able to charm a sixpence out of a woman's hand. To make matters even more mortifying, the woman did not have her sixpence tucked away under her left breast; she held it, temptingly shiny and new, between her thumb and her forefinger, ever so ready to give it away, if only Baines would show her something that she liked. He showed her shoes that he claimed were of the finest Spanish leather; she was sure they would pinch. He showed her a mirror; she wondered what possible use her own reflection would be to her, since she already knew herself. He showed her a pair of pillowcases, baby soft pink with delicate lace edges; she wanted to know where the pillows that went inside the pillowcases were (a question that he had never been asked before). Not quite defeated, he showed her the one thing that he thought no woman could resist—a crown fit for a queen, sparkling with rhinestones and the insincere glitter of cheap metal; she asked what kind of queen would wear a crown that only cost sixpence.

It was his turn to ask questions: What is your name? Prudence Ngoma. Where are your people from? Here. You obviously have traveled, where have you been? The City of Kings. Would you marry me?

An arched eyebrow let Baines know that she had heard his proposal. She asked him a question in return. Where are you from? Ezulwini. I have never heard of the place. But she said this in such a way that he knew she would not mind hearing more about the place and seeing it for herself someday. They married soon after and settled in Ezulwini.

The temptingly shiny and new sixpence never passed from her fingers to his.

Baines made a concerted effort to settle, but he could not cure his wanderlust. He had to travel, had to see the world, and, having seen his country, was now yearning to see beyond its borders. Like many other young men, he left for South Africa; unlike those young men, he was not headed towards the diamond or gold mines, but keen to do whatever job would allow him to travel. He almost immediately found a job as a traveling salesman for His Master's Voice gramophones. An easy job, he found, since people were enchanted by the magical machinations of a needle moving along the grooves of a black disc and making the most melodious sounds. They bought the machine without fully understanding it, but firmly believing in its magic.

Prudence worried that, like many of the young men who left for South Africa, Baines would not return. Although he sent her money religiously, for five years it looked as though she had every reason to worry. And then one day he returned with a His Master's Voice gramophone under one arm. He gave it as a present to Mr. Chalmers to thank him for his ennui-induced benevolence. For Prudence he brought the empty crook of his other arm for her to nestle her head in as she listened to his deep voice tell her tales of futures faraway, so allowing her to peacefully and contentedly drift off to sleep. His eyes were wide and bright with the wonder of all he had seen in South Africa. South Africa—one country that touched two oceans, imagine that. Prudence tried to imagine it, but, never having seen an ocean, was not able to. There was nothing left for it but to determine that Prudence would have to see South Africa for herself. Unfortunately, Prudence had to postpone the gratification of her desire because Baines' visit had left her with the expectation of a child, a baby boy whom Baines christened, via letter, Livingstone Stanley Tikiti. Prudence waited until after her son's second birthday to visit her husband. Not trusting travel the way her husband did, she left her son at home and traveled alone, eager to see Baines and the country he loved so much.

However, when Prudence arrived in South Africa, she found Baines in love with something else—a contraption that, like a bird, could fly through the sky. It was called an airplane. In the hostel, the four walls of his one-room flat were covered with pictures of this new love. Imagine being able to see the world—all the world—in a matter of days. Ships and trains were things of the past. The airplane was something of the future. Baines' eyes sparkled with a brilliance and his voice was weighted by an excitement that was contagious. While in South Africa, amid all the pictures and talk of airplanes, Prudence was able to imagine a life there with Baines and their son...a life in which they too would, perhaps, be able to fly away some day. She went back to Ezulwini and eagerly awaited the day that Baines would send for her and their son.

It took Baines almost five years to prepare a life for his wife and son because he wanted to make sure that their lives would not only be comfortable but also filled with travel. He bought a house in the newly built townships. He bought a bed. He bought a sofa. He bought a Welcome Dover stove. He bought a very-much-used convertible car. He could have bought any kind of car, but it had to be a convertible because not only did he want his family to have the best view as they traveled the country, he also wanted his family to be seen traveling the country. It was only once he was in possession of the convertible car that he sent for his wife and son. He proudly drove his convertible car, top down, all the way to the train station.

But unfortunately it was not meant to be. When Baines saw his son, he knew that he could not go traveling with him. His son's too-white skin, which seemed luminescent and translucent, made him vulnerable to the elements. They would always have to travel with the top up.

He watched as his son, awestruck, looked at the pictures of the airplanes on the walls. He watched as his son drew airplanes in the pages of an old His Master's Voice sales ledger. He watched as his son built model airplanes from the wires the workmen who had fenced the premises had left behind. Baines Tikiti was fascinated by the boy. He loved the boy but knew that they could not share in the same life. If only he had known of the boy's condition, then he would have prepared a very different life for them. Baines asked Prudence why she had never told him. Her heart breaking, she asked him why it should have mattered. His heart breaking, he sent his family back to Ezulwini.

Prudence could have returned home humiliated, but she did not. She returned home with only one regret—that she had not fully understood the man she had married. She also returned home unknowingly expecting another child, a daughter. When her daughter was born she named her Minenhle—"I, the beautiful one." Prudence left Ezulwini and returned to the place of her birth, which during her absence had become the Beauford Farm and Estate.

For his part, Livingstone Stanley Tikiti returned home with the memory of a distant father and a knowledge and understanding of flight.

Baines, although he understood that he could not live the life he wanted with his family, still loved them and continued to send money home religiously. Prudence, because she cherished the son that Baines had given her, found that she could no longer return the love of a man so blinded and foolish as not to see his own son's beauty, and just as religiously sent back the money that he sent her.

One day, Baines Tikiti, after receiving yet another return-to-sender, drove his convertible to the Indian Ocean, got out, walked into its waters, and allowed himself to be carried away by its waves. Never to return. When she received the news, Prudence hoped, for his sake, that this had finally fulfilled his wanderlust.

Prudence's union with Baines Tikiti had taught her one essential lesson—a person's character was the most important thing. It was all very well to be a charmer, to be able to make people love you, but charm did not have a very strong foundation. Charm was something altogether too dependent on others. Character was different. Character was something that you sowed, nurtured, grew, cultivated and then reaped. It spoke to an inner strength. It made a life into one that was lived with purpose. Prudence raised her children to have character, to be proud and strong, to not be afraid of humility and vulnerability, to hold their heads at a particular angle and never feel or look defeated by whatever life dealt them.

And so it was, under such sage and sanguine tutelage, that Livingstone Stanley Tikiti grew into a man. His self-possession made him a natural leader. His self-confidence instilled confidence in others. People gravitated towards him because he was not what they had expected him to be. They had expected him to be ashamed of his skin, to be cowed by life, to regret his circumstances. But when he held his head high they realized just what was possible. They believed that he saw into the future and that the future was good. He really did not have to do much, because just in *being* he held a promise and people were happy to follow him.

Livingstone was a man who thought about things deeply and liked to see things through. So when the war came, after having thought deeply about the issue, he decided that the freedom fighters' cause was just and that he would fight with them to the very end...or to his. To the war he took only the clothes he was wearing, his burning desire to fight injustice, the cravings of a half-full stomach, the beginnings of an unquenchable thirst and the His Master's Voice sales ledger with all his drawings of airplanes. He chose as his nom de guerre "Golide Gumede," which meant "fields of gold," because that is what he envisioned for his people after the war—lives of plenty, lives of comfort, lives of value, lives of substance, lives that mattered. When he shared his vision of the future with others, they were eager to follow him.

But before he could become the leader of men, it just so happened that one of his camp commanders saw the ledger full of airplane drawings and sent him to the Soviet Union to study aeronautical engineering. Golide happily endured the cold bitterness of the Soviet climate because he understood that after the war—when independence arrived—people would need to know that they were capable of flight.

When he returned he fought with purpose and determination, and his war was good. Having been raised to be content with what he had, Golide had long felt that his life was complete. Then one day, while on a reconnaissance mission at a beer hall in Victoria Falls, he caught sight of a woman's ankle through the slight opening of a door left ajar. The turn of the ankle was delicate. As he moved closer he saw that the ankle led to a foot clad in a dangerously heavy and high red platform shoe. Having seen the ankle, Golide was no longer content with just what he had. He wanted more. He wanted that ankle to be a part of his life.

There was a puff of smoke and a throaty laugh. He could not help but open the door wider...and there she was, suddenly upon him like a surprise—the woman who would determine the course of his life from that moment on. She had deep brown skin, the longest eyelashes he had ever seen, and a plumpness that his body would welcome. Her hair was plaited and parted with a precision that somehow did not belong to her; whoever had plaited her hair had not taken the time to get to know the woman, of this Golide was sure. The woman let a cigarette dangle precariously from her invitingly full lips as she reached for spun golden hair that seemed to stand suspended in the air and placed it ever so gently on her head. The golden hair made her perfect. If there was anyone else in the room, Golide did not see them. After an eternity, the woman looked at him through the mirror she was sitting in front of, took a deep drag of her cigarette, exhaled at her leisure, took the measure of him, shrugged her shoulders nonchalantly and then stood up. As she walked past him she said: "Waiting. That is definitely no way to treat a lady." Not auspicious words to be sure, but she had gently rested her left hand on his shoulder as she said them, and that had been enough to seal Golide's fate.

And so it began. The woman was Elizabeth Nyoni. She was a country-and-western singer, self-styled after Dolly Parton. She drew a large audience that spilled out of the beer hall and into the beer garden. She sang happy songs. She sang sad songs. All of them were love songs—love discovered, love lost, love regained, love unrequited, love remembered, love gone bad—and that afternoon she sang them all to him, Golide Gumede, the man who, without knowing it, had kept her waiting. There was also a song about a dog, which, from the way she cut her eyes at him while she sang it, he was sure was not about a dog at all.

As Golide watched the band pack away their instruments and Elizabeth spurn the advances of hopeful would-be lovers, he felt that they had already been on a journey together through the ins and outs and highs and lows of love—that they had always already shared a life with a past, present and future.

Golide and Elizabeth did not ask much of each other. She told him that she needed to make her way to Nashville, Tennessee, so that she could become a bona fide country-and-western singer, and he promised that he would one day get her there. He told her that after the war he intended to make a home on the Beauford Farm and Estate, and she promised that she would go ahead and prepare one for him. In all, they spent the better part of nine hours together that day, but that was all that was needed to lay their solid foundation.

After he met Elizabeth Nyoni, a part of Golide's life suddenly made sense to him. All those countless hours spent drawing and building model airplanes and trying to determine their aerodynamics had not been about trying to bridge the distance that his father had created, but had instead been about preparing himself to be useful in Elizabeth's life in the future.

In that future he saw himself building a giant pair of silver wings; he saw people come from all over—some fascinated, some disbelieving, some ready for him to fail—to witness him build them. Among the non-believers he saw a few believers who looked at him with such admiration, adoration and assurance that he knew, without a doubt, that he was a man capable of impossible things.

Golide knew that building airplanes was a costly business—that being capable of flight would come at a price. Parts either had to be bought or manufactured, people had to be educated and trained and the state's monopoly on manufacturing had to be destroyed and decentralized. These obstacles made Golide spend most of his time thinking of ways to make the people understand that they were still capable of flight, and at no cost to themselves.

The solution came to Golide one day when he looked up at the clear blue sky, saw a Vickers Viscount and suddenly understood what was possible. This Vickers Viscount was a passenger airplane that flew over the Zambezi River every day. Golide decided that he would strategically shoot down the passenger airplane so that it would land virtually undamaged in the guerrilla camp. This way he could teach people about how airplanes work before the war was over—before independence—at no cost. His commanders liked the idea because they could use the civilians on board as prisoners of war and hopefully broker an end to hostilities and finally realize the country that they had long been fighting for.

On September 3, 1978, as Golide sat looking at the magnificence of the Victoria Falls, as he waited for the airplane to fly overhead, he thought of how Frederick Douglass had, exactly 140 years earlier, escaped from slavery. He did not think this thought in order to justify his actions, he thought it because it was a thought one could think as one waited to shoot down an airplane.

As the Vickers Viscount flew overhead, Golide took aim with his anti-aircraft missile...and that was when they appeared with their formidable grace. Majestic. A herd of elephants raising dust beautifully in the savannah sunlight. The bull at the head of the herd raised his trunk and trumpeted terrifically and all the elephants came to a gradual standstill on one side of the Victoria Falls. The bull dived in close to where the waters plunge over the edge and swam across the Zambezi River. The ancient river and the mighty animal were in perfect harmony. This was a rite of passage made sacred by its sheer audacity. There was a wonder to it all...The possibility of the seemingly impossible. There was this feeling that Golide got...a knowing...He became aware of his place in the world. He understood that in the grander scheme of things he was but a speck...a tiny speck...and that that was enough. There was freedom, beauty even, in that kind of knowledge. It was the kind of knowledge that finally quieted you. It was the kind of knowledge that allowed you to fly.

Golide launched his anti-aircraft missile. The missile was followed by a vision: he saw Elizabeth going to Beauford Farm and Estate carrying a golden egg. The golden egg became too heavy for her and she dropped it. It cracked open and a girl emerged. The girl had a gap between her two front teeth, and that is how Golide knew, with edifying certainty, that he and Elizabeth had created a life together—a daughter, Imogen Zula...Genie.

The Vickers Viscount burst into glorious golden light.

PART II

—◆—

History

Beauford

As Golide Gumede watched the Vickers Viscount travel to the earth as a great ball of fire, he could not have known that retribution would be sought for this one act. This one act that made him a hero in the eyes of many and a villain in the eyes of many others. He understood the madness of war—that there was no rhyme or reason to its casualties, no clear lines between cause and effect. He could not have known that certain men with a jaundiced sense of justice would draw an undeviating line from the shooting down of the Vickers Viscount and follow it, like a river, to Beauford Farm and Estate, where their vengeance would flow like an everlasting stream.

But, truth be told, the line reached further still—through Golide Gumede and beyond him to connect him, in the inexplicable and inextricable ways that only geography can, to Beatrice Beit-Beauford, the heiress of the Beauford Farm and Estate and one of the survivors of the downed Vickers Viscount. Two separate lives lived on the same patch of land, brought to such proximity by an idea that had germinated, long before Golide and Beatrice came into being, in the mind of one Bennington Beauford as he sat in his armchair and smoked his pipe, watching the embers of a long-unstoked fire slowly die, trying to quiet the disquiet that resided deep in his heart.

The lush and verdant village of Guqhuka became the Beauford Farm and Estate in much the same way that most villages became settler farms in the colonies. Bennington Beauford, having had the misfortune of inheriting only the family name and none of its centuries' worth of fortune, dignity or honor—due to his father's wild speculations—and having had the fortune of, absolutely by chance, distinguishing himself during the Great War, had decided that perhaps a life in the colonies would be just the thing for him. He had always fancied that if he made a go at being a gentleman farmer, he would be a great success at it. He had then set about looking for some land he could acquire through very little effort and at no great expense to himself. There were many colonies to choose from and so it took quite a few years for him to find the right place. At one hundred hectares, the place he settled on—Guqhuka—was adequate for his needs.

Bennington was a fair-minded man and asked that the Africans who had lived on the land for centuries not be resettled. He had grand schemes for the Beauford Farm and Estate, schemes that would require a labor force. It was not lost on him that a readily available labor force would be less expensive than a labor force that came from afar. Bennington was a very enterprising man and he put the land and the people on it to good use. In just one decade he had made his farm one of the lifelines of the colony. He grew maize, sugar cane and cotton, reared cattle, sheep, pigs and chickens. He built refineries, butcheries and mills on his property. He turned the village into a modern compound, replaced the thatched mud rondavels with square concrete rooms under corrugated asbestos sheets. Everyone who lived on the compound worked in some capacity on the farm and estate. And because he was a generous man, he also built a school for the natives on his property.

Having thus established himself, Bennington married Rosemary Beit, a woman from the purest pioneer stock who had never quite recovered from the "tumble" from a horse she had taken when she was a child. Rosemary was considerate enough to die soon after giving birth to a baby girl, Beatrice, thus providing Bennington with an heir, perhaps not of the right gender, but an heir nonetheless. During a trip to the Netherlands with her father, his young daughter had shown a liking for sunflowers and so Bennington had dedicated a few acres of his land to growing them.

When the Second World War broke out, Bennington proved to be indispensable to the war effort—his cotton made the soldiers' uniforms, his canned goods fed the troops, and his leather made it possible to have boots on the ground. He became the wealthiest man in the colony. When he died in an unfortunate car accident in 1948, his only child and heir, Beatrice Beit-Beauford, then became, at eleven, the wealthiest person in the colony.

At thirteen, Beatrice went to Eveline High School with the distinction of being the daughter of the man most people thought instrumental to the colony's economic growth during and after the war. This guaranteed Beatrice respect and easy passage. However, Beatrice did not make it easy for those willing to grant her any privileges. She was a liberal-minded young woman whose ideas, especially on the rights and treatment of the African, terrified those around her—including Kuki Sedgwick, the girl who was to be her lifelong friend.

Beatrice questioned and challenged everything and everyone, whereas Kuki never had an independent thought. Kuki had accepted wholesale the opinions and beliefs of her family, community and country. She loved her family, she loved her community, she loved her country and she never once thought they could be wrong—that they could all have contributed to the establishment and preservation of a system and order that was at its very heart unfair and unjust. Kuki did not quite agree with Beatrice's notions, even thought them foolhardy, but she could not help finding Beatrice's irreverence for all the things that Kuki herself held dear seductive. Not quite brave enough to be as defiant as Beatrice, Kuki was happy just to live vicariously through her and know that an alternative way of thinking and being was possible. For her part, Beatrice never tried to make Kuki share her views. Beatrice was too self-assured, too convinced that her way of thinking was just, correct and right, to look for converts. And because they never tried to change each other and simply accepted one another, Beatrice and Kuki became the best of friends.

The only thing that threatened their bond was Emil Coetzee—a man whom Beatrice could never respect; a man whom Kuki loved and later married.

After Eveline, Beatrice left for Oxford University and returned five years later, perhaps predictably, as a hippie. It was the dawn of the Sixties—the age for the Beatrices of the world to finally come into happy being. Never quite comfortable with the grandness of her inheritance, Beatrice turned the Beauford Estate into a multiracial commune and artists' colony. She left the running of the Beauford Farm to the foreman and did not seem to care either way whether he did a good job or not.

But Emil Coetzee, Kuki's husband, did care about the Beauford Farm and Estate and how it was run. As head of the Organization of Domestic Affairs, he found enough incriminating evidence of interracial commingling to bring a charge of unlawful conduct against all those who lived on the Estate. Although equally appalled by the goings-on, the state was, however, hesitant to make them public and extremely reluctant to get on the wrong side of Beatrice Beit-Beauford, who was still the wealthiest person in the country and whose farm was still vital to the nation—especially now that it seemed to be gearing up for a civil war. In 1965, however, when Beatrice Beit-Beauford proudly gave birth to two Coloured twin boys, thereby flouting the state's anti-miscegenation laws, the state decided that she was not to be trusted. Beatrice and her guests were evicted for "unlawful behavior" and for being "unfit" residents.

When the war ceased to be a few skirmishes here and there and broke out in earnest, becoming a full-blown guerrilla war, Beatrice Beit-Beauford enthusiastically, vocally and publicly supported the terrorists ("African nationalists," as she called them) and believed, as they did, that the majority should rule.

When Emil Coetzee found out that Beatrice was financially supporting the nationalists whose military wing was conducting terrorist attacks across the country, he zealously and triumphantly brought charges of treason against her. Beatrice had been vacationing at Victoria Falls with her two sons when she received the summons to appear before the court. On her way back, tragedy struck. The airplane she was traveling in—the Vickers Viscount—was shot down by Golide Gumede. Many died. Beatrice's twin sons died. The policemen escorting Beatrice died. The air hostess, who had at that very moment been serving Beatrice a Malawi shandy, died. But Beatrice survived. Her belief in an equal society also survived.

There was such an outpouring of public sympathy for Beatrice Beit-Beauford that the treason charges were dropped and the trial dismissed. Emil Coetzee accepted this turn of events. This was not because he had forgiven Beatrice her past transgressions, it was because he had found another use for her—he used her tragedy to call for the imprisonment and execution of Golide Gumede. Daily images of the smoldering remains of the Vickers Viscount quickly turned public sympathy into public outrage and anger against Golide Gumede. The public soon joined Emil Coetzee in thirsting for Golide Gumede's blood, and Emil Coetzee promised to have his head on a platter within three days.

However, finding Golide Gumede did not prove to be easy at all. Although there were many reports of people having seen him, everyone had a different description of him: he was tall, he was short, he was heavyset, he was thin, he was handsome, he had the type of face only a mother could love, he was an African, he was white....And no one knew what his name had been before the war. When Golide Gumede proved elusive and thus impossible to capture, Emil turned to his most trusted man—Mordechai.

Mordechai Gatiro had grown up in Makokoba Township not knowing who his parents were or had been. The township was rough and, because he was a part of it, he was rough as well. He lived in an orphanage where he was bullied by the older children and where he looked forward to bullying the younger children when he was older. He was an angry child and, really, there was no alternative emotion for him to feel. He ended up, unsurprisingly, in a reform school that was even more "hard knocks" than the orphanage. Along the way, he adamantly refused to acquire a skill or get an education. He and everyone who knew him knew that he would die young because his was a life born of fire. He was always getting into fights—dangerous fights, with fists, knives and guns involved—but he did not die. Frustrated with living, he joined the war. He was a freedom fighter or a terrorist—you could think of him whichever way you wanted—he did not care. He was captured and this made him happy because he thought for sure he would hang for treason. Emil Coetzee, however, had other plans for him: he turned Mordechai into a spy, which was easy enough since Mordechai had never learned to have allegiances. He hoped he would get caught and killed, but that did not happen either. Instead, Emil Coetzee noticed a rare quality in Mordechai that made him officially employ him as a member of The Organization. For not only did Mordechai not care much for his own life, he did not care much for the lives of others either. Because of this, Mordechai became The Organization's best interrogator. He was so valuable to Emil Coetzee that his name was never recorded even within The Organization's files: Mordechai was simply known as C10.

It was through the unrelenting efforts of C10 that The Organization knew (months after Emil had promised the head of Golide Gumede to the public) that Golide Gumede, born Livingstone Stanley Tikiti, had a sister, Minenhle Tikiti, who lived on the Beauford Farm and Estate. And that is how Mordechai's and Minenhle's destinies became intertwined.

Minenhle Tikiti was picked up and processed by The Organization on December 24, 1978. But even though C10 was at his most persuasive—in a dark room, working and walking stealthily, attacking her from all sides, alternating gentle words with brute force, coming at her with a lit cigarette, a wielded knife, a heel of a boot, burning, cutting and crushing, secure in the knowledge that she could not see his face—Minenhle never gave up her brother. Nor did she give herself up, unlike most people, who usually offered up something (usually rather quickly) during their encounter with C10—a name, a story (true or false), a long-held dignity, an ingrained sense of self. Minenhle gave up nothing.

After days of torture, it was Mordechai who, in the exchange, gave up something—his desire to die. He had found in Minenhle Tikiti a new purpose in life. He had finally found something—someone—to have an allegiance to.

He would dedicate the rest of his life to undoing the pain

he had caused her.

It took Mordechai years to prepare himself for Minenhle. He left his job at The Organization (which was easy since Emil Coetzee had been greatly disappointed by his failure) and took a job at the National Archives repairing and restoring books and manuscripts—mending spines and fixing tears with great gentleness and care. He even changed his voice, making it more sing-songy. It was only when he was certain that she would not recognize him that he re-entered Minenhle Tikiti's life and never left it. Mordechai arrived at the Beauford Farm and Estate on a MacKenzie bus one unassuming Wednesday afternoon and departed two weeks later with Minenhle. They climbed aboard the MacKenzie bus and, as Mordechai paid the bus conductor, Minenhle looked up at the sky and marveled at its independent blueness.

The MacKenzie bus that Minenhle and Mordechai took in 1983 was the very same bus Thandi Hadebe had taken on the day she escaped from the Beauford Farm and Estate in 1974.

Thandi Hadebe was born on the Beauford Farm and Estate. Her father was the Beauford School's messenger boy and caretaker, a job that allowed her family to live a comfortable life—their housing was provided and they received substantial monthly rations. Both her parents were very Christian and very proper. They raised their daughter to stand out and be an example.

Thandi had known all her life that she was beautiful because almost everyone who saw her said so. At first she did not think much of her own beauty; she took it for granted. But as she grew older, she realized that her beauty afforded her a certain kind of ease, a certain kind of power. She never had to struggle. She made friends easily. Teachers tended to favor her. She got special attention and eventually she stopped trying to prove herself: she stopped trying to be anything more than what people saw.

And then, in Thandi's sixteenth year, Minenhle Tikiti entered her life as her Domestic Science teacher. Minenhle was not charmed by Thandi; she was not taken with her beauty. She pushed Thandi to have greater ambition in life than just being a pretty face. Thandi suspected that Minenhle, who had no beauty to speak of, was secretly jealous of her, and so she did not take Minenhle seriously...until the day the *sojas* came to Beauford Farm and Estate.

The *sojas* entered Minenhle's class while it was in session. The girls were busy making pretty dresses. One of the *sojas* asked the girls to strip naked and put on their pretty dresses. Because it was a preposterous thing to say, and because he sounded as though he was merely joking, most of the girls giggled. The *soja* made his request again, his tone more serious this time. The girls who giggled this time did so nervously and uncertainly. The *soja* made his request yet again and, to do away with any confusion on the girls' part, he shot two bullets from his pistol into the ceiling. The girls, trembling, stripped naked and put on their half made pretty dresses. Some of them cried silent tears. Then the *soja* asked Minenhle to choose who was the prettiest of them all.

For the first time in her life, Thandi did not want to be the prettiest girl...she did not want to be pretty at all. Her eyes pleaded with Minenhle, but Minenhle still did the unthinkable —she pointed a stubby finger towards Thandi. And when the *soja* took Thandi away, kicking and screaming, Thandi believed she saw a look of satisfaction on Minenhle's face. It was a look that she would never forget nor forgive.

The *soja* paraded Thandi in front of the whole school, calling her all manner of filth. When he led her to the toilets and they entered one of the pit latrines, Thandi thought for sure that he was going to rape her. She tried to prepare herself for the humiliation and violation, but instead he ordered her to jump into the pit latrine. He left her to drown in its putrid foulness. Now Thandi was sure that she would die. But she did not. Somehow she managed to tread the murky mire and keep her head above it. She desperately wanted to die, but, to her dismay and consternation, she kept on surviving until, after what seemed like days, but was in reality a little over two hours, her father pulled her out.

Thandi did not feel like she had been saved.

Her mother prepared basin after basin of scalding water and bar after bar of harsh soap for her, but Thandi could not feel clean. From then on she took to bathing multiple times a day. She became obsessed with dirt. She began to find the omnipresent dust of the compound oppressive. Whenever she was not cleaning herself, she was cleaning her surroundings. But one thing that she could not scrub clean was the air surrounding her, which had been contaminated by the putrescence of the pit latrine. The smell followed her everywhere.

Understandably, Thandi became desperate for a fresh start.

A fresh start came in the form of Elizabeth Nyoni, who one day descended in a cloud of dust on the Beauford Farm and Estate carrying a golden egg. She had traveled to a place she had only heard about, a place in which there was no one to take care of her and her egg, because she was certain that this place was where she was going to do the best living of her life. She was such a foreign concept on the Beauford Farm and Estate that Thandi could not help but be drawn to her. Elizabeth was the most singular thing that Thandi had ever seen: her blonde hair, her colorful clothes, her genuine self-confidence and self-esteem, her determination and drive, her believing herself to be a country-and-western singer, all showed that she marched to the beat of her own drum. In just being herself, Elizabeth presented Thandi with many possibilities.

For her part, Elizabeth took to Thandi and one day looked at the girl and simply said: "You are so pretty. Have you ever thought of being a model?" Thandi, who did not know what a model was, could not say that she had. Elizabeth reached for a magazine, flipped through its pages and pointed at a woman with ruby lips and penciled-in eyebrows who was looking into the distance as though it held a future in which she was not particularly interested. It was the model's nonchalance and detachment that Thandi found attractive... alluring. The model seemed removed from it all...above it... untouchable. "If you go to the city, I am sure you could make a living as a model."

The city—the place where no one would know or remember what had happened to her. The city—the place where she could start a new, unblemished, unbesmirched chapter of her life. The city—the place where she, with ruby lips and penciled-in eyebrows, could look into the distance as though it held a future in which she was not particularly interested. Thandi boarded the MacKenzie bus the very next day and headed for the city, determined never to look back.

It was in the city that, wearing a pink carnation in her hair, she danced in the rain and heard a young man sing "Don't let me down."

Perhaps the knowledge of what had happened to Minenhle at the hands of C10 gave Thandi some satisfaction, but this cannot be known with certainty. After Thandi left the Beauford Farm and Estate, she returned to it only once, during the war years, to deliver and leave behind a baby boy, Marcus Malcolm Martin. She only offered one word to explain her action: America.

Marcus grew up in the care of his strictly Christian grand-parents with one spiritual striving—to find something in his young life that would give him a sense of belonging. He found this something, a few days after his fourth birthday, in the form of a colorful woman who carried a baby on her back and sang songs of love.

"You treat her like an egg. I don't believe her feet have ever touched the ground. You carry her everywhere." Jestina Nxumalo—MaNxumalo to Marcus—said this in a neutral tone as she leaned against one of the fence posts, her left arm akimbo and a sliver of elephant grass in her mouth. Her eyes were on their target and on the most spectacular thing that young Marcus had seen in his entire life: Elizabeth Nyoni.

She was hanging her washing on a clothesline and had a baby—well, not really a baby anymore—strapped on her back not too tightly, but very securely, and she was humming a delightful tune. She was dressed in all the colors of the rain-bow—the "ladies' whip" his people called it—as if she had reached into the sky and retrieved each color with a gentle tug. And she had hair like no one else he had ever seen—long, straight, flowy, and, best of all, golden. Sometimes, Marcus knew, she assembled it all on top of her head so that it resembled a beehive. Sometimes she let it flow freely and dance gently in the breeze.

Marcus had been watching them for a very long time—he did not know how long because he had not learned how to count or tell time yet, but he knew it was a very long time. He was fascinated by these beautiful creatures. He had come to sit by the fence and watch this colorful woman hum through the day with her not-quite baby on her back often enough to pique Jestina's curiosity.

"And why shouldn't I treat her like an egg? She was a

golden egg for the five years I carried her. She was a golden egg until the third of September, 1978, when she hatched. Just because you see her like this in the flesh does not mean that she is not still a golden egg," Elizabeth said and then continued to hum her tune.

Jestina laughed a long and loud mirthless laugh. "Elizabeth, the things you say!" She brought her laughter to an end. "You are like a peacock. Proud."

"And why shouldn't I be like a peacock? Pride and all— when all that is mine is beauty."

"And vain too," Jestina said clapping her hands together, indicating that she was giving up and was washing her hands of Elizabeth. "Pride and vanity are sins, Elizabeth."

"Envy is an ugly thing too, Jestina."

Jestina made a sound of mock disgust deep in the back of her throat. "Anyway, I'm here about the boy."

Elizabeth made her way to the fence. The not-quite baby cocked her head to the side and examined him with such scrutiny that Marcus felt self-conscious for the first time in his young life.

"Thandi's boy. He is a thing of beauty."

"My eyes are not for beauty to see," Jestina replied with a shrug.

"What's your name?" Elizabeth asked, addressing him directly for the first time.

Marcus was too embarrassed to look at her directly, so he mumbled to the yellowish-gray silty soil and scratch of grass he was sitting on. "Marcus Malcolm Martin Masuku."

Elizabeth laughed heartily—a sound that came from deep inside her belly, genuine, free laughter. He had never heard anything like it. He felt his mouth spreading into a smile— ready to laugh.

"So you're going to be a revolutionary when you grow up?"

He had no idea what she was talking about. His smile became uncertain.

"I think he wants to be friends with your precious egg," Jestina said, coming to his rescue.

"You want to be friends with my Imogen?"

"Yes." He nodded, even though the thought had never occurred to him. He would have been happy to just sit by the fence, watch the beautiful creatures and wish that he belonged to them.

"Genie, you want to be friends with Marcus Malcolm Martin Masuku?" The little girl on her back neither nodded nor shook her head. She just looked at him.

"Well, Marcus Malcolm Martin Masuku, you can be friends with my Genie here if you promise me one thing. Can you promise me one thing?"

Marcus squinted the sunlight out of his eyes and nodded.

"What do you want him to promise? Not to break your egg?" Jestina asked.

"Promise me that you will not become a politician... promise me you will become a real revolutionary instead."

Since Marcus had no idea what she was talking about, it was very easy for him to nod his head, yes.

"I need to hear you say the words."

"I *pomise*," Marcus said, beginning to feel that this was a very important moment in his life. He stood up. He had seen his grandfather do this—offer his hand to another person. It seemed the occasion called for such a gesture. He stood on his tiptoes and strained to reach his hand over the fence and offer it to Elizabeth.

Elizabeth, laughing that belly laugh of hers, shook his hand.

She untangled the girl from her back and gently placed her on the ground. Little Imogen—Genie—was also embraced by the colors of the ladies' whip. Unsteady on her feet, she fluttered and braced herself by placing her hands on the fence.

Jestina clapped her hands. "Finally her feet touch the ground," she exclaimed before ululating.

Elizabeth ignored her. "I am trusting you with my most precious and cherished possession, Marcus Malcolm Martin Masuku. You will take good care of her."

This time it was Elizabeth who extended her hand. They shook the promise into existence.

Suddenly, a friend. Genie pointed at Marcus and made a delighted sound. There was a look of recognition in her eyes. She reached through the fence and grabbed hold of his hand. All she could utter were sounds—twitters really. She was yet to be gifted with language, but he understood her perfectly.

A gust of wind, carrying dust and billowing empty plastic bags, came their way. The wind lifted the colors of the rainbow. Genie fluttered. Marcus held her hand fast, afraid she would fly away. Unfazed by the wind, Genie giggled and continued twittering. She had so much to tell him. And he had all the time to listen. But the wind kept getting stronger and stronger until he had no choice but to let go of her hand.

After all the things that the Beauford Farm and Estate had witnessed and experienced in its recent history, the friendship that blossomed between Marcus and Genie was a much-needed balm.

Marcus & Genie

By the time Marcus and Genie were old enough to understand the world around them, the recent war seemed but a distant memory, for life on the Beauford Farm and Estate had taken great pains to become blissful again. Perhaps it was because their country was newly independent—and a country's independence is infectious and tends to permeate everything—or perhaps it was because both of them were too young to remember the particular horrors the civil war had visited upon the compound. Whatever the reason, Marcus and Genie both developed a strong sense of adventure and soon grew tired of the monotonous grayish-yellow of the compound. They were eager to explore the world outside, and because the farthest thing their eyes could see were the distant hills that looked like a hazy blue something on the horizon, they wanted to personally touch that hazy blue something.

If they had been able to tell the passing of time they would have known that it took close to six months to convince Elizabeth, who remembered only too well the horrors of the civil war, to let them walk out of the compound and down the long dusty road that seemed to stretch on forever only to lose itself in the distant hills. They never realized that she let them go only because she knew they could not go far.

And so it came to pass that on a clear day in December, Marcus and Genie left the compound for the first time in their lives. It never occurred to either Marcus or Genie as they set off down the dusty road armed only with a broken umbrella, a half-eaten packet of Lemon Creams and a bottle of water that they could actually climb the hills. From the stories they heard at night around the compound fire, they knew that what lived on the other side of the hills was terrifyingly wicked and relentlessly evil. They also knew from the around-the-fire stories that the hills themselves were innocent and that therefore there was absolutely nothing wrong with touching them and feeling their reassuring permanence.

Since they could see the hills, they thought it would not take long to reach them. They probably had not walked as far as they thought—Genie with Penelope (her handmade rag doll, whose dark brown skin and colorful dress her mother had made from scraps left over from material she used to make dresses for herself and Genie) tied on her back and secured there by a towel that was knotted around her waist, carrying a broken umbrella above their heads as Marcus drove his wire car along the dusty road, one trouser pocket stuffed with the Lemon Creams and the other containing the water bottle—when their dusty legs grew tired. As their determination to reach the distant hills rapidly waned, they were more than happy to discover to the left of them a field of yellow that stretched as far as the eye could see.

Sunflowers.

They had never been told that such a thing of beauty existed. Without hesitation, Genie ran giggling into the field, never stopping to think that it could contain anything harmful or dangerous. Marcus hesitated. He left his wire car on the side of the road in full view of any passers-by, just in case he and Genie got lost in there—disappeared in a sea of yellow, never to be found again. If anyone came to find them, they would know exactly where to look, and, if the two of them were never found again, at least people would know exactly what had happened. Marcus was a cautious but not particularly mor-bid child. He just knew from all the stories told around the compound fire that not all stories had a happy ending and that horrible things sometimes happened to people, espe-cially curious children who ventured too far away from home.

Playing among the sunflowers proved to be a happy dis-traction from the quest to reach the hazy blue something. Marcus and Genie ran laughing and zigzagging through the stalks, not really sure who was trying to catch whom.

And so it was that, day after day, they left the compound intent on reaching the distant hills, but, day after day, found themselves playing among the sunflowers. Then one day they gave up the quest altogether and simply made their way straight to the sunflowers. After that, it did not take long for the hazy blue hills in the distance to become a distant memory. When they were not playing catch-me-if-you-can, Genie sang songs she had learned from her mother and told stories she had heard around the compound fires to a very appreciative audience of sunflowers.

They continued to find pleasure in the sunflowers even as the petals began to shrivel, the stalks hardened, and the brown faces of the sunflowers became darker and downcast.

Then one day all laughter died. Just like that. Unable to comprehend, Marcus and Genie stared at all the sunflowers lying on the reddish-brown soil, no longer reaching for the sky. They had all been felled to the ground. Every single one. Genie desperately tried to get them standing again, and Marcus had no choice but to help her. With their hands they dug the reddish-brown soil and reinstated the stalks to their rightful places. Some stood but most fell down again. Genie was determined. She did not care how long it would take, all she told herself was that one day all the sunflowers would be replanted.

But when they arrived the next morning, the scene was worse than any they could have imagined. The sunflowers were gone—all of them, even the ones they had put upright again. There was not a trace—not a forlorn green stalk, not a withered yellow petal, not an abandoned brownish-black seed, no evidence at all that this had recently been a populated sunflower field. The barren scene truly broke Genie's heart and for the first time in her life she turned her face away from the sun. Wordlessly, Genie sank to the reddish-brown soil and cried silent tears—another first in her short life.

Marcus put his arm around her but at that moment became old enough to know that Genie's grief was something he could not console away. He was sad not for himself but for Genie because, although he understood that this was a loss, he knew that the loss was mostly hers. She had loved the sunflowers in a way that he had not. She had loved them deeply. He had not. She had loved them with every fiber of her being. He had not. In truth, he had loved the sunflowers only because Genie loved them. He saw that they were beautiful, but were it not for Genie he would not have seen that theirs was a beauty worth cherishing.

On that day, Marcus made another discovery. It was a discovery he could only have made because of the sunflowers' disappearance. As Genie planted her feet in the reddish-brown soil and sifted it through her fingers in a vain effort to find something that remained, a glint on the horizon caught Marcus' eye. In the early morning sunlight he made out the carcass of a car.

The abandoned car had been there all along, lonely as it listened to them play and laugh in the field, lonely as it listened to Genie sing and tell stories to the sunflowers, lonely as it watched them walk away without being discovered. The loneliness of the abandoned car filled Marcus with a sadness that made him want to run towards it without hesitation and touch it. It was only Genie's grief that stopped him from doing so.

In a show of solidarity he too sifted the soil through his fingers. But he could not bring himself to bury his feet in the reddish-brown soil. Every now and then, his eyes stole looks at the abandoned car.

Perhaps the biggest challenge that now presented itself in young Marcus' life was how to tell Genie about the abandoned car. Every day, secretly, he visited the car, a Morris Mini Minor that he christened Brown Car more for its rusty patches than for its original beige color. He found time for these secret visits in those moments when Elizabeth found it necessary to have her daughter close to her—when she washed their clothes and hung them to dry, when she cooked their meals, when she combed and plaited their hair, when she dressed them both in bright colorful clothes, when she wanted someone to sing to, or sing with, or when she simply wanted to have her daughter close so that she could pick her up whenever she felt like it and twirl her in the air and hug her fiercely and pepper her skin with kisses and listen to Genie giggle and giggle as though she knew no end to laughter and happiness.

Before they discovered the sunflower field and before he discovered Brown Car, Marcus' favorite time of the day had been bath time—not his bath time, which consisted of his grandmother religiously scrubbing his body with a coarse facecloth and harsh soap that was sudsy enough but stung his eyes and prickled his nose and made him sneeze repeatedly as his grandmother told him about the dangers of dirt and vanity while he stood in a zinc-galvanized steel bucket which was filled with just enough cold water to make him clean. No, not that bath time, but Genie's and Elizabeth's. They bathed together, and their bath time was filled with laughter and giggles and songs and warm water splishing and splashing in their enamel cast-iron tub, the warm and comforting scent of vanilla wafting out of the high window of their bathroom, under which Marcus stoically sat even though the other boys in the compound teased him mercilessly for doing so.

From under the window, Marcus could hear the conversations they had: "Ma, when I grow up, will I have breasts as big as yours?"

"Would you like to have breasts as big as mine?"

"Yes, most definitely."

"Then you shall."

"Ma, when I grow up, will I have a bottom as round as yours?"

"Would you like to have a bottom as round as mine?"

"Yes. Maybe even rounder."

"Then you shall," replied a laughing voice.

"Ma, when I grow up, will I be as beautiful as you?"

"No. You'll be much more beautiful than me. You'll be a true sight to behold."

"But I don't want to be more beautiful than you."

"Then you'll have to try very hard not to be."

"Ma, I know that I came from somewhere in your heart."

"Yes, you did."

"And that I was an egg."

"A golden egg."

"Does that mean...Marcus says that means that I don't have a father."

"Marcus knows as much as Marcus can know."

"Do I have a father?"

"It depends."

"On what?"

"On the future."

Marcus had fallen asleep many a time under that open

window, lulled by the warm vanilla scent, their soothing voices, generous laughter and genuine happiness.

But after he discovered Brown Car, he no longer spent time under the high window. He spent his time breathing in the surprisingly comforting smell of rusting metal and rotting seat cushioning. It was an old and somewhat familiar smell.

His fingers reveling in the curve of the steering wheel, Marcus imagined himself driving down the long dusty road away from the compound and towards the hazy blue hills—always with Genie by his side in the passenger seat and her beloved Penelope in the back. Marcus did all the driving because, from what he had seen on the compound, only men drove vehicles; it had never occurred to him that his imagination did not have to be bound by the reality of the compound. And as he fantasized about these journeys to and from the compound, he tried to devise a plan to tell Genie about his new love, Brown Car.

As it turned out, he did not have to. One day, as he imagined himself driving down the dirt road with Genie by his side, he smelled the warm scent of vanilla and woodsmoke and turned to see Genie looking at him from the passenger seat, a rare frown creasing her brow, her arms crossed and resting on her slightly distended belly.

"So this is it?" she said, looking over the interior of Brown Car with no hint of the admiration he felt when he looked at the car. "This is what made you steal away from me?" What was he supposed to say to that? The ever-present Penelope also seemed to give him a disapproving look from her secure position on Genie's back. He felt his heart sink. And then Genie's face broke into a smile, the gap between her two front teeth making him smile too, as it always did.

And from then on, that was how they spent most of their mornings and afternoons, slowly baking in Brown Car's carcass, together traveling to the places contained within their imaginations, places they had heard of—China, Egypt, England, the Soviet Union and America. In their imaginations the places all looked exactly like the compound, except China had a great wall running around it; Egypt had pyramids and sphinxes where the schoolrooms were; England had a stuffy and stiff queen looking very out of place in the grayish-yellow dust of the compound as she walked around in her bejeweled crown and heavy red cloak looking for someone called Margaret Thatcher but never finding her; the Soviet Union had the word communism (or rather, as Marcus and Genie spelled it, komookneezim) plastered on every building in the compound in big red letters; America contained Marcus' parents, who manifested themselves as younger versions of Marcus' grandmother and grandfather, the way they looked in their wedding photo—Christian, proper and unsmiling. The America that Marcus' parents lived in was filled with men riding horses and wearing Stetsons, and men driving fast cars and wearing fedoras—in other words, they lived in the America seen in the bioscope. During their many travels Marcus and Genie even visited Genie's father, Golide Gumede, in the future.

It was Genie's idea to borrow the world atlas from Marcus' grandfather's scant library so that they would have more places to visit. Unfortunately, it had been printed in 1965 and did not contain the name of their newly independent country. The world atlas therefore presented them with more possibilities as well as more challenges. Their newly independent country could have been any of those land masses surrounded by even larger masses of water. It could have been one of those teeny tiny shapes that seemed to be in grave danger of being swallowed whole by the masses of water. As a result, their newly independent country sometimes found itself in the center of the world map, sometimes in the north, sometimes in the south, sometimes in the east, and sometimes in the west. Marcus and Genie already understood that the world had a fluidity to it, even if they did not as yet understand their place in it. Worlds and possibilities unfurled before them, creating dizzying delights.

So engrossed were they in their travels that it took them a while to notice that shoots were beginning to rise out of the reddish-brown earth. The sunflowers were being reborn. This was how they learned their most valuable lesson about death—that after it there is life again, that things that perish will rise again, that after every ending there is another beginning.

And so, although they spent the days and afternoons traveling the globe, their eyes also patiently watched the sunflowers grow stronger as they reached towards the sun. They watched as the leaves appeared. They watched as a million blooms burst in unison. They watched as a million brown faces turned towards the sun, and Genie chose that exact moment to take her rightful place among them, welcoming the familiar itch of her skin as her arms came into contact with the stalks and enjoying the cool dampness of the reddish-brown soil as her toes burrowed in, rooting her in her place.

It was one day, while they were in the sunflower field, that the first truly strange thing happened. Through the stalks they saw a car sputter to a stop. Two men were inside. Neither of them got out. The driver simply rolled down his window and proceeded to smoke a cigarette, blowing smoke rings out of the open window as though he had all the time in the world. From their vantage point within the sunflowers, Marcus and Genie could see enough of the men to know that they did not know them: they did not belong to the Beauford Farm and Estate. After the war, strangers had been very rare on the

Beauford Farm and Estate. Even so, Marcus knew enough about strangers to hold on fast to Genie's hand—Genie who had a tendency to run towards everything without hesitation. They stood among the stalks for a long time holding hands, not moving, afraid to breathe.

Then the man in the passenger seat got out and walked towards them. Marcus and Genie held a collective breath, fearing something, though not really sure what. The man stopped right at the edge of the sunflower field and started unzipping his trousers. It was then that Marcus risked everything and moved. He lifted the hand that was not clutching Genie's hand and used it to cover her eyes. He shut his own. They heard the man's urine splash onto the reddish-brown soil. It was only when they heard the car door slam shut that Marcus removed his hand from Genie's eyes and opened his own. They felt too embarrassed to look at each other.

Not looking at each other is what allowed them to witness the astonishing thing that happened next. Just as the coolness in the air and the changing color of light through the sunflower petals was letting them know that the sun was beginning to set, the boot of the car popped open and out of it slowly unfolded an impossibly tall man, like a Jack-in-the-box that was taking its time to surprise them. This time Marcus and Genie held their collective breath in sheer awe.

The driver and the passenger got out of the car and joined the third man. They had a long, whispered conversation before they shook hands—grasping each other's upper arms with their free hands, a sure sign of something deeply felt. Without even having to say anything to each other, Marcus and Genie knew that they would be greeting each other like that from then on. The driver and the passenger got back in the car, which came alive without a sputter. It made a quick U-turn and raised a lot of dust in the air, so much that Marcus and

Genie had to strain to see what was happening. The driver said something to the third man that he responded to with a smile. Then all three men brought their right hands towards their foreheads at a very sharp angle. Then just as suddenly and just as simultaneously they brought their hands down in a sharp motion. Goodbye. Without even having to say anything to each other, Marcus and Genie knew that they would be saying goodbye to each other like that from then on too.

The car slowly drove away. The third man remained in the cloud of dust but started to turn towards the compound. His eyes quickly swept over the sunflowers. Then he stopped.

Genie immediately let go of Marcus' hand and ran towards the man. They seemed to share a mutual elation at having discovered one another. The man threw Genie into the air. Marcus was terrified. The man caught Genie with a smile. It was only when he saw the gap between the man's two front teeth that Marcus felt safe enough to leave the sunflower field. When the man shifted his smiling eyes from Genie to Marcus, Marcus was grateful to see that they did not lose any of their warmth. He basked in the warm glow of their welcome as he shyly and in a manly way, or so he hoped, shook the man's hand.

All three of them were so wrapped up in getting acquainted that they did not notice Elizabeth hurtling towards them with the speed and ferocity of a mother elephant that knows its calf is in danger. Dust rose in her wake as the many colors of her dress seemed determined to fly off her body. The blonde hair that often sat on top of her head had long flown off and been trampled by some of the other residents of the compound who were following her, sensing instinctively that something either spectacular or tragic was happening and that they would need to bear witness.

"Golide?" Elizabeth bellowed before coming to an abrupt

stop. Her eyes were wide with wonder, confusion, relief, joy and pain. Her body trembled with the force of feeling all these emotions at once.

Jestina strategically started ululating. Relieved to finally have something to do, the compound residents celebrated. The women ululated and danced a jig. Then the men did a very elaborate warrior dance, kicking their legs high into the air, humming and chanting a warrior song deep in their throats. The younger members of the compound did not do the jig or the warrior dance—they were too modern for that. They chose instead to do the twist, and the really gifted among them even braved the mapantsula. No one, not a single person, minded all the dust that the joy of the occasion raised as they made their way back towards the compound. Golide seemed at once both touched and embarrassed by the attention. However, this spontaneous excess of sheer joy was not unwarranted, for Golide Gumede, liberation war hero, had returned home alive and well, unlike so many others, who had returned broken or had not returned at all. The presence of life after the death and devastation of war was definitely something worth celebrating.

Marcus had never before felt such a deep sense of belonging as when he walked nestled between Elizabeth and Golide, each of his hands in one of theirs. He smiled up at Genie and she smiled down at him from where she sat, perched resplendently on her father's shoulders. This was to be the happiest day of their young lives.

It was while they were in Brown Car that the second truly strange thing happened. A few years had passed since Genie's father's return. Things all around had changed. There was more traffic along the dirt road. A mobile library came once a month, allowing residents of the compound to borrow one book each. Marcus borrowed a different volume of *The Adventures of Tintin* every month. Genie borrowed *The Firebird* and renewed it every month. Marcus enjoyed challenging his lips and tongue with Captain Haddock's alliteration-obsessed diatribes, and Genie was enamored of the pretty pictures of the beautifully colorful bird as well as the story of how it remained elusive for Prince Ivan and sent him on a tremendous quest.

In addition to the mobile library, a mobile clinic came once a week. A MacKenzie bus came twice a week from the city, resuming the schedule that had been suspended during the liberation war. Within Brown Car things had also changed. Penelope had been joined by Specs, a teddy bear who wore glasses that had been a Christmas present to Genie from her father. Penelope left the permanent security of Genie's back to be with Specs on the back seat.

The death and resurrection of the sunflowers was now something Marcus and Genie were accustomed to, so they were content to look on miles and miles of barren reddish-brown soil. They felt so secure in their happiness that when the second strange thing happened, it took them a while to realize that it was actually a threat to that happiness.

A flashy car drove up the dirt road at a very high speed, which was strange enough in and of itself because most vehicles had the good sense to travel slowly and carefully on the dirt road, knowing it was highly unpredictable and never to be trusted. The car whizzed by so fast that there was no way Marcus and Genie could tell who or what was in it. Truth be told, they did not particularly care to know. A few minutes after it had disappeared they ceased to think about it altogether.

Some time later the imprudently fast car made its way back down the dirt road. This time, though, it seemed to have learned its lesson and proceeded slowly and with caution.

Marcus and Genie were surprised when everyone they loved—Genie's parents and Marcus' grandparents—alighted from the back of the car. From the front, two people alighted, a man and a woman who looked too...shiny. Their clothes were shimmery, their skin (unburnt by the sun) looked burnished, their too-long hair (both his and hers) was glossy and incongruously curly as it glinted in the sun. Marcus was at first embarrassed for them, then he immediately felt guilty for being embarrassed, because he knew without being told that these were his parents, fresh from America.

The woman—he supposed he had to think of her as his mother now—came rushing towards him, arms outstretched, yelling "Honey!" Marcus got out of Brown Car, hesitantly, cautiously, reluctantly. Genie understood his apprehension, so she got out of Brown Car with him and held his hand.

The woman—his mother—frowned at Genie before hugging Marcus. "You're just as beautiful as I knew you would be," she said, covering his face with kisses. She smelled of something so sweet that it made Marcus and Genie sneeze at the same time. "Aren't you precious?" the woman said, looking at Genie and smiling a smile that did not reach her eyes or remove the frown from her forehead.

"Yes, I am precious," Genie replied matter-of-factly, which only deepened the woman's frown.

"Is her name Precious?" the woman asked no one in particular as she finally stood up and smoothed her shiny appearance.

"My name is Genie."

"Oh? How...precious."

The man—Marcus supposed he had to think of him as his father now—came forward but seemed not to know what to do next. Marcus strongly suspected that the man—his father —felt foolish, looking so shiny next to his grandfather and

Genie's father, who looked like real men. "Oh, Dee, you are hopeless. You both are," the woman said, laughing and pushing the man towards Marcus. Finally, the man—his father, Dee—offered Marcus his hand, and Marcus and he shook hands.

"Oh!" the woman squealed. "I wish we had brought a camera. We should have thought of it," she squealed some more. "Oh, this is just too precious," she said, clasping her hands together in sheer delight. "We have a surprise for you in the car," she announced, reaching out her hand to Marcus. When he took her hand hesitantly, she lifted him up with such surprising force that he had to let go of Genie. Without warning, his mother started walking rather quickly towards the flashy car and away from Genie.

Marcus looked at Genie over his mother's shoulder as the distance between them grew at an alarming rate. Even though his grandparents and Genie's parents were there, he felt that he was in danger and that something horrible was happening. "Genie!" he all but screamed. She ran after him, shouting, "Marcus?" The worry in her voice matched the fear in his.

"Perhaps there is another way to do this," Golide was saying.

"Surely you see how very attached they are to each other," Elizabeth added.

"I'm sorry," the woman—his mother—said, holding him tighter. "It is not our intention to be cruel. But you all know what's going on. It's no longer safe here."

"It never was safe, but we survived, we've always survived," his grandmother said. Marcus turned to look at her. Her voice had sounded hard but there was a tenderness in her moist eyes, which were fixed on Marcus. His grandmother had never looked at him like that before. His grandmother had never cried in his presence before. It was when he looked at his grandmother that the reality of what was happening to him became clear.

The surprise in the car was simply a ruse. This woman and this man—his mother and his father, his parents—were here to take him away. Suddenly feeling trapped by his mother's arms, Marcus struggled to release himself, kicking his feet and flailing his arms. He knew he was hurting her. Perhaps he even meant to hurt her. But his mother's hold on him only got stronger. He dug his fingernails as deep as he could into her neck and then dragged them. She let out a startled, sharp cry of pain but still did not let him go. "You'll thank us for this one day," she said. Marcus seriously doubted it.

Since he had no intention of leaving the Beauford Farm and Estate, he grabbed hold of one of her loop earrings and pulled as hard as he could. As the earring ripped through her earlobe and Marcus felt her warm blood ooze into his hand, his father opened the passenger door to the imprudent car. It was then that Marcus sank his teeth into his mother's cheek, but it was already too late, she was already sitting in the car and hugging him to her body. He heard the door lock after his father banged it shut. He saw Genie reach the door and try its handle before her own mother swept her up, saying: "Let him go. You have to let him go." It was then that he saw something enter Genie's eyes as she looked at him. It made him give up the fight entirely. Everything became a blur.

"I'm sure in time we'll be able to put all of this behind us," his father said, getting into the car. Marcus could not tell whether he was saying this to the people in the car or to the people outside. Marcus blinked away the tears in time to see Genie give him a smile. He knew it was not a genuine smile. It was a smile meant to give him courage. He did not want someone to give him courage. He wanted someone to save him. And then Genie did the unthinkable. She raised her hand in a sharp angle and brought it to her forehead. Goodbye. She waited for him to do the same. But he absolutely refused to say goodbye. Suddenly there was dust all over as the car sped away, and then Marcus could no longer see the sunflower field. He wondered for a long time afterwards if Genie, believing he had returned her salute, had completed the gesture by bringing her hand sharply down. Had she really said goodbye to him and let him go forever? Just like that? Or was she still waiting, her right hand at a sharp angle to her forehead?

In the car his mother pressed her cheek to the top of his head and rocked him gently. "You'll see. You'll thank us for saving you. You'll thank us some day." She repeated the words over and over again as though she was reciting a lullaby.

His eyes grew heavy. His body was tired from the fight. It was only as his eyes struggled to stay open that he noticed the other woman in the car—an older woman—and in her arms she held a sleeping child, a girl who seemed encased in frilly pink. "That's our surprise," his father's voice said. "She's your little sister and her name is Krystle."

Marcus looked at his father, who smiled at him, obviously happy about something. He looked back at the unsmiling older woman holding the girl.

"That is your grandmother. My mother."

"*We* are your family now," his new grandmother said, still not smiling. They all looked beautiful, the members of his family, but Marcus felt that their beauty was not to be trusted. It was a dangerous beauty. He was suddenly more terrified than he had ever been before. He let go of his bladder then, well aware that his urine would soil both his shorts and his mother's shiny dress.

Bhekithemba

In 1988, a couple of years after the Masukus took Marcus away from the Beauford Farm and Estate, Bhekithemba Nyathi drove stealthily, under the cover of darkness, up that same road. He had first driven up the road in the light of day a few months earlier, and it was because of that first trip that he was making this second trip. He parked his car some distance from the compound, walked through the barren sunflower fields and was astounded by the eerie silence of the place, where even the dogs refrained from howling at the full moon or barking at him. The life that was once here had disappeared. Bhekithemba shone a torch into a disused well when... something glimmered at the bottom, shocking him with its sudden unexpectedness. As he stole away from the com-pound feeling both relieved and wary that he had found nothing—no one in the well—he tried to reconcile the man he now was with the man he had thought that he would be.

The year was 1980 and Bhekithemba, perhaps for the first time in his life, felt rooted—connected to everything and everyone around him. A son of the soil, in a real, literal sense. He was something that had germinated and sprouted—broken through the earth—from this very spot. His eyes stung. His throat choked. His lungs filled with something heavy and bitter. People ran, helter-skelter, seeking safe spaces. Chaos. Confusion. Panic. Uncertainty. Fear. All around him. And yet here he stood unmoved. Rooted. Connected. Certain. The tear gas would clear, and when it did he would still be in this moment in history.

He had come all this way to see Prince Charles and hopefully shake his hand. His own grandfather had shaken the hands of various members of the British Royal Family: King George VI, the Queen Mother, Queen Elizabeth II and Princess Margaret. By the time his grandfather passed away he had lost most of his memory: he had forgotten his own name, which was Cosmos Nyathi; he had forgotten the name of his Christian wife and those of his two common-law wives; he had forgotten the names of his thirteen children and those of his twenty-eight grandchildren. He had even forgotten that he was a successful businessman whose enterprising spirit had seen him leave his life in the family village at the age of sixteen, to work as a stock boy for a Mr. MacKenzie at the MacKenzie General Goods Store.

By the time he died, Cosmos Nyathi had forgotten that at the age of seventeen he had suggested to Mr. MacKenzie that he open a bottle store. Although Mr. MacKenzie's General Goods Store was the only store for kilometers, his business was failing because people seemed to prefer the traveling goods men who always gave you a little extra something— a bonsella—as an added bonus for patronizing their business. Since the MacKenzie General Goods Store was located just outside a mission station, Mr. MacKenzie doubted that a bottle store would have enough customers, considering it would be within the ever-watchful purview of the mission-aries. But because Mr. MacKenzie was at his "wits' end" (a favorite phrase of his whenever he spoke of his relationship with the colony), he agreed to open a bottle store on condition that Cosmos would manage it himself. The MacKenzie Bottle Store proved so successful that Mr. MacKenzie soon decided to open another one in another village, and once again sent

Cosmos to manage it. Because of the popularity of the two Bottle Stores, "MacKenzie" became a household name and the General Goods Store became successful by association.

By the time he died, Cosmos Nyathi had also forgotten that when Mr. MacKenzie had come to another "wits' end," this time not with the colony but with the situation brewing in Europe, he suddenly returned to Scotland in 1938 and had been generous enough to bequeath the MacKenzie General Goods Store and the two MacKenzie Bottle Stores to the very man who had made them a success.

In 1938, most African men would have been very happy to own three successful stores, but Cosmos Nyathi was not. He grew his business to include the MacKenzie line of buses and the MacKenzie Bioscope. He was what was known in the colonies as a "good African"—primarily Christian, mostly hard-working, generally clean and sober—and because of this, whenever there was a royal tour, he was brought forward as an example of the progress the colony had made with its African population, which was how he came to shake the hands of King George VI, the Queen Mother, Queen Elizabeth II and Princess Margaret. Of all the things that he had done in his seventy-two years, he was proudest of the moments when he had shaken the hands of royalty, and so, as he entered the twilight of his years, he forgot all but these moments. When he passed away, he left his family with two inheritances: the MacKenzie businesses and his pride in the family's connection to the British Royal Family.

This was why, when Bhekithemba made his way to the stadium to see Prince Charles receive the Union Jack and witness the flag of the newly independent country being raised in its place, he was filled with the family pride and a great deal of sadness over the sun finally setting on the empire. At the age of eighteen, he had enough hubris to believe that he would have a private moment with Prince Charles to say: "My grandfather, Cosmos Nyathi, owner of the MacKenzie businesses, knew your grandfather and your mother. He was a good African. He shook their hands." And Prince Charles would say in turn: "Cosmos Nyathi, of course, my grandfather and mother talked of him often. He was indeed a good African, very enterprising for one of his kind." Then Bhekithemba would tell Prince Charles that he was strongly opposed to his country ceasing to be a British colony, that he had deliberately not joined the armed struggle led by the terrorists, and that he, at age eighteen, was very much saddened by the fact that he and all his future children would not be British subjects.

Of course, that is not how things had turned out. The Union Jack had indeed come down, been folded and handed over to the future king of England, and Bhekithemba had surprised himself by feeling absolutely nothing. He was confused by this, his lack of feeling. Prince Charles had seemed ill at ease, anemic, and far removed from everything that was happening around him; whether he was just above it all or whether he was simply uninterested, Bhekithemba could not tell. Instead of being a prince, he seemed to be playing at future king in his bright-white military regalia. Bhekithemba suspected that the shoes the prince was wearing were slightly too big for him. In all honesty, the prince had proved to be something of a disappointment.

Just as Bhekithemba was reconciling himself to an anticlimactic evening, a man in dreadlocks got on the stage, raised up a fisted hand and called out, "Viva!" The crowd went wild and Bhekithemba felt something stir within him—something nascent, a beautiful beginning. For the first time he became fully aware of the throng around him and of its elation and euphoria at finally being independent and free. He was jostled this way and that, but he did not mind—this closeness, this tight togetherness was actually comforting. The dreadlocked man, eyes closed, strummed his guitar. Three women, sirens really, made melodious sounds. The crowd moved as one and carried Bhekithemba along. For the first time Bhekithemba felt part of something larger than himself. The man opened his eyes and looked directly at Bhekithemba. "Viva!" the man called out again. The crowd went wild shouting "Viva!" in reply and Bhekithemba found himself joining them with his own "Viva!" even though he did not know what the word meant. Then he felt something travel through his body, a jolt of electricity that traveled from the top of his head to the bottom of his feet—grounding him, connecting him to the soil. The crowd, with Bhekithemba in it, became one moving, breathing, almost menacing force. Bhekithemba could do nothing but look at the dreadlocked man, mesmerized. It was the dreadlocked man who was doing this to the people. He seemed to possess a certain power, a power that Prince Charles did not possess—the power to move, unite and inspire people. Later, Bhekithemba would know that this power was called charisma. This dreadlocked man, Bhekithemba was certain, was going to lead him to something great.

The dreadlocked man closed his eyes again. There was a flash of light. The air grew thick with smoke that stung the eyes and filled the lungs with something bitter. The crowd panicked. Helter-skelter. Bhekithemba would not move; he felt too connected...too rooted. He waited patiently for the dreadlocked man to open his eyes again. If it so happened that he was destined to die here, on this spot, in his eighteenth year, so be it; he would gladly die, but only after the dreadlocked man had opened his eyes. The smoke cleared. The sting left his eyes. He took a deep breath. Clean, clear air filled his lungs. The man on the stage opened his eyes, looked straight at Bhekithemba again. Something like a smile—a lazy smile—played on his lips. A look of respect entered his eyes. The dreadlocked man's band and his melodious backing singers returned to the stage. It was only then that Bhekithemba realized that everyone else had run away as soon as the smoke had filled the air. "Now I know who is the real revolutionary," the dreadlocked man said, still looking directly at him.

Bhekithemba felt as though he had been anointed.

For the rest of his life he would feel a strong connection to that man. He would speak of his "encounter" with the dreadlocked man with just as much pride as his grandfather had had in speaking of shaking the hands of British royalty. Bhekithemba was known to find the perfect moment, whatever the occasion, to stand up in a gathering and regale them with the story of how Bob Marley had looked at him through the smoke of a tear-gas-filled stadium and told him that he was a real revolutionary.

That encounter changed him. It had filled him with a pride in his country and in his blackness that he had never had before. He wrote of this life-changing encounter as a "Letter to the Editor" for the local, state-run newspaper. The letter was printed and a few days later he received a call from The Man Himself praising his writing and offering him a scholarship to study journalism at the local, state-run university. Bhekithemba, the anointed one, happily took up the offer. Soon after graduating, he went to work for one of the local, state-run newspapers, his pride in his country making him a great mouthpiece for the state. He was a nationalist. He was a patriot. He was a revolutionary. He firmly believed that he lived in the country that Bob Marley had sung so proudly and so passionately about. And now he wrote about his country with equal pride and passion.

Truth be told, Bhekithemba felt the privilege of being so

singled out by The Man Himself. It was not lost on him that his connection to The Man Himself accorded him respect among his peers and helped him garner a reputation. If he had felt any guilt over being so cherry picked, he was able to do away with it by convincing himself that he was the man that his country needed at this particular moment. As a young man, it embarrassed him to admit he had been so colonized that he had not once considered joining the liberation struggle because, like his grandfather and father before him, he had so loved being a British subject. But he was sober enough now to reflect on that period of his life objectively. His country had not needed him *then*. Perhaps he would have been killed, and what good would that have been for the country? His country needed him *now*. He could write the kind of stories that would help build the new nation. He would be the one to change his country from a racist, divided country into a multiracial, unified country.

The Man Himself told Bhekithemba that because the country was still young and working out its differences, and because civil wars often had repercussions, conflict was inevitable. However, the country had an image to portray and protect, and Western countries were waiting for it to fail. It was Bhekithemba's job to ensure that the West did not receive any ammunition with which to destroy the country's image. Bhekithemba understood why the West should not be given reason to discredit or malign the country, but he also believed that the country should be given a chance to examine itself, because that was the only way it could understand itself fully, make necessary changes and create an equal society. That was the real revolution as far as Bhekithemba was concerned—the creation of an equal, discrimination-free, all-inclusive society. To this end he wrote award-winning articles on a woman's right to wear trousers, on the dignity of the disabled, on the plight of farmworkers, on the history of the Coloured people, on the rich cultural heritage of the Khoisan, on why women deserved equal pay, on the importance of commercial farming to the national economy. Often The Man Himself would call Bhekithemba and praise him on an article he had written, always making sure to quote a particular paragraph, turn of phrase or scintillating sentence. Bhekithemba always felt honored and humbled by such attention and strove to write and do even better. As a reporter he prided himself on his objectivity, his ability to present all sides of the story, and in providing his fellow citizens with information that helped them better understand their country and each other. His articles often led to very engaged exchanges of ideas and opinions in the "Letter to the Editor" section.

The Man Himself informed Bhekithemba that he was thinking of shaking things up at one of the local, state-run newspapers, which still had too many white journalists and therefore did not reflect the independence of the majority. Would Bhekithemba Nyathi like to be the new head of investigative reporting? Bhekithemba had just turned twenty-five and felt old enough for such a responsibility. He took the promotion.

When someone from a car assembly plant called him to tell him that state ministers were illegally reselling cars that they had received for free as part of their payment packages (one had resold as many as eleven cars), Bhekithemba thought it a good story to highlight corruption and make people think about why they elected officials and what kind of character an elected official should have. He could already see the conversation that would play out in the "Letter to the Editor" section. He wrote the piece, but it was not printed. He spoke to the editor-in-chief, who told him that from now on he could only report on things that The Man Himself told him to. The editor-in-chief laughed at the confusion on Bhekithemba's face. "Ay, you're green," he said. "The Man Himself also has illegally resold several cars, and you actually thought we would be able to run the story? The time will come for such a story. Trust me. But for now this is our free press."

Bhekithemba called The Man Himself and was told he was out of the office. He did so five times before he realized that The Man Himself was deliberately avoiding him. He went to work the following day awaiting the call from The Man Himself that would let him know what he could write on. The call never came. He reported to work for almost three months, receiving a paycheck every fortnight, but The Man Himself did not call.

Bhekithemba sat at his desk with nothing to do and watched as his colleagues bustled about. He noticed things—the wear and tear of the furniture, the cobwebs in the corners, the gray grime creeping up the windows, the smell of boiled cabbage that wafted up from the company cafeteria and remained trapped in the building—for the first time. He knew every chip and chink in the furniture, how many cobwebs there were, what progress the gray grime had made, and where the boiled cabbage smelled strongest and where it was overcome by the smell of sunbaked urine that rose up from the alley behind the building. He realized how much he had compromised himself through his association with The Man Himself. His colleagues would not talk to him, would not look him in the eye; he felt certain that they laughed at him behind his back for thinking that he had curried the favor of The Man Himself. He thought of seeking employment at another newspaper, but all newspapers were state-run and he was now wise enough to know that it would be a futile exercise. Perhaps if he had not received a paycheck every two weeks he would have felt better, but he did, and he knew that the paycheck for the services not rendered was The Man Himself 's way of communicating something: power.

That was when he heard the rumor. People in a particular region of the country were systematically being disappeared by the state. Bhekithemba refused to believe it, even when the rumors became more specific. It was a particular ethnic group, in this particular region of the country, which was systematically being disappeared by the state. Bhekithemba was steadfast in his refusal to believe the rumors. And then news arrived that his cousin—someone he remembered playing with as a boy, someone who, unlike Bhekithemba, had decided to cross the Zambezi River to become a freedom fighter—had been disappeared. He knew that the story of his cousin's disappearance would be forever uninvestigated, unwritten and unsolved. Something stung his eyes and filled his lungs with bitterness. He blinked his eyes, swallowed hard, and decided to ignore it.

By the time The Man Himself called Bhekithemba and gave him a direct assignment, he had learned his lesson well.

The Man Himself told him that there was a crazy man on the Beauford Farm and Estate who believed he was capable of flight and was cultivating a race of angels—followers who believed that they too were capable of flight. The man was building a giant pair of silver wings so that he could fly the woman he loved to Nashville, Tennessee. The man's followers touched the wings, prayed to the wings, kept watch over the wings, made offerings to the wings—all in hopes of one day having wings of their own. The Man Himself said that this would be the perfect story with which to amuse the masses during a difficult time. For Bhekithemba, the story of the crazy man and his cult was obviously one worth telling, not because it was amusing but because it was about the audacity to believe. He could already see the "Letter to the Editor" section abuzz with excitement. This was how he was going to redeem his fall from grace.

There was only one problem: Bhekithemba did not believe in love, at least not in romantic love. He understood the love one had for one's parents and for one's country—but that sort of love was born of respect and gratitude. It was a sort of giving back. There was a reason for that kind of love. It was only natural to love the things that had given you life, a sense of place, a feeling of belonging, a connection to things beyond yourself. You could not exist without these things and so of course you loved them. It was a selfish love: a love of self-preservation. Selfish love was understandable...reasonable. But romantic love had no reason. Bhekithemba had read somewhere that it was merely an invention, something that could preoccupy people, a yearning that could never be fulfilled, something that would make one's life a quest rather than a series of unrelated, mostly boring events. And so Bhekithemba did not quite believe that this man building a giant pair of silver wings was doing it for love—love of a woman. Bhekithemba suspected that there was another reason, more interesting, more real, more reasonable, and that in itself was story enough for him.

Intrigued, Bhekithemba made his way to the Beauford Farm and Estate. He drove up a dusty road surrounded by a sea of sunflowers.

Out of the sunflowers came a flash of colorful light that made Bhekithemba bring his car to an abrupt stop. In the middle of nowhere, anything was possible. He waited for the dust to settle before making his next move.

The dust cleared and there was a girl standing in front of the car, left arm akimbo, a teddy bear dangling from her right hand and a rag doll firmly secured on her back. Her face was knotted in a frown that was more curious than unfriendly.

She was mere inches in front of the car. Bhekithemba saw her mouth move, but could not hear her. He switched off the engine and rolled down his window.

"Who you coming to take away?" she asked, deliberately not coming any closer. What an odd question. "Who you coming to take away?" she repeated, still standing her ground.

"No one," he said, flashing his most charming smile.

She looked unconvinced.

"Is this the place, Beauford Farm and Estate, where the man is building an airplane?" he asked. Her frown became unfriendly. "I'm a reporter. I would like to do a story on this man."

"Why a story?" she asked.

How was he supposed to respond to that? Why a story? What else but a story? All he did was look for stories. It had never occurred to him to do anything else, to look for something else. "Well, I think the story is of interest. I think people will be...inspired by the story."

"Why inspired?" she asked.

Another question that he could not respond to. Did she even understand what it meant to be inspired? She was probably asking questions simply to ask questions, the way most children did.

"Who are you looking to inspire?" she asked.

Or maybe not, maybe she understood the conversation that they were having better than he did.

"A lot of people. Many people don't believe that we can fly. Many people need to believe that we can fly." He waited for her next question, but none came.

Instead, just as quickly as she had appeared, as a flash from the sunflowers, she disappeared as a flash back into the sunflowers.

Bhekithemba sat in his car, not sure what to do next.

A moment later he was not quite sure if a girl had really been standing in front of his car. He had been driving for hours and his mind had probably played a trick on him. She had been such a bright and...spritely thing. There had definitely been something otherworldly about her. Bhekithemba laughed at himself. What was he thinking? He was a man of reason. Of course the girl did exist...

Should he carry on up the dirt road, or should he turn around? As he was trying to decide, he saw them—a group of people coming down the dusty road, led by the girl. She did exist. Bhekithemba got out of the car, not quite sure if he was being welcomed or not.

"He says he is not here to take anyone away," the girl announced, before he could say anything. "He says he's here to tell the story of the man building the wings," she continued with authority. "He says the story will inspire people. He says people don't believe that we are capable of flight," she said and waited for whatever would happen next.

An impossibly tall man came forward. "I believe I am the man you are looking for," he said humbly. Bhekithemba doubted it. The man was painfully white.

"He is my father," the girl said, her chest puffing out with unmistakable pride. She looked at the painfully white man with reverence; all those who looked at the man looked at him with reverence.

Soon, Bhekithemba understood the source of their pride. Just looking at the man, Bhekithemba could tell that there was something different about him, something beyond the color of his skin. He possessed that certain something that Bhekithemba had witnessed in the dreadlocked man: power. But not just any power. Power of a special kind. The power to move, inspire and unite people.

Charisma.

The man told Bhekithemba how he had come up with his theory of flight on September 3, 1978, as he watched elephants swim across the Zambezi River. What had made the first elephant cross was that it could see the other bank of the river—the elephant would not have swum into the ocean, of this the man was certain. What made the other elephants follow was the successful passage of the first. The man wanted people to know that they were capable of flight, and at first he had erroneously thought that they would realize this if he taught them how to build airplanes. After watching the elephants, he understood that what was needed was merely his own belief in flight. If people saw him build a giant pair of silver wings, then they too would believe that they could fly.

Jestina

As Jestina watched people she had known all her life move through the yellowish-gray of the compound like automatons, she no longer recognized them. Something within them had changed, something fundamental. The residents of the Beauford Farm and Estate compound seemed to have expended every human emotion possible and were now simply exhausted. She could not help but wonder if the scene playing out in front of her was due to the fact that the journalist, Bhekithemba Nyathi, had written the story of Golide Gumede and his race of angels who believed they were capable of flight.

Mr. Vundile, her adult-literacy teacher, passed her by without seeing her. He carried his wife on his back. His wife's yellow and white dress was stained with a garish red. From the angle of her neck, Jestina knew that Mr. Vundile's wife, Mrs. Vundile, was dead. She knew this because she had seen the heads of dead birds, killed by the compound boys' slingshots, hang at that angle. She herself had wrung the necks of countless chickens, so she knew *intimately* the angle of the neck that marked death.

Mr. Vundile was not the only one carrying a dead person. Other residents were doing so too. Most helped each other carry a body. They all passed her by without seeing her. They all had a faraway look in their eyes that paradoxically seemed to be turned inward, as though they were searching for something deep within themselves—anything in the depths of their souls that would let them know what they had done to deserve this.

"This" was having to bury family members, friends and neighbors who, that very morning, had still been full of love, laughter, anger, greed, jealousy, resentment...something... anything but the emptiness, the nothingness that made a body offer no resistance at all to being carried and thrown into a disused well. Whatever it was that they had felt, be it love or hatred, it had not warned them that they would be feeling it for the very last time, had not urged them to savor the moment, to hold on a little longer to the feeling.

Jestina watched in stupefaction as people she had known all her life helped each other pick up the body of a person she had known all her life and carry it to the disused well at the edge of the compound. Then she noticed the silence. No one was crying. No one was screaming. No one gnashed their teeth. No one stomped their feet and tore out their hair. No one ripped off their clothes. These would all have been socially acceptable forms of grieving. But no one was doing what was socially accepted. When had they learned to do this, to bury their dead in absolute silence? Could an entire community learn a lesson so quickly and so completely?

There was a body that no one picked up. It was charred to brittleness, beyond recognition. The hands seemed gripped by the desire to seize something. The legs were twisted in a permanent dance of pain. The mouth gaped open, revealing crooked teeth. Jestina thought that in life this person must have had a crooked smile. She wondered if he had walked a crooked mile. She was filled with an overwhelming sadness because she could not recognize him. She had probably greeted him with a "Salibonani" many times. He had been part of the fabric of her life...of all their lives, and here he lay, reduced to nothing. They had carried fourteen bodies down the well to be buried underneath the water, Jestina had counted; the crooked man's body was to be the fifteenth. Everyone hesitated. The crooked man seemed ready to disintegrate and no one wanted to be the one to reduce him to further nothingness. Without saying anything, the surviving residents of the compound left the burnt remains alone and walked away.

They went to their respective homes, homes that were now broken—perhaps irreparably and irrevocably.

Having no other choice, Jestina went home too.

She entered the house through the kitchen and heard someone trying not to breathe. She turned to find Genie, terrified and trembling in the corner.

At some point Genie must have decided to run to Marcus' grandparents' house. She must have found them sitting at the table in their kitchen-cum-dining room the way Jestina had left them: opposite each other with a proper tea laid out between them—good china, scones, biscuits and sandwiches. The only thing odd about the scene was that both Mr. and Mrs. Hadebe were slumped over, their heads resting on the table, which was so unlike them since they were always upright and true. They were also holding hands, which was also so unlike them, since they vehemently believed that displays of affection were unchristian. Jestina wondered if it was the fact that the Hadebes were slumped over so carelessly or the fact that they were holding hands so openly that let Genie know that they were dead. Mr. and Mrs. Hadebe made the final death toll seventeen.

"Poison...rat poison in the tea," Jestina said in explanation as she went over to sit next to Genie. "They made me do it," Jestina whispered. "They made me put it in while the Hadebes watched. Then they forced them to drink the tea. And then they just left. Left them to die. And me to witness it."

Although Jestina was not crying—she was too shocked

and stricken to do so—Genie put an arm around her. It was the adult who was supposed to comfort the child; Jestina felt Genie was growing up before her time. She resented her having to do so. Why could those *sojas* in their red berets not have left them alone?

"I was in the sunflower field," Genie said. "I saw the *sojas* coming. I heard the noise. The rat-a-tat-tat. The screaming. The smell of burning flesh. When they were leaving, they stopped their army truck next to the field. One of them got out and lit a cigarette. He struck another match. I think he meant to set the field on fire but another *soja*, the one driving the truck, asked him what sunflowers had ever done to him and told him to put out the match. The other *soja* did as he was told and then got back into the truck. I ran here...to the Hadebes. I found this."

Eventually, the adult put her arm around the child. "They played Don Williams," Jestina whispered, her voice trembling, as though this was the real horror of the story. "They actually put Don Williams on the gramophone and then did what they did." Jestina looked at Genie, her eyes searching. "How could anyone who listens to Don Williams do such a thing?"

"They probably did not know that we also love Don Williams," Genie said, sounding almost certain. "If they had known, they wouldn't have done this. They wouldn't have done any of it." It almost made perfect sense.

Jestina looked at Genie with pity. "Oh, they knew. They knew we love Don Williams. They knew and *still* they did this."

At some point Jestina and Genie must have fallen asleep because a loud bang woke them up. Someone was knocking on the door. Before they could fully comprehend what was happening, the door was flung open. Jestina and Genie shrank further into the corner. Someone shone a torch into the room. A handful of the compound's residents strode into the kitchen but stopped short when they saw Mr. and Mrs. Hadebe slumped over the kitchen table—forever holding their peace. The torchlight swiveled and found Jestina and Genie tucked away in the corner.

"What happened here?" the torchbearer demanded.

Jestina was about to answer truthfully but Genie rushed to say, "It was the *sojas*...They killed Mr. and Mrs. Hadebe with rat poison."

There was silence. Then there was grumbling.

"Is that Golide's daughter?" an angry voice inquired.

"Yes," the torchbearer answered.

"She needs to come out here."

There was more grumbling. It sounded as if an argument was about to begin.

Genie was about to stand up but Jestina held her down.

"What do you want with the girl?" Jestina asked.

"Who is asking?"

"Jestina Nxumalo."

"You're Elizabeth's friend. You need to come out as well."

The grumbling outside got louder.

"None of this would have happened were it not for Golide. They were looking for him. They did this because of him," the angry voice outside called out.

"But the girl has done nothing. Neither has Jestina," said someone else.

"They probably know where Golide and Elizabeth are. They can tell us."

"Where are your parents?" the torchbearer asked.

"They flew away," Genie said.

"I told you. They ran away," the angry voice shouted. "They knew the *sojas* were coming for him and they ran away. And left us to...The girl needs to come out."

"Do you honestly think that if they knew the *sojas* were

coming they would have left their daughter behind?"

"Not all parents are made the same. Some are made to leave their children behind."

"It is simply not true that the *sojas* came here for Golide. Things like this...like what happened here today...have been happening throughout the region for years. We all know this," a voice said, trying to reason.

"Did you not hear them specifically ask for him by name? Did you not hear them shout, 'Where is Golide Gumede?' You are a liar if you say that you did not! How many of us were asked where we were hiding him? I was. If he had been here when the *sojas* came, none of this would have happened. They would have taken him away and that would have been the end of that. My son, Sikhumbuzo, would be alive and listening to a story around the fire right now, not in the well. This is all Golide's fault."

"I think they would have done what they did anyway. They just needed an excuse to justify their actions. Golide was that excuse."

"But they have been talking about unity for months now, talking about peace."

"Perhaps they only did so to make us relax...to lull us into a false sense of security...to catch us unawares."

"I don't care about unity. I don't care about peace. All I care about is that they asked for Golide Gumede by name," the angry voice said. "It is all because of what happened to the Vickers Viscount all those years ago. You cannot shoot down a plane and get away with it. The white man will not let you."

"No white man came here today."

"Golide is a madman, I have been saying it for years."

"But why would the *sojas* come all this way to kill a madman?"

"And his followers."

"Watch what you say. My son, Sikhumbuzo, was no fol-lower of Golide Gumede."

"I saw your son with my own eyes touching those giant silver wings and looking at them like he had seen the glory. You are a liar if you say he was not a follower."

"Those we buried were all followers—all died except the girl and Jestina."

There was more grumbling. The argument was becoming more heated.

"Hey...you...you...What is this girl's name again? Funny name...difficult name...English name...you...you..." the angry voice stuttered.

"What is your name?" the torchbearer asked Genie.

"Imogen."

"Imo...what?"

"Imogen."

"What kind of name is that?" a voice outside asked.

"They've always thought they were better than us, those two—Elizabeth with her blonde wig, always singing country-and-western music; Golide always tinkering with that mon-strosity of his and believing himself capable of flight—and giving their daughter a name fit for the Queen of England," another voice added.

"You can call me Genie if you like," Genie said.

There was a long silence.

"Jestina," the angry voice shouted, "you take this girl... Imo...Imo...this Genie...and the two of you go and never come back here again. Do you understand me?"

"Yes," Jestina said.

"What about my parents? When they come back?" Genie asked before Jestina clamped a hand over her mouth.

"You don't need to worry about them," the angry voice said with uncharacteristic calmness.

Genie obviously would have liked to say something to that, but Jestina would not let her speak.

The torchbearer and the handful of others that had entered the kitchen left. The crowd outside also dispersed. Jestina and Genie were left behind in the silent darkness with only each other and the resting in-peace Hadebes for company.

In the very early hours of the morning Jestina stood up. She grabbed hold of Genie's hand. Genie had no choice but to stand up as well. She looked at the Hadebes, hoping that they too would stand up.

"Don't look back. Never look back," Jestina said, looking resolutely ahead, leading by example. She dragged Genie along as they exited the Hadebes' house.

"What about my parents?"

"People will tell them where we've gone."

"Where are we going?"

"Somewhere over the hills. Somewhere far away from here."

"Will my parents be able to find me there?"

"Yes," Jestina said, without looking at Genie.

"Is that where Marcus is? Somewhere over the hills?"

"Yes."

"Isn't that where evil resides?"

"Evil?" Jestina said. "Evil has a way of finding you wherever you reside. Evil found us here today," she said, finally looking at Genie. "Then again, evil is everywhere...and in everyone, really. No one is inherently evil. But we are all of us capable of evil," Jestina said as she looked at the charred remains of the petrified man with the crooked teeth. He was still where the compound residents had left him.

"I see," Genie said, turning her head to look at the man.

The truth was that Jestina did not understand the work-ings of evil. She had always thought that evil was a thing that you cannot see. But now it turned out that evil could take the form of men wearing military camouflage and red berets who listened to Don Williams and had qualms about burning down sunflowers, but apparently none about making a middle-aged couple drink rat poison.

"If you had told me yesterday morning that by the end of the day I would have killed the Hadebes, I would have laughed at the ridiculousness of that notion. Who, after all, cuts off the hand that feeds them? And yet here I am...here we are," Jestina sighed, leading Genie towards the charred man. "There was a time, not so long ago, that we thought only white people capable of such hatred and anger, such evil. We know better now. We know different. Evil does not discriminate. It visits all of us with equal opportunity."

Jestina and Genie gently picked up the charred man, carefully carried him to the well, and let him free-fall to its bottom. If either of them noticed that the charred man's heart had calcified into a precious and beautiful something, neither of them let on—they had already witnessed too many things that defied articulation.

Jestina allowed them to make one stop: the Gumedes' home. They entered the house. It had been ransacked. The sofa cushions and the mattresses had been bayoneted and gutted. Pots and pans cluttered the floor. There was broken glass everywhere because the windows had been smashed, quite unnecessarily. The sight of Golide's Lovemore Majaivana LP collection, crushed into a million vinyl pieces that could never be put back together again, broke Jestina's heart. Golide always listened to Lovemore Majaivana when he was working on his silver wings. It was almost as if the *sojas* knew that and therefore let loose their fury on the vinyl. This was destruction simply for destruction's sake. Jestina watched as Genie pulled down a ladder and used it to climb into the ceiling. This should have surprised Jestina, but nothing could or would ever surprise her again. Genie re-emerged moments later carrying, in one hand, a suitcase that she had obviously packed for exactly such a moment in her life and, in the other, Penelope and Specs.

"We should not let this change us," Jestina said with authority as she took hold of Genie's hand again. "If we let it change us then they will have won."

As they walked past the sunflower field, Genie ran a hand over the closest stalks. "This is not an ending of my choosing. From now on I will choose my own endings," she said. There was a conviction and determination in Genie's voice that made Jestina believe her.

Holding hands and watching the day breaking, Jestina and Genie waited for the MacKenzie bus that would carry them away from the Beauford Farm and Estate.

PART III

The Present

Valentine

Valentine Tanaka looks at The Man Himself and cannot help but think that he does not quite fit in these surroundings—he is too large for the medium-sized office, too modern for the antiquated furnishings, and too shiny for the dust-covered surfaces. There was a time when the size of The Man Himself bespoke a presence to be reckoned with, but that was years ago when the country was newly independent and The Man Himself had just taken over The Organization of Domestic Affairs. He had carried his weight with authority, he had been nimble on his feet—a man of activity, dashing out of cars, bounding up and down stairs, never out of breath, a reminder of his predecessor, Emil Coetzee. But now here he sits, wheezing, sweating, unable to catch his breath; now his considerable weight, no longer athletic (time had seen to that), hangs off him, giving him a sagging appearance that promises to fold in on itself some day soon. This is why, even as he sits, he needs to prop himself up with a cane.

There is that familiar glint in the eyes of The Man Himself—mischief, malice, mayhem. Valentine can never really tell which one it is. The glint always makes Valentine wonder what kind of schoolchild The Man Himself had been. Because he has never been able to imagine The Man Himself as a boy, he always conjures up a miniature version of The Man Himself, sitting behind a desk (the old-fashioned kind that you opened and that had as its pride an immaculate inkwell) on a slotted wooden chair that pinches (not that the miniature

The Man Himself knows this because at this very moment his bottom is off the chair), his hand eagerly raised as he screams "Me, me, me," leaning over his desk, trying to get the attention of a colonial schoolmaster whose studied lack of interest lets everyone know, without a doubt, that he is British. "Me, me, me," the miniature The Man Himself screams. "Absolutely no need for all this excitement, I assure you," the disinterested schoolmaster says. "A hand quietly raised will get my attention. But I suppose it cannot be helped, it is in your natures to make a cacophony...empty vessels and all that." Valentine watches as the eyes of the miniature The Man Himself glint—mischief, malice, mayhem.

"I suppose you are wondering to what you owe the pleasure of my company," The Man Himself says as he wipes his face with a pristine white handkerchief, interrupting Valentine's reverie. "

"Yes...sir."

The Man Himself looks at Valentine, long and hard. Valentine knows that it is best not to look away. The Man Himself reaches into his pocket, his eyes never leaving Valentine's, and places something carefully on the table.

"You owe it to this."

Valentine looks at the thing on the table. It is the most precious and beautiful something that he has ever seen. Its beauty makes him want to touch it. He only realizes that he has reached out his hand to touch it when The Man Himself snatches it up and secrets it away in his pocket.

"I would like to think that you and I are friends."

Valentine cannot help but think that The Man Himself starts many conversations in this way, conversations that do not end particularly well for the listener.

"Or am I wrong? Are we not friends?"

"We are friends."

"Good. That is what I thought, why I knew I could trust you." The Man Himself looks at Valentine long and hard again. "I can trust you, can't I?"

"Yes, yes. You can trust me," Valentine says, not particularly liking who he is at this moment—a man so uncertain that all he can do is try to please.

"Good. I knew I could," The Man Himself says as he once again removes the precious and beautiful something from his pocket, places it between his thumb and forefinger and rolls it back and forth, making it glimmer like a beacon. He no longer trusts Valentine enough to place it on the table between them. "As soon as I saw it, I thought, Valentine Tanaka will be the man for this job. He is someone who can be trusted...a friend."

Valentine is too mesmerized by the precious and beautiful something to look at The Man Himself.

"You'll never guess where I found it," The Man Himself says, looking particularly pleased with himself. "The Beauford Farm and Estate."

"The Beauford Farm and Estate?" says Valentine. And with these words, he feels as though a spell has been broken.

"Yes. The farm has been taken over by the war veterans, of course."

"Of course."

The Beauford Farm and Estate being taken over by war veterans had made the headlines some years before. The Organization had not intervened in any way... until now.

The Man Himself shifts his gaze away from Valentine to a pile of dusty papers resting on a window ledge behind Valentine. "While I...we...appreciate their service to this country, their self-sacrifice during the war, they are squatting on the land illegally and something will obviously have to be done about that," The Man Himself says to the pile of papers.

"Obviously."

The Man Himself shifts his gaze back to Valentine.

Mischief. Malice. Mayhem.

"I knew you would understand," The Man Himself says. "I knew you were the man for the job."

The Man Himself leans heavily on his cane and then struggles to stand up. The scrape of the chair along the floor takes Valentine back to the classroom where the miniature The Man Himself is screaming "Me, me, me," trying to get the attention of the ever-disinterested British schoolmaster.

"Beatrice Beit-Beauford still has the title deeds. Legally, the farm belongs to her," The Man Himself says as he returns the precious and beautiful something to his pocket.

"I see."

"I knew you would."

Kuki

Kuki Carmichael puts her hand on the door handle and takes a deep breath. She does this once every week and it never gets any easier. She looks at her liver-spotted and wrinkled hand and grimaces. When did she become so bloody old? How did she allow this to happen to her? She studies her reflection in the rear-view mirror—a shriveled, sunburnt face with a smear of strawberry-red lipstick. "Ugh!" It is a sound that comes from the back of her throat in disgust. Perhaps she looks good for eighty-one, but to be honest, she has no idea what a good-looking eighty-one-year old should look like. It had never occurred to her that she would live this long. And if it had occurred to her, she would probably have thought she would be a blithering idiot by now. But no, unfortunately Kuki has all her wits about her—a brain as sharp as it was fifty years ago. Sharp enough now to let her know that she looks like a prune.

"Enough of that, Kicks!" she says out loud, clapping her hands together to snap herself out of it. She lifts her cardigan and the biscuit packets that she has concealed in it off the passenger seat. She places the package securely under her arm before pushing open the door with some effort. When did the door become so damn heavy? She gets out of the car as quickly as her years allow. Standing in the bright sunshine, she takes a deep breath and without allowing herself to give it a moment's thought she marches towards the building. The Princess Margaret Retirement Home. She supposes it is a kindness to call it a retirement home instead of what it really is: a home for the old, abandoned, misbegotten and forgotten.

The pastel-colored decor and Vera Lynn singing "The White Cliffs of Dover" make Kuki want to turn right back around as soon as she enters. But she steels herself and forces a smile.

"Good afternoon, Mrs. Carmichael," a bevy of black beauties, all smiles, say from behind the reception desk.

"Good afternoon, ladies," Kuki says in her gruff, I-used-to-smoke-a-pack-of-Everests-a-day voice.

"She's waiting for you," the bevy of black beauties say in unison.

"Thank you!" Kuki says, her strawberry-red smile still plastered on her face, the strain of it beginning to show. She strongly suspects that there is lipstick on her two front teeth, but she cannot stop smiling. She has to answer every single "Good afternoon, Mrs. Carmichael" that will inevitably accompany her down the corridor with the same strained smile and a "Good afternoon" of her own.

Time was the staff at the Princess Margaret were all white. Now they are all black. Time was Kuki would not have cared either way. Now she does. The past ten years have had her talking about "them" more and more. Kuki does not want to be misunderstood. She is not a racist. She does not have a racist bone in her body. She is a liberal; has been ever since she married Todd Whitehead Carmichael in 1981. So no, she is not a racist. She is just a frustrated liberal.

"Good afternoon, Mrs. Carmichael."

"Good afternoon."

They always seem so nice and friendly, but they are really wolves in sheep's clothing...and if you give them an inch they will run the country into the ground and let it go to the dogs.

"Here goes," she says under her breath as she inhales

deeply before opening the door.

The room looks warm and wonderful in the sunlight that streams through the peach curtains. This is why Kuki always comes in the afternoon: for the blushing light. She once came in the evening and the room had been positively depressing.

The room is furnished well. All the furniture belongs to Beatrice. Kuki is sure that this is what the inhabitants appreciate about The Princess Margaret—it allows them to bring their former homes to the Home. This does not stop their furniture from seeming more and more like museum pieces, or their bodies from seeming more and more like relics as time goes by, but it is still a considerate gesture.

"Kicks?" a voice says from within the folds of a peach curtain. It's Beatrice Beit-Beauford.

Kuki genuinely smiles at her friend and stretches her arms out for a big, satisfying hug. "Yes, B. It's me."

They hug. Kuki avoids Beatrice's eyes as they both sit down on the sofa. She does not want to see the faraway look that will inevitably enter Beatrice's eyes. It has been six months now and Kuki has yet to reconcile herself to the fact that Beatrice has Alzheimer's. Today is a good day. Today started with recognition. But Kuki now knows better than to hope that the entire visit will be good.

"My nails are such a mess," Beatrice says, looking at her hands. "I've been waiting for Genie. But she has not come." She smiles apologetically as her hands pat her hair. "I must look awful."

Kuki pats Beatrice's hand reassuringly. "You look lovely, dear. Absolutely lovely." Suddenly feeling cold, she unfolds her cardigan and reveals the packets of stowed-away biscuits. "Look what I brought you," Kuki says, holding up the biscuits like treasures. "Highlanders and Tennis Biscuits."

Beatrice makes a sound of pure delight. "Oh Kicks, you're

the bestest friend a girl could ask for."

"Let me pop the kettle on," Kuki says, as she makes her way to the electric kettle that sits on a table in the corner, surrounded by sachets of teas with exotic names, teacups, saucers, teaspoons and a small bowl full of sugar cubes. Electric kettles are rare at the Princess Margaret. Only the "good" patients are allowed to have them. As Kuki clicks on the kettle, she takes comfort in the fact that her friend is considered a good patient.

"My nails are positively grotesque. Imagine what Matron Stinkerbockers would say if she saw them," Beatrice says, her voice carrying laughter within it.

Stinkerbockers. It has been many years since either of them used the word. Its unexpectedness makes it even funnier. Kuki laughs heartily. Tears sting her eyes. She wipes them away. What do you know? It is going to be a good visit after all.

"I think we should go visit her," says Beatrice.

"Visit who, dear?" Kuki asks, suddenly apprehensive, but trying to sound nonchalant, as she pours the just-boiled water over the teabags in the teacups. The aroma of jasmine fills the air. Stinkerbockers, or rather Matron Pulvey, has been dead for decades.

"Genie."

"I told you that Valentine Tanaka from The Organization is coming to talk to you about the farm. We spoke about this over the phone earlier today. You remember?"

"Of course, I remember. But I refuse to be in this disheveled and unkempt state any longer. I need grooming. I need Genie."

"Perhaps we can visit Genie after we talk to Valentine," Kuki says, delicately handing Beatrice a teacup and saucer.

From the moment Beatrice had entered The Princess

Margaret, Genie and Kuki had made an agreement with one another. Genie would come to visit Beatrice, Miss B to her, twice a month and take her on a "girls' day out" to the spa or to the hair salon. They would have manicures, pedicures, massages, incongruous hairstyles, giggles and thick, generous slices of chocolate cake. And once a week, Kuki would come for tea and sympathy. Kuki would have loved to come more often, but it broke her heart to see her friend, her best friend, in here, like this. Genie could spend time with a Beatrice who forgot more than she remembered because Genie had not known Beatrice when...when Beatrice would not have cared a jot about her nails, her hair, or Stinkerbockers.

It seemed to Kuki to be more than a simple twist of fate that Genie was the daughter of Golide Gumede, the very man who had shot down Beatrice's plane during the war. When Kuki had shared that news with Beatrice, she had had no idea that it would lead to a beautiful friendship between Beatrice Beit-Beauford and Imogen Zula Nyoni. They had too much in common—a love of sunflowers, a childhood lived on the Beauford Farm and Estate, a hero for a father, and a brave, defiant spirit—for their differences in age and race to matter.

There is a hesitant knock on the door before one of the black beauties, apologetically so, lets a man into the room.

"Valentine," Kuki says, automatically pouring him a cup of tea.

"What is all this business about Beauford all of a sudden?"

"Kuki...Beatrice," Valentine says, accepting the cup of jasmine scented tea and sitting himself on the chair facing Beatrice.

"Why the interest in Beauford?"

"Well...As you know, war veterans have settled on the farm."

"Have been settled there for years."

"Well...that...that is an illegal act."

"We know it is."

"We would like to evict them from the land."

"Who is 'we'?"

"The Organization."

"You mean your boss?"

"I mean The Organization."

"Why now?"

"Well, as they say, there is no time like the present. All we need from Beatrice are the title deeds—"

"Don't have them," Beatrice says.

"What do you mean, you don't have them?" Kuki asks.

"I mean just that. I no longer have them. I sold the land."

"To whom?" Kuki and Valentine ask simultaneously.

"The Survivors."

"The Survivors?"

"The Survivors. They bought the land fair and square for a dollar, not a penny more, not a penny less."

Genie

The discovery of the precious and beautiful something lets Genie know what she needs to do next. She needs to send the 1965 world atlas to Marcus. She needs to send a post-card with the image of the Victoria Falls on it to Krystle. She needs to trust in the efficacy of the postal system to get these things safely to America. She needs to send a colorful bird to Minenhle and Mordechai. She needs to take Beatrice for a spa day. But first of all she needs to stop taking her medication without Vida noticing.

PART IV

———◆———

Teleology

Marcus

In 1988, on a crisp and brilliant day in the city, Marcus found himself in an elevator with his mother, father and a lanky man in a maroon uniform, complete with matching cap and socks, who took off his cap whenever he greeted someone and called everyone sir or madam—even eleven-year-old Marcus himself had been called "sir," which had pleased him. The man's gloves were a brilliant white and Marcus was amazed that they did not have a speck of dust or dirt on them. So impressed was he by the man that he briefly entertained dreams of becoming an elevator operator himself. He whispered this ambition to his mother, who had only frowned in return.

His father held his hand and squeezed it when the elevator operator told Marcus that he could press the button for their floor—which, his mother informed him, was six. The building had ten stories in all and it seemed rather grand. Marcus felt the importance of the occasion as he pressed "6" and the button lit up. Pleased with himself, as if he had just performed magic, he smiled at the elevator operator, who chuckled, reached behind Marcus' ear and retrieved a sweet, which Marcus only took after his father had nodded his approval.

He had been told by his parents not to take sweets from strangers. Not to talk to strangers. Not to accept lifts from strangers.

All these were new rules. On the Beauford Farm and Estate he had learned to make friends of strangers.

On the sixth floor, his father pressed the button outside a door and moments later the door opened. The man who opened the door was eating a fruit—a marula—with care, which is the only way to eat a marula fruit.

"I believe you've been expecting us," his mother said to the marula man.

"The Masukus, I presume. Yes, please do come in. Mordechai Gatiro," the man said, gently spitting the slippery marula pit into the palm of his left hand and offering his right hand for them to shake.

Marcus heard his mother make a sound in the back of her throat before shaking the man's hand.

"You've found me indulging in a guilty pleasure, I'm afraid," the man said with a broad and generous smile.

Marcus had no idea what the words meant, but he liked the way they rolled off the man's tongue like the beginning of a song. He liked the beginnings of songs. He liked this man.

They entered a small room where the man offered to take his father's coat before entering a modestly sized living room.

The furniture consisted of a six-piece living room set, three overladen bookshelves and two flowerpots from which two climbers were already making good progress towards meeting halfway along the ceiling. Everything looked squeezed in and cozy.

There were books on the coffee table, covered in cloth, ancient with broken spines and torn pages, in various states of repair. There were papers—yellowed and fragile—a breath away from disintegration. Marcus knew not to reach out and touch them even though the temptation was great.

Marcus sat on a love seat sandwiched rather snugly between his parents.

The man with a song for a voice sat on an armchair opposite them and started the kind of conversation that grown-ups liked to have about the weather, traffic, relatives, and the price of this, that and the other (which seemed to Marcus to always be rising, never falling). These conversations could never hold Marcus' attention.

Luckily for Marcus, there were some voices coming from another room—feminine voices. These voices held his attention, they made him feel that he was on the threshold of a surprise. He was excited because you never knew...you just never knew what a surprise could hold.

Before he knew it, he had stood up and was opening the door to that other room.

Sitting in front of a mirror having ribbons and flowers put in her hair by a woman leaning on crutches was Genie—as colorful as ever. He ran to her.

"Oh Marcus!" Genie said, looking at him in the mirror. "You've spoiled the surprise." Smiling brightly, she was far from disappointed. But for some reason her smile was no longer like the Beauford smile that he remembered; it was like his mother's smile: a smile that did not reach her eyes.

Eunice

There is a knowing that happens in the bones. As Eunice Masuku got down on her knees, she knew deep in her bones that the girl would be no good.

She remembered the girl as a proprietary slip of a thing that held on to her grandson's hand a little too tenaciously. She remembered the girl as belonging to a family that had dabbled in politics and rightly suffered the consequences.

The Masukus did not do politics.

Why did the girl have to become a part of her family? She had a crushed and broken aunt, Minenhle, who was very willing to take care of her. Even the woman she had been found living with, Jestina, had been prepared to take care of her. So why did the girl have to become part of her family?

Dingani was adamant. The girl must be welcomed, must be lived with, must be a part of their family. Eunice had always been the one to say how things must be, but with the introduction of the girl, power had shifted: Dingani was the one who determined things now. Her son, who had dedicated his entire life to not disappointing her, seemed hell-bent on disappointing her now.

Did he not understand that they were perfect just the way they were: father, mother, son, daughter...and her, the grandmother, the overseer of their happiness? Four was the perfect number for the modern family, all the magazines said so. Four fitted so beautifully around her yellow Formica table.

The girl would make five...

Eunice had no other choice but to get down on her knees and divide the room in half in preparation for the girl—the girl she knew deep down in her bones would be no good.

Krystle

———•———

At first Krystle had thought...no, felt...no, known that she would not like the girl. The girl that her parents insisted she remembered from the day that they had gone to collect Marcus from a place called Beauford Farm and Estate. A place whose name Krystle liked because it sounded like the kind of place from where a prince would come. A place that Krystle did not remember ever having visited and therefore imagined as a grand castle with a gloriously impenetrable fortress. If this girl coming to live with them, the girl she had met but no longer remembered, came from the Beauford Farm and Estate of Krystle's imaginings, it was very likely that she was some sort of princess whose fortunes, as the fortunes of many princesses did, had suddenly changed.

Krystle did not want to live with an unfortunate princess. She wanted to be the princess. She imagined a girl with fair skin, long hair, large eyes and rose-colored cheeks, and envy filled her heart as she realized that her own light complexion, her thick hair that her mother only seemed proud of on Saturdays after a trip to the hair salon and a painful session with the hot tongs, and her overall prettiness that her grandmother told her of daily, would be nothing compared to the girl's.

She watched as her father and grandmother argued about the girl. She watched as her mother worked herself into a frenzy buying all manner of pink things for the girl and promising Krystle that she and the girl would be the best of friends.

She watched as Marcus gave his opinion, with the supercilious air of an expert, of what the girl would and would not like. But Krystle knew she would not like the girl.

On the day of the girl's arrival, Krystle folded her arms, turned her face away and knotted her lips with a determination to show the girl and make her feel that she was not liked... not wanted. But the girl who came to stand in her bedroom, wearing tattered clothes, carrying a battered suitcase and two raggedy toys, was definitely no princess—unfortunate or otherwise. Her dark skin and kinky hair would never have permitted it. Krystle instantly liked the girl for the obvious reason that she would always be her inferior. And so she unfolded her arms, turned to face her and unknotted her lips to say: "You and I will be the best of friends." And they were. They shared everything, on Krystle's terms of course, and were soon like sisters. The only thing that interrupted their happiness was Marcus.

When Marcus came home on holidays from the all-boys boarding school he attended, he was always the hero. Bounding up the stairs, two at a time, making his short legs do impossible things; throwing his purple cap in the air; tearing his purple blazer off his chest, unable to get it off fast enough; struggling to loosen his purple-and-gray striped tie while kicking off his shoes; the maid and the gardener smiling up at him indulgently as they struggled to carry his oversized black school trunk, stenciled with his name in big white letters, MARCUS MALCOLM MARTIN MASUKU, up the stairs, picking up the clothes that lay strewn in his wake; Marcus would scream at the top of his lungs: "I am the cop and you are the robbers!"

Or, "I am the cowboy and you are the Indians!"

Or, "I am Knight Rider *and* Kitt and you are the bad guys!"

Or, "I am Six Million Dollar Man and you are the bad guys!"
Or, "I am He-Man—"

"Then I am She-Ra," Krystle would offer.

"No. No She-Ra! Just bad guys. You girls are the bad guys."

Krystle did not like this, but Genie did not seem to mind.

"You let him bully us, Genie!" Krystle complained to Genie one night in the darkness of the pink bedroom they shared.

Bully. Krystle had liked the word as soon as she heard it, even though the girl who had used it had meant it as an insult aimed at her.

"He does not bully us," was Genie's patient reply. "He spends so much time away from home that when he is here he likes to feel important."

"But he is *not* important!" Krystle turned her back on Genie. An impotent gesture since Genie could not see her in the dark, but one that allowed Krystle to feel self righteously wounded all the same.

"And if we didn't play the bad guys, then he wouldn't have four o'clock tea with us."

Krystle frowned, confused by this. What did Genie mean? Her four o'clock teas were a privilege. Privilege—another word she liked. She knew what a privilege was because Mrs. Ketz, the headmistress of the all-girls primary school that she and Genie attended, would, during assembly, particularly and pointedly, look at the row of black girls, the handful that the school had recently admitted, and say: "You should *all* feel honored. This is a school of great renown. It is a privilege to be allowed inside these hallowed walls."

Mrs. Ketz herself had attended the school as a girl. Many of the girls who had attended the school had grown up to become the successful wives of politicians, businessmen and farmers. One had even grown up to become the wife of a prime minister.

"Marcus should feel honored to be invited to my four o'clock teas. So should you. They are of great renown. It is a privilege to be allowed inside their hallowed walls," Krystle said into the darkness.

Four o'clock tea was an elaborate event that usually lasted until dinner time, which was at 6.30 p.m. It commenced with the consumption of tea and biscuits. The "tea" was diluted blackcurrant syrup. The biscuits were invariably Choice Assorted. Everything was served on Krystle's fancy pink tea set that her grandmother had bought her for her fifth birthday. It was perhaps because she owned the tea set that Krystle was always the hostess. Genie was the neighbor who always somehow dropped in at exactly four o'clock, just in time for tea. Marcus, when he was there, was another neighbor who miraculously chose four o'clock as his visiting hour as well. His long absences during the school term were explained away by Marcus being a "secret agent" who was often assigned to the Soviet Union to do what he called "spy work."

Krystle had four teddy bears and five dolls—nine children in all. Three had been bought in America and six in South Africa. None, and this was a point of pride, had been bought locally. Her children were always there for four o'clock tea. Her husband, the father of her nine children, was an ar...chi... tect. She had met him when she was a jet-setting, internationally renowned ballerina. They had quickly fallen in love and married; a whirlwind romance. Now he was never at home because he was always flying all over the world building gorgeous buildings. Krystle did not seem to mind his absence.

Genie always attended four o'clock tea with her two children—the love-worn Penelope and the no-longer bespectacled Specs. Krystle felt sorry that this was all Genie had to show by way of children, but Genie was more than happy with her lot. Genie had no husband and had never been married.

She simply came with her two children to every tea party and never explained how it was possible to have children without a husband.

Marcus always attended alone. He was a bachelor, he said with pride, as though it was a mark of distinction. He had no children. But he had lots and lots of cars—the perks of being an international spy. Sometimes he came to tea on his model Lamborghini, sometimes his model Jaguar, sometimes his model Rolls-Royce.

And so it was. And so it had always been...Then, one Saturday afternoon, when Genie was thirteen years old, she went to a double feature of *Who Framed Roger Rabbit* and *Dirty Dancing* at Kine 600 with Suzanne Da Silva and came back transformed.

Suzanne was the only addition Genie had made to her life since moving in with the Masukus. She came from a place called the Philippines, a place that Krystle was still to locate in her world atlas, and therefore a place she doubted existed at all. Suddenly best friends, Genie and Suzanne spent all of break time at school giggling as they paged through *Archie* comics and *Sweet Valley High* novels that Suzanne had smuggled into school.

Krystle had not been allowed to attend the double feature because, as Genie explained, both films were PG-13 and Krystle was only ten years old. Krystle understood enough about rules to know that they were there to be strictly obeyed, so she was totally persuaded by Genie's explanation. What she did not understand was how the same rule did not apply to Suzanne, who was only twelve.

"Because Suzanne can pass for thirteen," Genie said, a little too matter-of-factly for Krystle's liking. This matter-of-factness was all the evidence that Krystle needed to prove what she had suspected from the moment Suzanne befriended Genie—Suzanne was not a good influence on Genie.

"I'll tell you all about it when I get back, I promise," Genie said as she walked out of their room with a flourish.

It did not seem to have occurred to Genie, the way it definitely had occurred to Krystle, that this was the first time in the three years they had known each other that one of them would be going to the movies without the other.

And Genie kept her promise: she told Krystle all about it —*everything*. Where they sat (front row), what they ate (chocolate-covered peanuts, Milko bars, and Freddos), whom they sat next to (an elderly couple who smelled delightfully of antiseptic soap on their right, and a group of teenage boys from Plumtree High School on their left who whistled for a long, long time when Jessica Rabbit came on the screen). "Who is Jessica Rabbit?" Krystle asked, although what she *really* wanted to know was why the boys had whistled at her.

Genie removed a packet of chocolate-covered peanuts, two Milko bars and two Freddos from her pink, heart-shaped purse, lay on her stomach next to Krystle, took a deep breath and for the next two hours told Krystle all about Roger and Jessica Rabbit and Johnny Castle and Baby, as they shared the chocolates. Genie spoke with the excited energy of someone who has just discovered something important.

Afterwards, Genie stood up and started humming and dancing. The only word that came to Krystle's mind as Genie hummed and danced around the room was...buzzing. She was suddenly like a bee—noisy, restless and forever busy...buzzing.

After that day, everything changed. Genie now bathed in their shared bathroom with the door locked. She no longer changed in front of Krystle. She emerged from the bathroom fully clothed. She no longer had time for Vaseline fights or lip-syncing in front of the bathroom mirror. Krystle suspected that this new occurrence had something to do with the two small lumps that had suddenly made themselves at home on Genie's chest.

In addition, Genie's vanity soon became cluttered with Impulse, Anaïs Anaïs and Mum 21, an impossible amount of lip gloss, every imaginable color of scrunchy and Alice band, and a rainbow of bangles. Neon green and shocking pink became her favorite colors; if an article of clothing had polka dots, she had to have it; and the only denim she would even consider wearing had to be "stonewashed." Genie would stand in front of the mirror trying on clothes that she now called "outfits," striking various poses, and, as though that were not enough, she spent an unforgivable amount of time talking to Suzanne on the phone.

Way too easily "Krystle and Genie" became "Genie and Suzanne." The entire situation was made even more unbearable by the fact that whenever Krystle asked Genie to explain something about her new transformation, Genie would say: "You're too young to understand." Their three-year age difference had never mattered before. It appeared to make a world of difference now.

Worse still, this new transformation seemed to require that Genie no longer attend Krystle's four o'clock tea parties because, as Genie explained, she no longer played with dolls. Penelope and Specs sat on Genie's bed, seemingly content to be mere decorations as they smiled pleasantly at nothing in particular. Krystle pouted for days and let herself feel the rejection that Penelope and Specs would not allow themselves to acknowledge. Her mother explained with a sad smile that Genie was now a teenager and on her way to becoming a woman, and as such was leaving childhood things behind.

Her mother's explanation would have made perfect sense had Genie left *all* childhood things behind, but she had not.

She had left all childhood things behind except *Button Moon*. Genie was obsessed with *Button Moon*. She watched it religiously every Wednesday at 3:05 p.m. Her obsession with the television puppet show had always surprised Krystle, who had never understood the attraction of the obviously handmade puppets attached to visible strings as they walked and gestured jerkily through their imitation of life. Krystle had never been able to suspend her disbelief and travel across Blanket Sky with the Spoon family—Mr. Spoon, Mrs. Spoon, Tina Tea-Spoon and Tina's friend, Egbert—to *Button Moon*. She instead preferred *She-Ra*, *Dungeons & Dragons* and *Danger Mouse*— she liked her cartoons to have definite heroines and heroes and definite villains, or "bad guys" as Marcus called them. But Genie loved *Button Moon* with a steadfastness that Krystle suspected had to do with bigger things that she was not privy to. She had never asked what these bigger things were because she strongly suspected that they had to do with the "time before," the time Genie and Marcus had spent on the Beauford Farm and Estate. She did not ask now because she was afraid that Genie was going to tell her that she was too young to understand.

One Wednesday, the two of them were waiting near the main gate of their school for their mother to come pick them up. Pickup time was between 1:00 and 1:30 p.m.

Krystle sat on her brown school suitcase. It had her name, misspelled KRYSTEL MASUKU, stenciled carefully onto it in white ink that did not interfere with the design of road traffic signs printed on the suitcase. Genie alternately stood or paced...buzzing. Finally she fished out two Everlastings—a black one and a brown one—from somewhere in the depths of her satchel. She held them both towards Krystle, giving her the first choice—licorice or toffee. Krystle made as though to grab both of them. They both laughed. And then Krystle chose the toffee. They each ate their Everlasting methodically. They both bit off a chunk of candy big enough to fit comfortably in the mouth. But whereas Genie would suck on the sweet, savoring the anise flavor of the licorice, Krystle munched through hers, chomping the toffee flavor to nothingness before quickly taking another bite.

As always, Krystle finished her Everlasting first, looked up at her big sister, then at her remaining half of the Everlasting. Smiling, Genie bit off a comfortable chunk and gave the remainder to Krystle. "Come on, get up. Let's go," Genie said, glancing at her shocking pink digital wristwatch.

"Where to?" Krystle asked.

"We'll go to your father's office."

If Genie had just said, "We'll go to dad's office," perhaps things would have happened differently. But she had not. And things had happened the way they had.

When Genie had first arrived to live with the Masukus, she had been asked to think of Krystle's parents as her new mother and father. Then she had been asked to call them mum and dad. Then she had been *told* to call them mum and dad. She never did.

"I don't wanna go," Krystle said, sitting back down.

"*Button Moon* starts in half an hour," Genie said, heading towards the padlocked gate.

There was a waiting room outside their father's office. And in that waiting room, mounted on a wall, there was a black-and-white, slightly snowy television set that would have to do under the circumstances.

"I'm not coming," Krystle said, folding her arms.

"Suit yourself," said Genie, prying open the loosely chained gate and squeezing through. "I'm sure your mum will be here to pick you up soon."

A school bell sounded and almost instantly there was the cacophony of laughter, running and general chaos. Krystle watched as girls in white shorts and t-shirts ran down the courtyard steps and towards the field. What if she was coerced into playing a sport she absolutely did not care for, like volleyball—all that irritating sand in your takkies? She got up in a flash and followed Genie out of the gate.

As soon as they were out of the gate, Genie took Krystle's suitcase from her, grabbed hold of Krystle's hand and started running as fast as she could. They ran down Borrow Street, zigzagged on pavements and crossed the street at Ninth Avenue in a dizzying dash that Krystle had to admit was thrilling and exhilarating. Luckily, 2:35 p.m. was not a popular time for traffic. By 2:45 they were at the clinic.

But as soon as Genie and Krystle turned the corner to their father's office, still hand in hand, they realized that something was wrong. One of the two nurses who assisted their father—the pleasant one who always smiled at them indulgently and gave them lollipops or Sugar Babies—was ushering patients out and looking very embarrassed. "Please go wait in the main lobby. I will come and call you in a little while, I apologize for the delay," she said, smiling nervously. She looked at Krystle and Genie, confused to see them there. Without knowing what else to do, she allowed them to follow her into the waiting room.

It was their mother's voice that greeted them. She was speaking so loudly that even the shut door to their father's office could not muffle or mute the sound of her voice.

"It is the sheer disrespect. The utter disregard that I take umbrage with."

"Umbrage?" Krystle and Genie were now close enough to hear their father's voice as well.

"Yes, umbrage. What? You think you're the only one who

is smart, because you have MD after your name? Smarter than the housewife? You forget, Dee, that I was on my way to being somebody when you knocked me up. Twice. And this man...this associate of yours...The Man Himself...he comes into my house, my home, and says because he owns you, I'm his property too."

"You must have known." Their father's voice was soft, conciliatory. "The house, the lifestyle came at a price—you must have known, Tee."

Their mother's voice was broken as she responded. "How dare you put me in a position like that. How dare you... you compromise me in that way. He didn't touch me. Not this time. But next time..."

"There won't be a next time. I promise."

"Oh, there'll be a next time. He wanted us both to know that. He wanted us to know that there will be a next time, and that neither one of us would be able to do anything about it. In prostituting yourself, you've prostituted me too. You were supposed to not let me down, Dee. What happened to not letting me down?"

Suddenly Genie grabbed Krystle's hand and they were off running again.

"Mum's crying."

"I know."

"Where are we going?"

"Suzanne lives close by. Maybe we can watch *Button Moon* at her flat."

Krystle did not like Suzanne da Silva at all. Understandably. "No. I'm not going."

"You want to go back there?" Genie asked, pointing a shaky finger in the direction of their father's office.

"You just want to watch stupid *Button Moon*."

"*Look & Listen* says this is the very last episode," Genie said, looking at her shocking-pink wristwatch...buzzing.

"Go. You don't care about me. You don't care that *my* mum is crying. You don't care that *my* mum and dad are fighting. You don't care about us at all."

"I care."

"Liar."

Genie bent down and put an arm around Krystle. "Parents sometimes fight. Don't worry. Everything will be fine."

"Did your parents fight?" It was the first time Krystle had ever mentioned Genie's parents.

"No," Genie said honestly. "All parents are different." She hugged Krystle. "If you're not coming with me, then promise me you'll not go back to the waiting room. Go sit in the lobby." She hugged her again. "I'll bring you something nice. Suzanne's mother likes to bake. I'll bring you some biscuits."

"I want a Cornish pasty."

"You always want a Cornish pasty," Genie said with a smile. "Remember to stay in the lobby. Make sure the receptionist knows you're there," she added before running off.

Krystle went back to the main lobby. It was chock-full of people; stifling. A man next to Krystle gurgled a cough that sounded highly contagious and she decided it was best to follow Genie after all.

She ran out. By the time she turned the corner Genie was ready to cross the street opposite the Sun Hotel. She waited impatiently...buzzing...for the traffic to whizz by. Krystle ran along the pavement as fast as she could, trying to catch up. Traffic cleared. Genie started running across the street. Krystle called out her name. Genie successfully crossed the street. Krystle called out her name again. Genie turned around. Saw Krystle approaching. Ran back across the street and...

That was when it happened. There was the screech of

tires as Kuki Carmichael's car came to an abrupt stop. And the next thing Krystle saw was Genie flying through the air, looking like something truly wondrous. There was a collective gasp of shock, awe and horror from the lookers-on. Before Krystle could even comprehend what was happening, Jesus swooped in and carried Genie away in his Scania pushcart. And as Krystle followed Jesus to the clinic, she believed that everything would be fine.

When Krystle returned to her father's office the waiting room was populated again. Someone had turned on the television and *"Button Moon"* had already started.

Her mother came out of the office just then, a mauve lipstick smile freshly painted on. Her father was close behind her with a smile on his lips as well. It was as if nothing had happened. "Chris! What are you doing here?" her parents both exclaimed at the same time, and then together they looked behind her expectantly.

"Where is Genie?" her father asked while her mother looked at her watch. "Oh dear...I was supposed to pick you up two hours ago," she said. "But where is Genie?"

Krystle told her parents what had happened—that Genie had flown briefly through the air like something truly wondrous, on her way to *Button Moon*. "She is all right though," she said to the worried frowns that had suddenly creased their foreheads. "Jesus saved her."

Kuki

As Kuki Carmichael watched Jesus walk along the pavement of Tenth Avenue pushing a Scania pushcart, she thought, and not for the first time, that he was the bravest man that she had ever known. It was while she was watching him that it happened. A girl went flying through the air and Kuki knew that all the important moments of her life had been leading to this exact moment and so, quite naturally, her life flashed before her eyes.

Her life, it seemed to her, had not begun at the moment of her birth, but on the day she gave birth to her son, a beautiful, golden-haired boy.

Perhaps because she could not find much strength in herself, Kuki had been attracted to brave people. Emil Coetzee had been a brave man. He had never been afraid to face danger and, actually, more often than not, had seemed to go in search of it. By the time Kuki met him, he had already wrestled a crocodile, dived through a waterfall, had an automobile drive over him and hunted a lion the good old-fashioned way, with an assegai, none of that monkeying around with rifles and shotguns for him. He had done all of this simply because he could.

Emil had been twenty-five at the time. He was tall. He was muscular. He was blond. He was a daredevil. Kuki at fifteen, with her freckles, her red hair cut in an unforgiving bob, her slightly overweight body, could not see how any girl could resist falling in love with Emil. And so she fell in love with him, even though Beatrice thought Emil Coetzee was a popinjay and a buffoon, a man too enamored with the idea he had of himself to be of any real use to anyone. Kuki knew that it was going to take some doing to get Emil Coetzee to marry her. He did not know her and she only knew him through his exploits in the paper. Added to which, he was an Afrikaner, and Kuki's parents, whose veins ran blue with the blood of good pioneers, would never countenance Kuki's marrying "one of those."

But although Kuki was not brave, she was very determined where Emil Coetzee was concerned. Having been born with very little beauty and no grace at all, Kuki gave herself three years to become beautiful and graceful enough for Emil. And she succeeded. Soon after her eighteenth birthday, she attended a dinner that she knew he would also be attending and had the satisfaction of turning every head when she entered the room, including Emil's.

Having vowed to be a bachelor for life, Emil Coetzee found himself seriously considering matrimony in his twenty-eighth year. He was an ambitious man with an ambitious plan. He had just proposed a program for a state domestic affairs unit—one that would gather all necessary intelligence on the citizens of the country. The country was changing rapidly, the African no longer knew his place. It was no longer enough to simply have a decentralized Native Affairs Commission, with commissioners scattered countrywide. There needed to be a centralized intelligence unit and Emil Coetzee wanted to be its head. He knew the proposal was appealing. Even so, the state hesitated. They talked to him about the expense of the thing, but he knew the real reason for their hesitation.

There were two reasons, actually: he was a single man, and he was an Afrikaner born and raised in South Africa. Being an

Afrikaner could be passed over, but as a single man, he would never be seen as serious and settled enough to head an entire state department. In order for his proposal to succeed, he needed to be married.

Kuki Sedgwick walked into his life at the right time.

He remembered her as a girl who, for years, had had nothing to recommend her; she had not blossomed the way most girls did. She had had to painstakingly cultivate what for most girls came naturally. However, whereas Kuki Sedgwick had had nothing to offer him during his avowed bachelor days, during which he had only had one use for women, now she did: her name. Sedgwick—proud, proper pioneer stock. Marrying a Sedgwick would fast-track his domestic affairs proposal. And so Emil Coetzee and Kuki Sedgwick got married.

When Kuki accepted Emil's proposal, she could not have known his reasons for marrying her. He told her of them during the course of their troubled marriage, whittling down her already fragile self-esteem.

For Kuki, the only good thing that issued from her union with Emil was a beautiful, golden-haired boy.

Kuki had known for years that her beautiful, golden-haired boy was not like most other boys. A mother knows these things. She just does. Even when she refuses to acknowledge them. She understood that her son was "artistic," but she loved him anyway. Emil, however, did not, in fact, *could* not, understand a son who was so very different from him. A son who wrote poetry that he shared publicly and who proudly sang at eisteddfods. A son who refused to go hunting or fishing because he thought killing a living thing for mere sport was inhumane—barbaric, even. A son who, although he had Rosamond for a girlfriend, was too "chummy" by half with Vida, the Coloured De Villiers boy.

When their son was eighteen, he was called up to defend his country against the terrorists. The son, who did not believe in killing living things, had no desire to fight. It was not a war in which he believed. Kuki did not want her son to fight in the war, not because she did not think it was a war worth fighting, but because he was her only child and he was beautiful and precious. In Emil's mind there was no doubt that his son would fight to defend his country. It would be just the thing to make him a man—to make him worth his salt. The delicate balance within the Coetzee household gave way. Words were uttered by the father that let the son know that he was deficient in some way. Words were uttered by the son that let the father know that he was deficient in every way. The mother lacked the courage to do anything other than watch as the father and the son deliberately broke each other's hearts and left the pieces on the floor for her to pick up and mend where possible.

Eventually, the son went to war and never came back, choosing instead to step on a landmine and be blown to pieces that not even Kuki could put back together again.

At first, Kuki did not see how she could continue living in a world that suddenly found itself without her beautiful, golden-haired boy in it. To continue living would be a kind of betrayal, she thought. She felt that the rest of her days would have to be lived out in bed, wrapped in unrelenting emotional pain and unbearable sadness. But she did carry on living. In fact, she became active: making funeral arrangements, attending her only child's funeral, moving out of Emil Coetzee's house, moving into her own apartment, filing for a divorce, being (finally) granted a divorce. In all, she spent only three days in bed wrapped in unrelenting emotional pain and unbearable sadness. Instead of standing still, her life seemed to propel itself forward. Now, she actually had the courage to take initiative. Still, she could not help but think that this was the courage that could have saved her son's life. It had come too late and in its belatedness it seemed like a mockery.

Living alone for the first time in her life, Kuki prepared herself to welcome a crushing loneliness. Loneliness would be the perfect commemoration of her son. Loneliness was not what she welcomed, however; what she welcomed was the friendship of one Todd Carmichael.

When terrorists attacked his homestead while he was in Geneva, Switzerland, trying to bring a peaceable end to the war, Todd Carmichael lost his entire family—his wife, his son, his daughter, his dog, his maid and his gardener. This friendship with Todd Carmichael was Kuki's second betrayal, the first being leaving her mourning bed. He made her laugh, which was the third betrayal. Kuki started caring enough for Todd to care what she looked like in his eyes: she started jogging, she put herself on a series of strict diets, she tried (unsuccessfully) to kick her pack-of-Everests-a-day habit, and she put her face through numerous regimes to get rid of the wrinkles that were yet to appear. Trying to be attractive to a man was the fourth betrayal. The fifth betrayal was that she became comfortable in Todd's presence. Todd asked her to marry him and she accepted, perhaps a little too readily, and Kuki thought this sixth betrayal to be the biggest of them all. This last betrayal—one allowing the unrelenting pain and unbearable sadness to gradually give way to the selfish and immeasurable joys of living—was so great that Kuki felt certain that she would never forgive herself. She tortured herself with images of her golden-haired boy every night, as soon as she closed her eyes, and every morning, just before she opened her eyes.

One day Kuki woke up and could not quite readily remember the beautiful, golden-haired boy's face and the many expressions it had held. She surreptitiously looked at his photograph on the mantelpiece so that she could remember what her son had looked like on the day he had left for war. But the picture on the mantelpiece was not to be trusted. He, who had always worn his hair rather long, had a buzz cut. His face, which had always been soft and gentle, was more angular, mature and stern. In that picture he seemed to be everything he was not: proud of his country, proud to defend it, proud to be the kind of man who defended his country. In other words, proud to be his father's son.

The photograph on the mantelpiece was not a remembrance at all. The boy she had seen kissing Vida de Villiers and then looking at him with such love was not in that picture. The boy who sang with the voice of an angel at eisteddfods was not in that picture. The boy who wrote award-winning poetry was not in that picture. Her son was not in that picture, but Kuki could not bring herself to throw away the photograph. It was the last photograph that had been taken of him. And this too, this not being able to throw away the photograph of her not-quite son, this too was betrayal.

Years after the war had ended, an army buddy—that is how the young man had identified himself, as an army buddy—had brought to Kuki what he must have thought was a gift. The young man had been on the verge of leaving the country for Canada and, while packing, had come across a photograph of the beautiful, golden-haired boy. In the photograph the golden-haired boy was leaning against a Jeep, shirtless save for the dog tags hanging from his neck, cigarette dangling dangerously from his lips, arms crossed. His fatigue trousers and military boots seemed too big for him. He looked as though he was just about to laugh or had just finished laughing.

Kuki did not know quite what to do with the photograph. The man—and he was a man indeed, no longer a beautiful, golden-haired boy—the man in the picture did not resemble her son at all. He seemed like a younger version of Emil... and proud of it. There was an iconic photograph of Emil Coetzee, taken when he was about the same age, leaning against a car and reveling in his youthful invincibility. It was not rational, she knew, but she felt that the beautiful boy had demanded that the picture be taken because he wanted her to see the result of her lack of bravery. Though the black paint he had put on his face made him look fierce, and even though a smile lingered on his face, his blue eyes looked dead. The gift photograph let her know that, even if he had survived the war, her beautiful, golden-haired boy would never have fully returned.

Not allowing herself to think too much about what she was doing, Kuki had taken the photograph of the son she did not recognize and thrown it into the fireplace. She had watched as the photograph contorted and the image blistered and distorted before it burnt to ashy nothingness. The burning of that photograph was the only thing she did after the death of her beautiful, golden-haired boy that did not feel like a betrayal.

Perhaps her many betrayals would not have seemed so great had Vida de Villiers not become a vagabond. He too had loved her son. He too had lost him. He, however, had chosen not to carry on without him, choosing instead to vacate the world in his own unique way. Whenever she saw Vida on the street, wrapped in his unrelenting pain and unbearable sadness, resolutely refusing to propel his life forward, so far removed from everyone around him, even as he pushed his Scania pushcart among them, she envied him for having found a way not to betray the beautiful, golden-haired boy that he had loved. She envied him his bravery. She always stopped to look at him, fascinated by his ability to do what she could not do, and that was what she was doing when she sent a girl in a blue and white uniform flying through the air.

Everleigh, "he is sun-kissed perfection. Such a delight." She leaned forward and kissed Vida on the lips.

Vida was confused. He had reconciled himself to the fact that he liked boys. He had come to realize that he was not alone—that there were others like him here, there and everywhere. There were names, most of them unpleasant, for people like him. These names, no matter how much they were meant to injure and vilify, gave him comfort because they acknowledged (whether they wanted to or not) the existence of someone like him. Without a name something does not, cannot, will not exist. With a name, something cannot help but exist. He was a moffie and that was that. He existed.

But here was Rosamond presenting him with something else entirely: something without a name. It terrified him. It threatened his existence. Since he liked both boys *and* girls, what did that make him? He had never heard of a name for such a person. Did such a hybrid thing even exist? If it did not exist, then what did that make him: an aberration, an anomaly, an abnormality...something wrong?

"Don't worry. It's simple," Everleigh said, kissing him on the shoulder, understanding, as always, what he was going through. "Don't complicate it."

And in that moment Vida knew he was not alone.

He felt content and fulfilled and complete.

It was a charmed life. Everleigh was eighteen, Rosamond seventeen. They were young and felt justified in not having any care in the world save the pleasure of each other's company. But there was a war raging. Everleigh was called up. Not long thereafter he stepped on a landmine. Rosamond went to seek refuge in a convent. Vida prematurely joined the army, hoping that he would die too. He did not. Instead it was his parents who died. Together. In a car crash. And just like that love ceased to exist in his life. In its place came anger. He had

had no idea that life could be so devastating, God so uncaring, and the world so cruel.

He was so filled with anger that he could not even cry. The closest he came to crying was listening to Janis Joplin's raw and wailing voice. In that voice he could clearly hear hurt that was deep and still festering. He used her voice as a surrogate. When he was deployed to Tongaland to help patrol the border to ensure that the terrorists did not cross into or out of the country, he took his small cassette player with him and listened to Janis Joplin every chance he got. He did not care if Janis Joplin alerted the terrorists to his whereabouts; in fact, he wished she would. Tongaland was known as the "hot seat" of the war because of its proximity to the border, so Vida had been convinced that that was where he would meet his end and he awaited it with a determined resolve.

However, he found Tongaland uncommonly calm and peaceful for a war zone and the natives too hospitable for a people so heavily policed, constantly under surveillance and regularly mistreated by both the soldiers and terrorists alike. He soon learned why. The Tonga people grew and consumed two crops in abundance—marijuana and moringa. The former left them feeling peaceful and easy, the latter made them feel satisfied and content. They had found a way to live with devastation, uncaring gods and an oh-so-cruel world, and they generously shared their knowledge with Vida.

And that was how Vida spent his war—in Tongaland, listening to Janis Joplin and feeling peaceful, easy, satisfied and content. He still felt the loss of love but numbed himself to the pain of that loss. He would never love again—of that he was determined, certain. He owed it to those he had loved and lost to never love again. To love again would make meaningless the love he had already received and the love he had already given. If he survived the war, and he really hoped that he would not, then he was determined to live a life that would make love impossible.

One day, September 3, 1978, to be exact, standing camouflaged in the tall, yellow, almost golden elephant grass of Tongaland, a feeling came over Vida that he could not put into words. He was standing in the field alone, but he no longer felt alone. He could somehow feel the sway of the elephant grass tingle in his fingertips, the flap of a bird's wings overhead whisper in his ear, the richness of the soil coat his tongue. He was in the presence of something that filled him with a sense of wonder. He liked the feeling, but could not put it into words. It was something that he could only experience, not name, and for that he liked it better.

He did not feel it for long, however. Before he could comprehend what had happened, he was squinting down the barrel of an AK-47. This is it, he thought. Finally, the end. Perhaps that was what the feeling had been...a heralding...a way of knowing before the fact...an experience of wonderment before dying.

But instead of shooting him, the man carrying the AK-47 lowered it and looked Vida straight in the eye.

"My name is Golide Gumede," the man said. "You will remember me."

"My name is Vida de Villiers," Vida said before he could stop himself.

"You think you are telling me something I do not already know," the man, Golide Gumede, said with a gap-toothed smile that oddly seemed to Vida to be all too familiar.

When the war ended, Vida made his life on the street. His hair and beard grew long from lack of care, and the people of the street christened him Jesus.

During the day, Vida roamed the city streets and at night

he slept in the alleyway behind Downings' Bakery. For a bum, a vagrant, a vagabond, a derelict, a homeless person, a stray —whatever you chose to call people like him—the alleyway behind Downings' Bakery on Grey Street was prime real estate. It was best during winter, when the heat from the ovens, which were turned on at 3:00 a.m., seeped through the bakery walls and made for a comfy and cozy second half of sleep. He particularly liked to rest his back against the bakery walls, letting the heat invade his body while the warm smell of baking bread enveloped him.

For Vida, there was nothing like waking up to the warm smell of freshly baked bread. It made every day seem as if it would have infinite possibilities. The smell was like a promise, a contract even, the city's pledge to take care of its citizens— a guarantee, almost, of its ability to do so.

He could not believe his luck when he found the Downings' Bakery alleyway unoccupied when he returned from the war. Granted, in 1980, with the country newly independent, there had not been many bums, vagrants, vagabonds, derelicts, homeless persons or strays—just a lot of optimism and fresh starts. But what street dwellers (and that was what Vida pre-ferred to call bums, vagrants, vagabonds, derelicts, homeless persons and strays) there were, were extremely territorial, cordoning off entire sections of the city as theirs—the privi-lege of having plenty because there are only a few of you.

The original colonial street dwellers had been exclusively white; the colonial city had, after all, been exclusively white. The original colonial street dwellers were comprised of poor whites, retired prostitutes, people who would have been better served in a mental institution, and a few old-timers that time and empire had forgotten.

The post-war period saw a considerable increase in street dwellers. Some, like Vida, had belonged to the armed forces, some had been freedom fighters or terrorists (depending on who was talking), others were civilians who had been traumatized by the war but whom the overflowing mental hospitals could not accommodate, others still had left the rural areas when the war heated up and marooned themselves in the relative safety of the city. Most of them had seen things that made them retreat into an inner world that they had absolute control over. These postcolonial newcomers learned to coexist with the colonial settlers. The post-war street dwellers were a truly multiracial lot and probably the country's best example of post-war tolerance and reconciliation.

During the day, they were joined by a slew (some called it an onslaught) of blind and otherwise handicapped beggars. They walked or hobbled around with Kango enameled tin plates or mugs in their hands, shaking them in order to clink and chink the coins at the bottom. They were often led by their able-bodied children. The beggars sang or played an instrument, or both, singing or playing mostly religious songs, while their children actively asked for money, both beggar and child stopping to say "Thank you" when the sound of a coin chinked onto the tin surface. It was a harmony that quickly became a part of the postcolonial city. The beggars were extremely gifted singers and musicians, one and all.

Vida's favorite musician was Shadrack, a man whose legs had been amputated below the knee when he was a child to stop the spread of leprosy. Shadrack traveled the city streets on his hands—he pulled himself forward in a swinging motion and crossed the streets faster than anyone Vida knew. Shadrack had fashioned cushions for his hands out of pantyhose stuffed with plastic bags, strips of fabric and cotton wool. He always had an Olivine-can guitar that he had made himself strapped to his back. Shadrack played it in a way that would have reduced Jimi Hendrix to tears. And, man, what a voice.

What he could do to The Beatles' "While My Guitar Gently Weeps"....For Vida, there was nothing like being high on premium Tonga dagga while listening to the twang of Shadrack's Olivine-can guitar. That made a good day phenomenal.

The blind and otherwise handicapped beggars were not street dwellers per se, because every evening they left the city with the rush-hour throng heading westward towards the townships. They had homes, families, responsibilities. And that was what made them leave the townships every morning with the rush-hour throng heading eastward: they came to make a living.

That was the fundamental difference between the street beggars and the street dwellers: the street dwellers did not beg. They did not need to. They were not trying to make a living, educate children or be productive members of society. Besides, they were always well provided for.

The Salvation Army doled out clothing twice a year, at the beginning of winter and at the beginning of the rainy season, for anyone who wanted something new—well, something new to them. For food there were restaurants, bakeries and butcheries; if you were not actually handed a plate (usually at the service entrance), you were sure to find something in the rubbish thrown out every night after closing. A street dweller could actually eat better than your average productive citizen.

That was in the 1980s.

In the 1990s things began to change. Suddenly there was an onslaught—an actual onslaught and not just a slew—of a new breed of street dwellers. And they were all children. The state chose to call them "street kids." The street kids came to the city to both beg and live.

There had been a code of ethics among street dwellers and between street dwellers and street beggars. There was no camaraderie, at least not on the part of the former. You did not take to the streets because you wanted to make friends. Friends (like families) had expectations and created obligations. You took to the streets to free yourself of expectations and obligations. You took to the streets because you wanted to be left alone—or rather because you wanted the privacy that could only come from living publicly, from having people pretend not to see you. No, there was no camaraderie, but there was a code of ethics, a social contract that governed life on the street: you respected other people's property, zones, marks, clients and customers; you neither interfered nor intervened; you lived your life however you wanted and left all else well enough alone.

The street kids did not abide by any of these codes. They formed cliques that more often than not became gangs, got high on glue, which they pilfered from Hassamals and Esats, and then set about doing whatever they needed to get by. Everything and everyone was fair game. They had no respect —none whatsoever—for anything or anyone. Vida did not really blame them. Most were the orphaned children of parents who had died during the liberation war or because of the AIDS pandemic. Life had dealt them a particularly cruel hand. Their glass was definitely empty. If they chose to say "Up yours" back to the world, so be it. But their presence definitely made being a street dweller less quiet and comfortable.

It was because of the street kids that a lot of the old-timers were displaced. Mick, Vida's occasional companion, was pushed out of his cushy place behind the Colcom Butchery and lost with it his steady diet of pork pies, sausages, bacon and polony. Before Mick was forced out, he and Vida had had an understanding: Mick would provide cold slices of polony and Vida would provide warm bread. There are very few things in life that come together as perfectly as warm

Downings' bread and cold Colcom polony—and together Vida and Mick would feast like kings, which was only fitting since they lived in the City of Kings.

Those days were gone. Mick was not happy. Many of the old-timers were not happy.

Vida worried—and Vida did not like to worry because it felt too much like caring—about the future of things.

The street kids' arrival created so many disturbances that, after twelve years of living by the street code, Vida had been forced to break it. Because of the street kids, he found himself doing something he had vowed never to do: involving himself in the lives of those around him.

When Joseph Pereira—one of the old-timers, a real veteran of the street—had told one of the street kids, a girl of about fifteen who had taken over his particular corner of the Main Post Office's courtyard, to go home to her parents, she had told him, "Go back home to England." When Joseph had retorted that even though his ancestors had originally come from Portugal, his family had been in Africa for so many centuries that Portugal had long ceased to be home, the girl had replied: "My home can never be your home." She punctuated her point by putting her arm as close to his as she could without actually touching him. And Vida had had to watch the heart of a man well over seventy years old break. As consolation, Vida had offered Joseph a ride down Selborne Avenue on his Scania pushcart. Usually Joseph jumped at the chance, but this time he just smiled sadly and put a hand on Vida's shoulder and said, "I'll see you around, my son." Joseph was found the next morning having hanged himself in the Main Post Office courtyard next to the "P" plaque commemorating those who had died defending the British Empire in World War II. He was dressed in full military regalia. It was Vida who cut him down and waited with his body until the police came. The police reprimanded him for interfering with the scene of the crime. Vida understood their anger, but he was not sorry for intervening because he firmly believed that Joseph Pereira's death deserved dignity, and a man whose body is left hanging for too long loses his dignity.

Then there had been the fight between David and Goliath.

David had become a street dweller a few years after Vida. Unlike most postcolonial street dwellers, he was not a casualty of war. His story was unique, and perhaps because it was unique, it was the most unfortunate that Vida had heard. David lived on the street because he had not been able to go overseas to finish his education. It was the simplicity of his circumstance that made it tragic. A brilliant boy, with a scholarship to attend Harvard University, but a family too poor and resourceless to get him there. A stroke of luck presented itself when the community and church rallied and came up with most of the money for his airfare. Nonetheless, at the embassy David's lack of funds proved to be an issue— although he had a scholarship, he still needed money for living expenses, which, in Cambridge, Massachusetts, were prohibitive, the bespectacled lady behind the desk sadly informed him...before denying him a visa. His prospects were dashed. His brilliant mind, having touched the cusp of something beautiful, disintegrated.

From that day, David estranged himself from his surroundings and eventually took to the street. He talked to himself, kept to himself, and occupied himself by reading *The Chronicle* from front page to sports page every day—silently mouthing every word. He religiously completed the daily Target and did both the easy and cryptic crossword puzzles. All the street dwellers knew to leave him alone. All, that is, except Goliath, the puny but dangerous and malicious leader of the most notorious gang of street kids, "The Survivors."

The Survivors were organized and they engaged in every base activity—they broke into cars to steal radios and whatever else they could get their hands on, they picked the pockets of the office workers, they snatched the purses of unsuspecting old ladies, and, for whatever reason, they liked to beat up the boys from Milton Junior School and shout obscenities at the girls from Townsend High School. Of course there had always been gangs of car thieves, pickpockets and purse-snatchers, but these gangs had tended to be amorphous. With his many years on the street, Vida had witnessed a purse snatch here, heard a car alarm go off there, occasionally seen a pocket picked , but he had never seen any gang worthy of the name. Goliath, to be sure, was the leader of a gang, and the members of his Survivors were known to all who lived on the streets.

On the day of the fight between David and Goliath, one of the members of The Survivors snatched *The Chronicle* from David while he was reading it. In the blink of an eye, David had his fingers wedged on either side of the kid's windpipe. Then there was the sound of glass breaking and Goliath was wielding a broken brown bottle of Castle Lager, jabbing the jagged edges towards David's face. Goliath lunged. David flung the street kid against the wall. For once, they both were after the same thing: blood. Vida knew that he had no choice but to intervene. For his troubles, he got the jagged edge of a Castle Lager bottle embedded in his right shoulder, but at least the only blood that had been shed that day had been his.

Another time Vida had tried to intervene was when he had seen a girl (she could not have been more than eleven years old) enter the car of a well-known Indian businessman who had a penchant for streetwalkers. He mostly preferred the black prostitutes (Vida liked to call them The Painted Ladies because of their pink lips, blue eyelids and dangerously long, red, tapered fingernails) who stood outside Kine 600 and Elite 400 and did especially good business after a Stallone or Norris or Seagal or Van Damme late-night double feature when testosterone levels were predictably high, along with the desire to conquer something, anything. But sometimes the Indian man liked to mix it up. He had picked up Vida once or twice. Picking up such a young girl, however, was going too far in Vida's book. When Vida tried to remove the girl from the passenger seat, she slapped him across the face and told him that she also needed to survive on the streets and slammed the door in his face. He heard the Indian businessman chuckle and say "Next time, Jesus, next time" before driving away. The next day the girl was beaten to within an inch of her life by The Painted Ladies. They took the money (twenty dollars) that she had made. The girl joined The Survivors after that and did not look happy about any of it.

Whenever Vida intervened in such affairs that were not his own, he was reluctant to break the street code. Once, though, Vida had willingly intervened in something happening on the street—when he had seen Golide Gumede's daughter, Imogen Zula Nyoni, fly through the air like a thing of sheer beauty...a wondrous something in the sky. She would have landed broken on the ground but instead she had landed in his Scania pushcart, her fall cushioned by the quilt his mother had made for him. He had no idea how he had managed to get to her so quickly but he had.

She had looked up at him.

"You're Jesus, aren't you?"

"Yes," he had said, hesitating slightly.

"You don't look like Jesus."

"I know."

"Why they call you Jesus then?"

"I think it is because of the long hair and the beard."

"And the kind eyes."

He had smiled down at her. She had smiled up at him.

"Maybe you should cut your hair and shave off your beard."

"Maybe I should."

"Maybe you are afraid that people will stop calling you Jesus if you do."

He had seen her clearly then for the first time. "Maybe I am."

"No matter. You'll still have the kind eyes," she had said. He had smiled down at her. She had smiled up at him.

"You will remember me"—that was what Golide Gumede had foretold. Vida looked at the gap between Imogen's front teeth and he did remember. He remembered the feel of the sway of the elephant grass tingle in his fingertips...the presence of something that filled him with a sense of wonder...a heralding.

And then Vida noticed Genie's blood blooming on the quilt and at that very moment he wanted no other meaning for his life but to save her.

Marcus

It was the day after Krystle's thirteenth birthday party that Marcus discovered the truth between Genie and him.

They were sitting under a jacaranda tree that was fully in bloom. She was making something out of its purple flowers and he hoped that whatever she was making was for him. He was lying beside her—watching, content.

It was a lazy Sunday morning, the best kind of morning.

He had just finished telling her that he had managed to sneak a drink at the birthday party when none of the adults were looking, whisky he thought it was, when she said: "Did you know elephants can swim?" He shook his head, no. "You'd think it impossible, wouldn't you? But it isn't. They float. I saw them on the Zambezi River when I went to visit my grandfather last year." Her voice was filled with awe. "Imagine that. Elephants floating as though they were as light as feathers."

Marcus just looked at her, aware that something was changing between them.

"They are magnificent. You should see them. Promise me one day you'll go to see them."

He found himself nodding his promise.

"It is the most beautiful thing you will ever see."

Marcus doubted that very much, because at that very moment he was witnessing the most beautiful thing he had ever seen: Imogen Zula Nyoni surrounded by the bluey purple of jacaranda flowers. He doubted very much that he would ever see anything more beautiful.

"The ancient river and the mighty animal in perfect harmony...a rite of passage made sacred by its sheer audacity." Genie, at sixteen, was able to construct such sentences because she unashamedly read and understood Shakespeare, loved Jane Austen's novels and frequently read poetry without any prompting or provocation. "There is a wonder to it all...the possibility of the seemingly impossible...And there's this feeling that you get...a knowing...You become aware of your place in the world...You understand that in the grander scheme of things you are but a speck...a tiny speck...and that that is enough. There is freedom, beauty even, in that kind of knowledge...and it is the kind of knowledge that finally quiets you. It is the kind of knowledge that allows you to fly...You have to experience it for yourself," she said, smiling at him, her face brilliant and beatific.

For his part, Marcus, at seventeen, was able to appreciate her words because he loved beautiful things.

He had at some point stopped breathing, but he could hear his heart beating strongly.

So this was how it was going to happen for him? For him it would not be about sunlight or moonlight, about a gentle breeze lifting the skirt of her dress just so, a flower in her hair, a peal of laughter. No, for him it would be about swimming elephants under a jacaranda tree. "Genie." His voice could not be more than a whisper. She looked at him then. He took a breath that was sharply cut short. So this is what is meant by "take my breath away," Marcus mused. She smiled at him. "Genie I—"

Then laughter entered her eyes.

Marcus immediately lost his courage. If he told her what he felt and she laughed at him, he would never recover. He needed to find something else to say. Retreat somehow.

"Welcome," she said, the laughter still in her eyes.

He was confused.

"I think we're on the same page. Finally."

Without really knowing what he was doing—or preparing for it—he kissed her smile. She kissed him back briefly and then stopped. All laughter gone. She left him, amid those bluey-purple jacaranda flowers, confused about everything but the swimming elephants.

Krystle

On the day after her thirteenth birthday, Krystle had woken up to a sound of something that she had never heard before in the house; the sound was so foreign that for a moment she believed that she was still dreaming. Someone was speaking with a raised, angry voice. Marcus. Why was Marcus, the good child, angry? The question was too tantalizing for Krystle to leave uninvestigated. She had long made plans for this morning, the morning that would usher her into womanhood. She had spent most of the morning in bed, feeling every bit the lady, but when she heard the commotion downstairs she quickly tossed the bed linen aside and jumped out of bed. As she was putting on her slippers, the thought occurred to her that her sudden appearance in the kitchen would put an end to whatever was going on there. And so she carefully and stealthily made her way down the stairs.

The house still smelled delicious and inviting from all the party food that had been served the day before. Krystle entered the kitchen to find the most extraordinary scene: her parents, in their matching satin nightclothes, were sitting... no, cowering...at the yellow Formica table, with Marcus (who in the last two years, to his utter relief and probable disbelief, had had a rapid growth spurt) towering over them, looking at the tops of their heads. "I want to hear it from the both of you," he said in a way that made her parents huddle together. Even though they were sitting in the center of the kitchen, they seemed cornered by Marcus. Their eyes were downcast, refusing to see anything other than the yellow surface of the Formica table. They both looked...guilty.

When Krystle saw her parents' look of guilt, she knew instinctively that something was changing, and that the change would be irreparable.

Genie was sitting in the breakfast nook, her legs folded beneath her, her arms wrapped around her body; she looked as though she was trying to occupy as little space as possible. She was not looking at anyone in particular—she seemed to have withdrawn into herself. She had obviously been crying. This terrified Krystle more than her parents' guilt. Genie had never cried: not when she first arrived to live with the Masukus; not when Marcus decided that his first real girlfriend was to be Anesu, his second Buhle, and his third Coleen; not even when Kuki Carmichael sent her flying through the air. Genie had never cried. Until now.

Krystle's grandmother, Eunice, stood by the oven in her trusted terry cloth nightgown, wig slightly askew, arms resolutely crossed under her breasts, her mouth twisted into a tight and determined knot, and her eyes looking quizzically, almost critically, at the yellow-and-gray checkerboard pattern of the floor as though seeing it for the first time and finding irredeemable fault with it.

They all looked like actors in a play, but Krystle could not tell, as yet, if she was one of the actors or part of the audience.

"Say it," Marcus said.

"Marcus, please," her father said, reaching out to touch him.

"Say it!" Marcus screamed, stopping her father's hand before it reached its destination.

"Genie is HIV-positive," her grandmother said, generously untwisting her knotted mouth.

"So you keep saying. But I want to hear it from them. It has been *their* secret."

"I am HIV-positive, Marcus," Genie said, still not looking at anyone.

"But how?" Marcus asked. "HIV is a sexually transmitted disease and Genie has never..."

Marcus sat down, defeated, opposite his parents, but now that his eyes were level with theirs, he chose not to look at them. He placed his hands on the table carefully instead, almost delicately, and watched them tremble.

Just at the point when the silence was threatening to become oppressive, her father said: "HIV/AIDS can...can be transmitted sexually, but there are other...other ways." As always her father was trying to reach for facts in a time of uncertainty, but that was all he said before realizing that he could not bring himself to say more.

"Like between mother and child," her mother added, supporting her husband, but her voice lacked the certainty and authority that his voice would have conveyed.

"My mother was not HIV-positive," Genie said with an unshakeable firmness in her voice.

"No...no one, I'm sure, was suggesting that...that she was ...As I said there are other...other ways. Blood...blood transfusions with contaminated blood, for example. Many...many other ways," her father explained, more to the yellow Formica table than to Genie.

Silence filled the space between them again.

Suddenly there was sound; a...buzzing. At first Krystle believed that the buzzing was in the room. Then she realized that the buzzing was coming from within. It was inside her. She heard her voice call out Genie's name. She saw Genie turn and run back across the street. She heard the screech of tires as Kuki Carmichael's car came to an abrupt stop. She saw Genie flying through the air for a brief moment before landing in Jesus' Scania pushcart. She saw Jesus smile down at Genie. She saw Genie smile up at Jesus. She saw her ten-year-old self smile too, fooled into thinking that everything was all right.

She realized now that Genie and Jesus had deceived her.

She looked around the room and realized that her family was deceiving her now.

Krystle looked at her family—her parents looking at the yellow Formica table, Marcus looking at his trembling hands, her grandmother looking at the yellow-and-gray checkerboard floor, and Genie looking at the nothingness in front of her—and realized something: it was not that they were actively not looking at each other, it was that they were determined not to look at her. They were shielding her from what lay in their eyes. Accusation.

She suddenly felt hot. Her body tingled...buzzing. She felt something liquid and warm ooze between her thighs. She knew she was leaving childhood things behind. In their place she welcomed guilt as her constant companion.

Krystle ran out of the kitchen and up the stairs, aware that whatever was oozing out of her body was staining her lily white panties, embossed with the word "Sunday" in dainty cursive letters. Sure enough, when she got to her pink bedroom and removed her panties, she found their lily whiteness stained with a brownish-red liquid. Womanhood...not at all a pretty sight. She got into bed, determined not to tell her mother or grandmother of this latest occurrence and wishing with all her heart that the brownish-red liquid oozing out of her would soak the bed linen, seep through to the mattress and leave an indelible stain that would have to be reckoned with forever.

She willed herself not to cry, but, of course, she cried. She willed herself not to wait for someone to come and comfort her, but, of course, she waited for someone (any member of her family, she was not feeling particularly particular) to come and comfort her. No one came. Not in time.

Hours later, Genie entered the room with a smile on her face and sat on the corner of Krystle's bed as though the scene in the kitchen had never happened.

"Please forgive me," Krystle whimpered.

"There is nothing to forgive," Genie said with a smile that Krystle knew was deceptive.

From that day, Krystle had learned a truth about her family —they were not to be trusted. Not one of them. For if there was really nothing to forgive, why had her family never talked about Genie's accident and Krystle's role in it? If there was really nothing to forgive, why had her family never brought up that incident in the kitchen, which they all knew Krystle had witnessed?

In her more generous moods, Krystle allowed herself to entertain the thought that her family probably meant to be kind. But did they not know that it was cruel to not allow her to talk about the accident and her role in it; to go to such great lengths to make her not feel responsible for Genie's illness, the illness that would some day surely kill her; to make her suffer under the weight of her guilt silently and alone?

Every time Krystle said, "Please forgive me," the answer came back the same, "There is nothing to forgive." Every time.

And Genie, perhaps unwittingly (Krystle was never quite sure), added insult to injury by returning to her old kind and caring self, by playing the role of the loving older sister. Perhaps Genie had always put on a persona, from the very moment she became part of the family, and had simply been whoever the Masukus wanted and needed her to be—the unproblematic daughter, the patient peacemaker, the humble high achiever, the grateful charity case that made the rest of the family feel good about their wealth and privilege, the brave young woman absolutely unfazed by the devastating news of being HIV-positive.

Krystle began to suspect then that Genie was like Scheherazade herself, but instead of trafficking in tales, she trafficked in performances: a thousand and one performances. There was no real, original Genie to be found. Perhaps there had never been a real, original Genie. Only iterations.

For the next two years Genie laughed, loved and lived as though nothing in her life had changed...until one afternoon, on the day of her eighteenth birthday, without warning, she picked up all the belongings with which she had entered the house and made her way to Jesus. Genie had entered the room as a ten-year-old girl with Penelope and Specs held under one arm and an old suitcase under the other. Those were all the possessions she had, and to her they were precious. When she left eight years later that was all she took—Penelope, Specs and an old suitcase stuffed with clothes that no longer fitted, still her most precious possessions.

PART V

———◆———

Epidemiology
Love in the Time of HIV

Vida

———•———

There was sunshine. And then there was no sunshine.

"Jesus," a female voice said.

Vida opened his eyes, squinted and looked up. She was so... incandescent. He had to shield his eyes. The sun behind her made her reddish-brown hair look like a flaming halo. It took him a second to realize who it was. It was Golide Gumede's daughter, Imogen Zula Nyoni. The girl he had caught as she went flying through the air what seemed to be a lifetime ago. She inclined her head to the left, bringing the sun suddenly back, directly into his eyes. He shut his eyes tightly and swore.

"You saved my life once. Thank you," she said, then waited.

What was he supposed to say to that? He had nothing to say. But she was obviously expecting him to say something. He did not like people expecting things of him. "There's no need to thank me. I just happened to be there. Just at the right place at the right time, I suppose," he said finally, his eyes still closed.

Suddenly he felt the warmth of the sun full on him. Had she walked away? He hoped she had, hoped his indifference had let her know that he was a lost cause. But even as he was hoping she had left him alone, he knew he was not going to be that lucky. He felt her sit down beside him.

"You saved my life. And now I'm here to save yours," her voice said.

The scent of vanilla...and something else...woodsmoke. He held his breath. He did not like smelling people. He tried very hard never to do so. He always held his breath when someone passed by too close. There is something highly intimate about smelling another human being. It is a taking-in of sorts—a sharing, an absorbing, a consuming of another. It is just one step away from taste. Hearing, seeing, touching, smelling and tasting: that was the hierarchy of the senses in ascending order according to Vida. He liked to delegate most of his human interaction to the first two senses. But here was Golide Gumede's daughter, and after only a few seconds of acquaintance the scent of vanilla had already invaded his body and become a part of him. He exhaled and, having held his breath for so long, had to open his mouth. The scent of vanilla in his mouth was obscenely close to the sensation of taste. Something fluttered in the pit of his stomach and made him uneasy.

He had no choice but to open his eyes, turn his head and look at her. His eyes still adjusting to the sun, he saw her in a haze. She was sitting on a suitcase and in her arms she unabashedly held a rag doll and a teddy bear. How old was she? Too old to be walking around with toys in her arms, in broad daylight, in the city. She smiled at him, revealing the gap between her two front teeth, which for some reason made that something flutter in the pit of his stomach again, which in turn made him angry.

"You've come to save me?"

"Yes," she said, nodding her head and smiling.

"Who says I need saving?"

She just looked at him and continued to smile. Perhaps something was wrong with her. Maybe she was not right in the head. She had, after all, suffered a head injury.

"Thank you, but I don't need saving."

"Oh, but you do," she said rather too quickly and matter-of-factly.

He did not like the way she stared at him. The way she held his gaze. The way she made him be the one to look away first. How old was she? She could not be older than eighteen and yet she looked at him like she knew things—things about him that he did not know himself. He closed his eyes again, hoping she would be discouraged and walk away. Instead he felt her settle in and make herself more comfortable beside him.

"Who's the company?" Mick's voice said, speech slurred, as he staggered back to his rightful place next to Vida, reeking of alcohol and tobacco.

Vida, eyes still closed, shrugged his shoulders and turned his face up towards the sun. Maybe Mick was just what he needed to chase the girl away. But just as he thought the thought, he felt her reach across his chest. Vanilla...woodsmoke...No, too strong. He held his breath.

"Imogen Zula Nyoni. It's a pleasure to meet you."

"Shakes hands too," Mick said, sounding both amused and surprised. "I'm Michael Macintosh. It's a real pleasure to make your acquaintance."

Mick laughed, as did Vida. Vida felt foolish and childish because he knew that the only reason he was laughing was to hurt her feelings. Mick was probably laughing because he was drunk, or high, or both, and anything at this point was either very sad or very funny.

"Friends call me Mick."

"Not Mike?"

"No...Mick the Tick...bush name...Mick for short."

"You have an accent."

"Originally from the United States of America. I came here as a mercenary—a soldier of fortune. The country hasn't been able to shake me off since. I'm the tick for sure." Mick laughed heartily at his own joke.

"Friends call me Genie."

"So what's your story?"

"She says she's here to save me," Vida said, eyes still closed.

"I wasn't aware that you were in need of saving," Mick said, sounding suddenly serious.

"Neither was I."

"You're Jesus. Shouldn't you be the one doing the saving?" Mick went on, still sounding serious.

Vida shrugged.

"How do you intend to save him?" Mick asked.

"I'm not altogether sure yet."

Vida laughed mirthlessly. "Some savior you are."

Mick started snoring beside him. Vida felt the sun begin to set behind the City Hall clock tower. It took its time. The brick wall of the free public toilets against which his back rested slowly began to cool. The clock chimed six times. The city became quieter as the bustle of the rush hour subsided. This was his second-favorite time of day—his first being when the city woke up in the morning to the scent of freshly baked bread.

Vida got up suddenly, too quickly. He felt dizzy. He saw stars. He had to brace himself against the brick wall for a minute, which gave Genie enough time to stand up too. He had almost forgotten that she was there. Almost. He took his first unsteady step away from her and had to brace himself against the wall again, fighting all the while not to entertain the thought that he had almost forgotten that she was there because he had already grown accustomed to her *being* there.

"I'm off to Scobie's for my sundowner." He pretended he was telling this to Mick, who was still snoring loudly.

He walked off without looking at her.

And, of course, she followed him.

He turned around suddenly, causing her to walk right into him.

Touch. "Go back home, Genie," he said, stepping away.

She took a step towards him. She was a stubborn little so-and-so.

He had thought it was the sunshine at first, but he saw now that he was wrong—*she* was radiant. It was as though she had a light within her that made her luminescent.

He took a few steps back. "I don't know what you're thinking. I don't know what you've got planned, but whatever it is, it is probably not a good idea. You need to go home. I am sure your guardians are wondering where you are." He regretted the words immediately. He should have said "parents." The word "guardians" revealed that he knew about her—knew the particular details of her life.

He turned and walked away again. He knew she was following him. He felt her close behind. Suddenly a thought occurred to him and he turned to her. This time she avoided bumping into him—a fast learner.

"Did something funny happen at home?"

She frowned and then looked down.

Anxious, he grabbed her arms. Touch. He let her go. He stuffed his hands in his pockets. "Did something funny happen at home?" he repeated.

Her eyes flew up at him—confused. "Funny how?"

"Did something you didn't want to happen, happen?"

"Something like what?"

He ran a trembling hand through his hair and avoided looking her in the eye. "Did someone touch you in a way you weren't comfortable with?" The words rushed out of his mouth.

"No."

"You need to go back home," he said, hugely relieved.

"It's not my home anymore."

"Did they kick you out?"

"No."

"Then what?"

"Like I've already told you, I've come to save you. It's time."

"Well I'm going to Scobie's. If you're still inclined, you can save me after that," he said with resignation. He made his way to Scobie's with her in tow.

She shivered. Her skin goose-bumped. The evening air probably had a bite to it that he could not feel. The advantages of living on the street—one became impervious and immune to so many things.

"Don't you have a jacket or a jersey in there?" he asked, pointing at her suitcase.

"The clothes in here no longer fit." She said this as though it made perfect sense.

Why was she carrying a suitcase full of clothes that no longer fit? There was definitely something wrong with her. He removed his faded army camouflage jacket—well aware that it unapologetically reeked of smoke, beer, the street and him—and handed it to her. He intended to spend quite a bit of time at Scobie's. The evening air could be chilly, he guessed. "You can't come in. No one under twenty-one. If you decide to go home, just leave the jacket outside the door."

He nursed two beers for two hours. When he came out, she was not sitting outside the bar as he thought she would be—or rather, as he feared she would be. Instead of feeling relief, he felt panic. But only for a moment. He saw her suitcase a few meters from the doorway, basking in the glow of a street light. His eyes quickly scanned the area. She was leaning into a car window—a light-green Pulsar—on the other side of the street. The rag doll and teddy bear were still held in the crook of one arm; without knowing it, she was probably playing into some pervert's fantasy. Then again, she could simply be asking for a ride and the kind gentleman inside the car might be willing to oblige, Vida tried to convince himself as he ran across the street. But he had lived on the streets long enough to know better. Before he could stop himself, he was yanking her away from the car window and reaching in to grab the driver by the collar. He satisfactorily landed a few punches before the driver wised up, started his car and sped away.

"He was only asking for directions."

"Nobody asks for directions at eight thirty in the evening," he said, dragging her back across the street. Touch. He did not care. He held on to her. "The fact that you're naïve enough to believe he only wanted directions is proof enough that you need to go home." He picked up her suitcase and handed it to her. "Go home before you see things you were never meant to see." He tried a little tenderness. He gently touched her arm. "Please." He smiled a weak smile, but a smile nonetheless. "These streets are not what they seem to be during the day. You can't stay here. You don't belong here. Please go home."

"I am already home," she said with a smile of her own.

The warm and comforting smell of baking bread gently eased Vida awake. He opened his eyes to look at the latest addition to the community of street dwellers—a street kid, Imogen Zula Nyoni. Genie.

She was sleeping soundly and rather contentedly for someone who was lying in a strange place next to a stranger. Looking at her, one word came to Vida's mind—responsibility. Vida felt the flutter in the pit of his stomach yet again and recognized it for what it was: fear. He did not want to be responsible because responsibility meant one sure thing— he was going to disappoint whoever was relying on him. He felt the tension in his body build, his hands clench into two fists, his lips seal in determination. Resistance was rising.

The street changed everyone and never for the better.

He would be damned if her metamorphosis into something hardened, callous, cruel and selfish would be his responsibility.

"Please go home," he had said the night before, as convincingly as he could.

"I am already home," she had replied matter-of-factly, and apparently more convincingly, for here she was.

Home. The heart of the city.

Genie opened her eyes suddenly, as though she had not been sleeping at all and caught Vida looking at her.

The way she looked at him made him no longer feel at ease in his own environment. She seemed to see him, to already know who he was. He remembered the look her father, Golide Gumede, had given him in the field of elephant grass—all-knowing and all-seeing. Vida had no desire to be seen. He had no desire to be known.

He got up. He had to put some distance between them. He felt that their lives were already intertwined and he had a very strong desire to extricate himself, now, before it was too late. Their eyes met and held.

Belief...that was what shone from her eyes. She believed he was capable of doing impossible things. He walked away from her but it was already too late...Intertwined, interwoven, imbricated.

At first they seemed an incongruous pair—he with his pale skin and military fatigues, she with her dark skin and colorful clothes. He was quiet and broody, she was always on the verge of laughter, with an ever-ready smile. He let the world pass him by, she was constantly finding ways to involve herself in it. But soon enough their incongruity developed its own harmony and it was as though Vida and Genie had always been walking together.

Although Vida had a very public existence, he had a very

private life and quite a few secrets, which was no small feat as everyone made it their business to know everybody's business. Although he lived in what was technically a city, socially it functioned very much like a small town. Before you finished thinking a thought it had already traveled half-way across the city. Everything you said always came back to you distorted, everything you did was dissected, weighed and judged.

Because they were such rare commodities, Vida valued his privacy and his secrets above all else. People saw him on the streets and thought he did nothing more with his life than eat warm, freshly baked bread from Downings', bask in the sun at City Hall and drink his sundowners at Scobie's. When they saw him salvaging metal all over the city, which was what he spent most of his time doing, they simply thought he was doing what all other bums, vagrants, vagabonds, derelicts, homeless persons and strays do—collecting stuff for no reason whatsoever. He liked that no one suspected anything when they saw him push his Scania pushcart laden with scrap metal, which he unsuccessfully tried to hide from their view by placing the gently folded quilt his mother had made for him on top.

Vida's best-kept secret was that he did not salvage metal simply to have a collection of metal. And now that Genie had entered his life, he strongly suspected that his secret would not be secret much longer. Because she was always by his side, and since she liked involving herself in all that was around her, Vida had had no choice but to co-opt Genie into salvaging metal with him. He knew the moment would come when she would ask him what he did with it and he dreaded that moment because he knew he would have no choice but to tell her the truth.

Genie actually proved very useful when he went salvaging —she had an eye for the colorful, the unique and the precious.

She saw beauty and value in things that he would have disregarded or discarded. Together, they combed the streets from the townships to the city center to the industrial sites to the suburbs. He led and she followed. But not for long. Soon she was walking beside him, even on the narrowest of walkways. She walked beside him and made her presence felt. On a few occasions she actually charged ahead towards something glinting in the distance; she would reach for it, hold it firmly in both hands and then show it to him—an offering that would inevitably find a place in his Scania pushcart.

But not once did Genie ask him what he did with the metal.

Apparently, if he wanted to, Vida could keep his secret safe.

So he was surprised by the ease and casualness with which he came to share that secret with Genie. In doing so, he introduced her to the workings of his inner life—the life you would not know he had just by looking at him.

The secret was that he had his own warehouse behind the De Villiers, Mendelsohn and Sons' Auto Repair and Panel Beaters Garage. In it he wielded his welder and reshaped scrap metal to create larger-than-life statues of the people that made up his life on the street: Mick laughing in the sunshine, Shadrack strumming his guitar, Joseph Pereira standing tall and proud, David and Goliath in their life-or-death struggle, The Painted Ladies strutting their stuff, The Survivors in all their undignified glory—his fellow street dwellers in deed and action. He had been tinkering and welding for years without ever tiring; it was a true labor of love. He thought of the welding as the thing that kept him honest. He loved shaping metal, building structures, recreating life. He loved...the delicateness of it...the care it required...the time that needed to be spent. His love for what he did kept him true to himself. He did what he did as a way of establishing his place in the world, of giving his life meaning. He was a man who could bend metal to his will and mold it to fit his vision, and that was enough for him.

It was only when he saw Genie looking at the things he had created with awe and wonder, only when he saw one hand traveling to her mouth to cover an "O" that had already escaped, only when he saw the other hand reaching out to touch him gently on the shoulder, only when she looked at the things he had created as things of utter beauty, only when she whispered, "I knew it. I knew you were special. I knew it," her brilliant eyes never leaving the sculptures, it was only then that he realized that the things he created could actually have lives of their own—beyond him.

When he was younger he had been told that he had a talent as an artist, and he had entertained the possibility of becoming an artist when he grew up. However, when he grew up the country was reeling from war, and art did not seem to be the order of the day—and he, having been ravaged by war, thought art too precious a thing to be culled from his own hands. The look in Genie's eyes let him know that perhaps he had been wrong, that something precious, something beautiful for the eye to behold, could perhaps be created by these hands that he had deemed unfit. At the time, he felt that Genie had entered his life for this exact purpose—to let him know this particular truth about himself.

Then, one day while they were salvaging scrap metal, she cut herself badly—a gash in the thigh, blood everywhere. He moved to help her but she told him to stay away. She would not even accept the hand he offered her to help her stand. He knew he was being tested. This was the moment of truth. She stood up on her own, looked him straight in the eye, and, without warning, told him about sunflowers, *sojas*, saviors and secrets. She told him the story of her life. And then she waited for him to respond.

"So, I didn't save you at all," he said without thinking, and realized, too late, that that had not been the right thing to say. He felt her retreat. Suddenly terrified of losing her, he knew he had to proceed with caution. He knew what she was waiting for. And he knew that it was something that he could give. He heard his father's voice say: "There are many ways to be a man. Always remember that." He knew that in uttering these words his father had prepared him for precisely a moment such as this. His father had spoken the words at a time when Vida had needed absolute understanding and acceptance. And this was a time in Genie's life when she needed absolute understanding and acceptance.

At thirteen, walking down the streets of Thorngrove on his own for the first time, Vida had felt like an adventurer—until a group of boys he had known all his life, boys he considered his friends, had followed him and started calling him "moffie." They screamed it for all to hear, "Moffie! Moffie! Moffie!" He had never heard the word before but immediately knew what it meant, knew that it was not a nice word, knew that it was meant to shame him, knew that it had something to do with the fact that he had let Robbie McKop kiss him behind the school tuck shop one Thursday afternoon.

It had been a dare; it had not mattered. Well, it should not have mattered. Robbie McKop had done the right thing and said "Sies man" as he wiped his mouth in disgust. But Vida had kind of liked it. Maybe it had showed. Maybe he should not have closed his eyes. They had laughed then, these boys he had known all his life. They were not laughing now. They had not called him a moffie then. They were calling him a moffie now. Now he understood that they, like vultures, had been waiting for the moment when he would be alone and vulnerable.

He walked at an even pace. He was proud of the fact that he did not run. He was proud of the fact that he did not cry. He was strong until he saw the carefully cultivated hibiscus hedge of his home—then his endurance started to crumble. A stone whizzed past his ear. "Moffie!" one boy called out for the last time before they all ran back laughing and jeering, seemingly proud of themselves.

To his mortification, when he opened the gate he saw his father, Ezekiel de Villiers, sitting on the steps of the stoep, wearing his overalls, beer in hand and red toolbox, as always, by his side. It was what his father did with his Sundays, the only day he found himself not working at the De Villiers, Mendelsohn and Sons' Auto Repair and Panel Beaters Garage: he took apart the engines that lay in their front yard and put them back together again. Vida stood some distance from his father and blinked away the tears. He did not wipe them off but stood still and waited for the air to dry them before advancing. He hoped, futilely, that his father had not heard what the boys had called him. He had recently begun to understand that his relationship with his father was changing— that his father now had expectations of him. He had no idea what those expectations were but he felt overwhelmed by them nonetheless. He felt that he was going to disappoint his father in some way.

His father looked at him as he stood there waiting for his tears to dry. Ezekiel did not say a word, only moved to take a swig of his Castle Lager, his expression hard to read. Then he got up from the stoep and went into the house. Vida took the opportunity to wipe the traces of tears from his eyes. Having done so, he did not know what else to do. His father came back, stood by the front door and opened a bottle of Stoney Ginger Beer using the door frame. He sat back down on the stoep and held out the bottle to Vida. Vida let out a breath—

only realizing then that he had been holding it in—and went to sit next to his father. With the red toolbox between them, they drank in silence for a while.

Eventually his father spoke. "You can cry if you want to. I'm your father. Nothing you do will change that. Nothing you do will change my love for you."

Vida tried to be strong and stoic but the tears came anyway. He wondered if his father would love him if he knew about Robbie McKop and the kiss. If he knew that he had closed his eyes? If he knew that he had enjoyed it?

His father did not put his arm around him. His father simply took off the Ivy cap that had been a permanent fixture on his head for as long as Vida could remember and placed it on his. He opened his omnipresent red toolbox. In it were the many tools that seemed to be an extension of his father. There were also two pairs of gloves—one big and worn, the other smaller and brand new. His father handed Vida the second pair.

"There are many ways to be a man. Always remember that," his father said.

Vida felt his chest swell with a mixture of love, pride and gratitude. Being the son of Ezekiel de Villiers was indeed a wonderful thing.

"Let's get to work," his father said, getting off the stoep. Vida followed him, and it was then that his father introduced him to the things he loved: a spanner, a ratchet, a socket, a screwdriver, a vice grip. Together they took apart an engine and together they reassembled it. And when the day was over, they both knew that it had been a day well spent.

Now, looking at the girl who had just told him her story— her story of sunflowers, *sojas*, saviors and secrets—he realized that it was not just his father's words that had mattered; it was both what his father had *said* and what he had *done*. His father had shown him by word and deed that he accepted him just the way he was.

Now Vida had to find the thing to say and the thing to do to be the right man for this moment. He reached out and wiped the tears from Genie's eyes. Touch. She let him. He told her his own story: the enchanted childhood, the violent and tragic death of his parents, the boy he had loved and lost, the girl he had also loved but not lost...not quite, the war he had fought, the battles still raging within, the anger, the anger, the anger, meeting her father in a field of elephant grass... experiencing the heralding. He poured it all out until there was nothing left. They stood there with nothing standing between them...no secrets. Genie reached up and wiped away his tears. Touch. Laid bare and armed with the knowledge of each other's truth, they had no choice but to accept each other as they were.

It was a liberation.

Genesis

Finally, Vida took Genie to The House That Jack Built.

The House That Jack Built was the house that Vida's eccentric Afrikaner great-grandfather, Jakob de Villiers, had built at the turn of the twentieth century. In keeping with Jakob's personality, the double story house had been built into a hillside—nature and culture coming together to create an incongruous but ultimately spectacular structure. Victoria, Jakob's very English wife, had lived long enough to plant a very English garden that would one day be the pride of the country, before she succumbed, as most very English wives did, to some very tropical disease.

Vida's grandfather, Frederick de Villiers, the son of Jakob and his maid, Blue, had been born in the house but had only been able to live in it as a servant, given the zoning laws of the land at the time. Vida's father, Ezekiel de Villiers, like his father before him, had also been prevented by law from residing in the house as anything other than a servant. However, unlike his father, he had had no desire to reside in the house and had left it at the age of thirteen never to return. In 1980, at the age of eighteen, Vida had come back from the war to learn that his great-grandfather had bequeathed the house to him. He had done absolutely nothing to deserve or earn it, but suddenly The House That Jack Built was his. It was a weighty inheritance and Vida felt burdened by it. His was a definite embarrassment of riches.

It was not a rare occurrence at Scobie's to hear the otherwise taciturn Vida curse his great-grandfather, his grand-father, and his father for not having had the good sense to have more than one issue each and thereby leaving it to him, a bona fide moffie, to carry the weight of both the family name and the inheritance. Whenever a bartender heard the word "issue" issue from Vida's lips, he knew that it was time to tell Vida to leave. Sober, Vida often wished that he had some of his grandfather's attachment to the house, or some of his father's aversion to it, to help him decide what to do with it. He had neither. If he sold the house he felt that he would be disappointing his grandfather. If he stayed in the house he felt that he would be disappointing his father. Whatever he chose to do, one or the other was sure to roll in his grave. Vida thus decided to neither live in it nor sell it. This resolution had worked well enough until Imogen Zula Nyoni decided to share her truth with him.

Together, Vida and Genie pushed the ancient and weather-beaten teak door that creaked open with an asthmatic croak and revealed a dusty, crypt-like interior. Everything in The House That Jack Built was from a bygone era—old, faded, rusted and more than gently used. Everything seemed to have a special story to tell: the collection of assegais in the display case in the sunroom; the frozen, fiercely growling heads of a menagerie of animals in the trophy room; the demure Victorian Rose furniture in the sitting room; the overladen crystal chandeliers in the ballroom; the stately and somber oak table with its twenty matching chairs in the dining room; the dignified Welcome Dover stove in the kitchen.

Although initially overwhelmed and somewhat frightened by all that lay before them (especially in the trophy room), Vida and Genie soon found a way to live with the house. Since the house had a surfeit of rooms, the two of them were spoilt for choice. Genie chose the room that had the most sunshine and put her suitcase on the bed, opened it, carefully retrieved Penelope and Specs, and placed them on the pillows, in this way claiming the room as hers. She did not seem to care that the lace covering the four-poster bed was yellowed and moth-eaten or that the wooden floor slanted a little; all she cared about was that the room received the most sunshine. Vida chose the room at the end of the hallway simply because it was the room at the end of the hall and would allow Genie and him to coexist privately.

Luckily, after Jakob de Villiers's death in 1975, members of the Antiquarian Society and members of Victoria's Own, a special branch of the Settler Society's Women's Auxiliary that oversaw the proper implementation of English gardens in the city, had successfully persuaded the City Council to declare The House That Jack Built and Victoria's Garden city treasures. As a result, both the house and garden were well looked after by a loyal housekeeper, Matilda, and gardener, Stefanos, who were in the employ of the City Council. The house and the garden were both local and tourist attractions—very popular with people who enjoyed reliving romanticized versions of a colonial past by having four o'clock tea in Victoria's Garden, seven-course dinners in the stately dining room, photographs taken in the trophy room, or dancing the night away in the ballroom, all while being waited on hand and foot by liveried black servants with beneficent and beatific smiles. Generously, the proceeds from such events went equally to the Settler Society's Women's Auxiliary, the Antiquarian Society, the City Council and the De Villiers Family Trust.

However, in 1995, The Man Himself—who had once or twice dined in the stately dining room and who had proudly hung in his office a picture of himself standing triumphantly with one foot on the head of one of Jakob de Villiers's trophy lions—reprimanded the City Council for its collaboration with the Settler Society's Women's Auxiliary and Antiquarian Society in the maintenance of The House That Jack Built and Victoria's Garden, saying that these societies smacked of colonialism. The Settler Society's Women's Auxiliary and Antiquarian Society were then left to maintain the property themselves. Unfortunately, by that time membership of both societies had dwindled due to death, exile in old age homes or repatriation back to Britain; and so, the once robust but now frail societies were no longer able to maintain The House That Jack Built and Victoria's Garden. As fortune would have it, Matilda and Stefanos decided to stay with the property, but without their regular paychecks from the City Council, they could only do so much to keep up with its upkeep.

So when Vida and Genie arrived to live in the house, there was much work to be done; since it had seen no social life for a couple of years, the house was long overdue for a good and thorough clean. They kept busy and they were happy to be busy. When they were not cleaning the house, with the assistance of Matilda, or trying to right the garden, with the assistance of Stefanos, they were out salvaging scrap metal, or in the workshop behind the De Villiers, Mendelsohn and Sons' Auto Repair and Panel Beaters Garage, Genie assisting as Vida bent and shaped metal. At night they both happily collapsed onto their separate beds.

With all their hard work—it could not be helped—the house started becoming a home. A previously unassuming chair stopped simply being a chair and became Genie's favorite because she liked the way she could fold herself into it; Vida started taking a moment out of every day to watch the sunset from the tranquility of Victoria's Garden; the Welcome Dover stove became the place where Genie would lightly burn her custard to give it more flavor; and it became impossible for Vida to fall asleep without listening to his grandfather's meager collection of records on a His Master's Voice gramophone.

While Vida's great-grandfather, Jakob de Villiers, had left behind a plethora of things, Vida's grandfather, Frederick de Villiers, had left behind only three records of classical music, a worn copy of the King James Bible, a thin, neatly folded blanket, a bowler hat, a well-worn suit, and a collection of seashells placed carefully in a rusted tin can. Vida had accidentally made the discovery of his grandfather's belongings when he forced open the swollen door to what he thought was an old tool shed but soon discovered to have been his grandfather's living quarters—the servants' quarters.

Vida remembered his grandfather, who had infrequently visited them in Thorngrove, as a proud man who always wore a suit and a bowler hat and always sat upright, his hard-working and determined hands placed firmly on his knees. He could not reconcile the memory of that proud man with the things he found in the servants' quarters. Surely there must have been more to his grandfather's life than what he had left behind. Vida busied himself looking in The House That Jack Built for other things that might have belonged to his grandfather, and, in not finding them, was filled with a sadness that made him cry. He would often spend time with the things his grandfather had left behind: sometimes he treated them like clues that would reveal the mystery of who his grandfather had been, sometimes he treated them like points on a road map that would lead him to an understanding of his grandfather's life, and sometimes he treated them like pieces of a puzzle that he could put together again in order to reveal his grandfather's true self. Yet whichever way he handled his grandfather's belongings, they did nothing to make his grandfather more legible or tangible to him.

Whereas Vida was preoccupied with his grandfather,

Genie was curious about the true matriarch of the De Villiers clan, Blue, Jakob's Khoisan—or, as the parlance of the time would have it, Hottentot—maid. There was absolutely no trace of her in the house. There was no way of knowing what she had looked like, where she had lived, what she had loved, what she had hated. All that was left of Blue were questions: How had she come to cross paths with Jakob? How long had she lived here? What had she thought of her circumstances? How had she been treated by Jakob? Had she loved her son, Frederick? Had she loved herself? Had she cared about love at all or had she given herself over to something else entirely? Had it been her decision to live a life that could and would end without a trace? What had her original name been—the name she responded to as a child, the name she had held long before she crossed paths with Jakob? Genie liked to imagine Blue as a child the way she remembered herself as a child, playing in a field of sunflowers. Had sunflowers even been introduced to this part of the world back then?

In a house filled with the proud collections and clutter of Jakob de Villiers's life, Blue's absence seemed like a haunting.

All Vida knew about his great-grandmother was that she had traveled with Jakob in the guise of a man and had lived with him for many years as his manservant before becoming pregnant with Frederick and revealing her secret. A delicious crumb of information that led nowhere. Genie scrutinized Vida's face, hoping to find some trace of Blue, but there was none. Had Blue simply chosen to make her life not matter, or had the choice been made for her? Blue's absence was both intriguing and frustrating for Genie, perhaps because it contained a truth that she did not want to acknowledge—that one could come into this world, live a life (full, empty, contented, unfulfilled) and leave it without a trace. The very idea filled her with a sadness she did not know what to do with.

Then one day Genie found a pair of small, gently worn, baby-blue silk slippers in a chest at the foot of Jakob's bed and quickly convinced herself that they had belonged to Blue. Perhaps it was their size, perhaps it was their daintiness, perhaps it was their unassuming appearance, perhaps it was their color, perhaps it was just a knowing she felt when she touched them that convinced Genie she had found something that had belonged to Blue. Something so soft, so delicate, that still remained of her.

Vida, Genie & Marcus

On a bright and sunny day in May, as Genie and Vida drove to the Thomas Meikles Hyper, Vida was still wondering how the simple purchase of a mattress had turned into such a production. Genie had had them test all manner of mattresses, looking for the one that was just right, until the salespeople had given them a knowing look that Vida found presumptuous. He had been ready to leave after the second mattress, but Genie kept on finding ways to co-opt him into her decision-making. Was there really any difference between mattresses except how much they cost? When Vida had first suggested the purchase of a mattress, he had thought they would take no more than ten minutes to find the most affordable one and purchase it. But Genie obviously had other ideas.

A man who called attention to himself because he had a hump on his back and a beautiful woman by his side walked into the store. Almost immediately, Genie found herself standing next to him and pointing at two mattresses.

"Which one do you think we should choose?" It was as though she had been waiting all along for him to come and help her. The beautiful woman was clearly taken aback, but the man looked at Genie with...recognition.

"You are Golide Gumede's daughter?" the man with a hump on his back said. It sounded more like a statement than a question.

"Yes, I am Golide Gumede's daughter; although that fact is not helping me make a choice at this very minute." She gestured towards Vida with her head. "And this one, who is useful for all other things, is being absolutely useless for this."

The beautiful woman smiled apologetically at Vida, and the man with a hump on his back looked at him with eyes that said "Women, hey?" With that look Vida suspected that the man was offering something that he rarely offered: friendship.

More than an hour later, the man with the hump on his back helped Vida secure the finally chosen mattress to the top of the Austin Mini Cooper. When they were done he offered Genie and Vida his hand, another rare offering, Vida was sure. "Valentine Tanaka," the man said as they shook hands.

But that had not been the end of it. Genie had then been determined that they go to the Thomas Meikles Hyper to get the ingredients for custard. So, to Vida's chagrin, they had driven through the city with the telltale mattress on top of the car.

Getting out of the Mini, Vida looked at the mattress, which looked exactly like the other mattresses that they had not chosen, wondering if it had been worth it.

"Don't worry," Genie said as she made her way towards the store. "Given everything that it has and does, it was worth it."

"What does a mattress do?" Vida asked.

But before Genie could answer, Marcus ambushed them.

Vida did what he did best on the street: he did not interfere. He let this moment in Marcus and Genie's lives play itself out to its predestined end. He stepped a respectful distance from them, to where he was sure he would not hear what was being said. As an added measure, he forced himself to have a conversation with Goliath, the puny leader of The Survivors, who now considered himself friends with Vida because he had made friends with Genie. Or rather, to put it more accurately, because Genie had made friends with him.

Vida looked back over his shoulder at Genie and Marcus. He watched as Marcus gestured towards the car that was laden with the mattress, a gesture that communicated one thing: despair. Suddenly, even from a distance, Marcus' desperation became palpable to Vida and made him briefly ponder the thought—one, now unwelcome—of someday, perhaps, finding himself without Genie.

Genie had taken the news of Marcus' leaving for America rather well—too well for Marcus' liking. He had been cherry picked by his employer to undertake an apprenticeship in the finance department of one of the nation's Fortune 500 companies.

"You should come with me," Marcus said. This was a new idea, even to him. He had only wanted to take her back home, away from Vida. That was before he saw the mattress weighing down the Austin Mini Cooper. The mattress changed everything, made him anxious, made his hands itch to do something he could not do in public. He was not quite sure what that something was. "I love you," he told the frown that had creased Genie's brow.

At his declaration, Genie smiled.

"You want to love me, but wanting to love me is not the same as loving me."

He realized then that her smile had been the harbinger of false hope.

"You've never forgiven me, have you?" Marcus asked, sounding almost triumphant in his sadness.

"Forgiven you? What is there to forgive?"

"You've never forgiven me for that morning in the kitchen. Never forgiven me for letting go of your hand. For...for what I did after."

"There is nothing to forgive."

Genie took his hands gently in hers, finally giving them something to do.

"Remember how I used to burrow my feet in the soil of the sunflower fields?"

It was Marcus' turn to frown.

"Remember how you never did?"

Genie let go of his hands.

"My letting you go is my way of loving you."

Vida & Genie

Vida was still breathing her in, her taste was still in his mouth and his fingertips were still tingling from having touched her. His arm was carelessly thrown over his eyes as he made a valiant effort to catch his breath, which only moments ago had been happy to leave him. He could hear her struggle to catch her breath as well. He listened to her breathing normalize and calibrated his to match hers.

"This beautiful thing is something that the body needs," Genie said.

He felt her sit up.

Vida raised his arm from his eyes and looked at her. She was hugging her knees to her body and looked iridescent with the glow of what he had made possible within her.

"Promise me you will never speak to me of love," she said. She looked at him and ran the back of her hand idly over his chest. "To not have to speak of love is such a freeing thing."

"I promise," Vida said. It was an easy promise to give because he remembered looking into a pair of startlingly blue eyes and feeling so content...so fulfilled...so complete.

In that moment, he felt relieved that Genie was not looking for that contentment...that fulfilment...that completeness from him.

Vida

Vida had left the city with its smell of freshly baked bread because a change had taken place. Uninvited and unwelcomed...in the beginning. But then he had grown accustomed to the change—to the way it was always accompanied by the scent of warm vanilla and woodsmoke; to the way it always laughed at the beginning of The Carpenters' "Calling Occupants of Interplanetary Craft"; to the way it always made sure to slightly burn custard to give it extra flavor; to the way it seemed all-knowing and yet, paradoxically, always questioned everything; to the way it was fiercely independent and sometimes stubborn; to the way it faithfully consumed the marijuana baked goods and moringa tea that he made to fend off the ravages of HIV; to the way it offered no resistance to the suggestion that they share the same bed; to the earnestness with which it went about buying a mattress; to the way it propped its body against his to reduce the rumble in its chest; to the loneliness it left behind when it went to Mater Dei Hospital for six weeks to be treated for tuberculosis; to the way it valiantly defeated pneumonia with antibiotics; to the happiness it shared when the antiretroviral medication became available; to the way it became something he reached for in the night; to the way it always entwined its legs with his when they slept; to the way it whispered his name in his ear in the dead of night; to the way it made him feel like a man standing alone in a field of tall yellow, almost golden, elephant grass—a man who could not put into words the sense of wonderment he felt upon discovering that he was never truly alone.

Vida and Genie never defined their relationship. They never spoke of love. They were just *together*. And because they were together, Vida became a well-known artist. Genie encouraged him to show the Street Dwellers to Beatrice Beit-Beauford, who, in turn, purchased them for a ridiculously exorbitant sum and then donated them to the city in a lavish ceremony where Vida and the mayor had to hold an enormous pair of scissors and cut a gigantic yellow ribbon, after which the mayor presented Vida with a golden key encased in red velvet—The Key to the City. The city planner decided to put the sculptures on the median of Selborne Avenue opposite Centenary Park. The street dwellers felt honored, the city was proud, and the sculptures soon became a tourist attraction, which benefited the city economically. Tourists liked taking pictures of the sculptures with the very street dwellers who had inspired them. The Survivors turned this into a lucrative business for themselves, especially since they accepted payment only in foreign currency. One of the tourists turned out to be a Dutch music producer, Shadrack was "discovered," moved to Amsterdam and became a rather successful world music recording artist. Just like that, the winds of change blew and everything seemed to fall into place.

Vida became an overnight sensation, the toast of the town. Journalists, art critics and academics wrote articles about him and his work. They called him a "truly postcolonial artist." As he understood it, being a postcolonial artist simply meant that he was an artist working after independence, which was true enough. But when journalists, art critics and academics used the term he got the impression that they meant more by it. They interviewed him and published articles in which his life on the street had been interpreted to mean more than it was. According to them, the Street Dwellers represented the "postcolonial condition," and he, in being able to capture that condition, was a truly postcolonial artist. Apparently, when he bent and shaped metal, he was doing more than just that, he was expressing something truly postcolonial. But more than anything the critics were in rapture over his use of scrap metal: he was a genius for understanding so implicitly how salvaged metal depicted the condition of postcolonialism as no other material could.

Genie continued to go salvaging with him and spent hours with him in his workshop. They spoke about the work he did in words he understood: spanner, ratchet, socket, screwdriver, vice grip, welding machine. This helped to ground him, and he needed grounding because it was a very heady time; it would be easy to get carried away by the idea of being a truly postcolonial artist. Instead, he just opened the red toolbox that he had inherited from his father and Genie handed him the tools that enabled him to do what he loved.

It was in this way that he created what would become his most famous work of art: "The Theory of Flight: In Three Movements." It was a sculpture that consisted of three pieces, namely "Golden," "Lady in Waiting" and "The Firebird." He dedicated the sculpture to Genie for reasons that were obvious to him. The journalists, art critics and academics all agreed that Vida had moved beyond realism, and because they interpreted the piece differently and could agree on very little, they all agreed that "The Theory of Flight" was post-postcolonial. One critic wrote that "'The Theory of Flight' bravely signals the way forward." The way forward to where, Vida could not help but wonder.

"The Theory of Flight" successfully toured the world before finally returning home and settling at the National Art Gallery. This time, The Man Himself wielded the enormous pair of scissors that cut the gigantic yellow ribbon. History seemed ready to repeat itself.

But now the winds of change were blowing differently and, just like that, everything seemed to fall apart. The state became politically unrestful and tourists stopped coming. The city's fortunes changed and people started vandalizing the Street Dwellers on Selborne Avenue, finding other uses for the salvaged metal. The city had no choice but to construct barbed-wire barricades around Vida's creations. Then The Man Himself decided that Vida de Villiers was "too white" to be a truly postcolonial artist and ordered that the sculptures be dismantled and thrown away. The city had no choice but to comply.

Luckily, there was an international outcry, and various art collectors, galleries and museums around the world offered to buy Vida's work. The city happily sold them. Mick laughing in the sunshine ended up in the Cleveland Cultural Gardens in America; Shadrack strumming his guitar ended up in the Middelheim Open Air Sculpture Museum in Belgium; Joseph Pereira standing tall and proud ended up in the Kirstenbosch National Botanical Garden in South Africa; David and Goliath frozen in their life-or-death struggle ended up in the Changchun World Sculpture Park in China; The Painted Ladies strutting their stuff ended up in the Windsor Sculpture Park in Canada; and The Survivors in all their undignified glory ended up in the Hirshhorn Museum and Sculpture Garden in America.

The Man Himself then commissioned work from artists he considered to be utterly postcolonial in order to replace the Street Dwellers. These postcolonial artists made sculptures of The Man Himself, which he placed outside select state buildings. However, the statues were vandalized and graffitied so often that The Man Himself enacted a law that made it a crime punishable by life imprisonment to be found defacing any of his statues.

The only time Vida and Genie were apart was when Vida went by invitation to an artists' retreat in Stockholm every year. Genie imagined Stockholm to be too cold a place to welcome her and stayed at home. Every year Vida would return to find Genie waiting for him on the veranda. She would open her arms wide. "Vida. Finally. Home," she would say, beaming, before hugging him and kissing him full on the lips.

And so it should have been when he returned from Stockholm just before his fiftieth birthday. But it was not. Instead, he found Matilda and Stefanos waiting anxiously on the veranda. Before Vida could even ask where Genie was, Matilda blurted out, "Madam, sir. Something is wrong."

"Matilda, how many times must we tell you? We're not madam. We're not sir. We're Genie and Vida," Vida said, surprised by the calm in his voice.

"Yes, sir. Of course, sir."

"Madam...she is not eating," Stefanos said, nervously crushing his hat in his hands. "We are trying to feed her and she is saying she have got no appetite."

"We are not knowing what to do, sir," Matilda said, almost in tears.

"For how long?"

"Five days," Matilda and Stefanos said simultaneously.

"I'm sure all will be well," Vida said, reassuring them both with a smile.

"It is good to be having you home, sir," Matilda said with relief.

"Very good, sir," Stefanos said as he opened the front door for Vida.

When Vida saw Genie, he was shocked by the difference

five days had made, but he did not show it. He found Genie sitting on her own: she was calm as she looked at something that he could not see. It seemed to reside in one of the corners of whatever room she happened to be in. He felt she was giving herself over to this something and that giving herself over to it made her calm. This something was rapacious. It ate away at her body. It stole the light from her eyes. It made murky the luminescence of her skin. It was obviously intent on taking her away from him, and she was letting it. Vida felt that her giving in was a betrayal.

Genie had been gravely ill before but had always bounced back. Vida took a lot of comfort in that. He tried his trusted regime of marijuana and moringa again, but Genie would take neither. A change had taken place in Genie herself.

She had fought everything that HIV had put in her path. Even when she outwardly looked healthy, he knew there were battles raging within. So why had she given up the fight?

He might have accepted it years ago...in the beginning. In the beginning, they really had thought that their time together was borrowed. When they were being realistic they expected to have three, maybe five years together. When they were being dreamers they had imagined being together for ten years. But that was before the ARVs.

They had survived so much before. Why could they not survive the something in the corner? The answer was simple—they could not survive it because Genie did not want them to.

Frightened, Vida stood in her field of vision, obscuring the something in the corner. She slowly adjusted her gaze and looked at him, not because she wanted to, but because he had made her. She made him feel the obligation of looking at him.

The something in the corner was an uninvited and unwelcome guest that came between Vida and Genie. After years of being together, it came, settled between them and seemed intent to leave only when Genie left with it.

The something in the corner made Vida desperate. He had accommodated abrupt changes in his life before, but he would not accommodate this one. Not without a fight.

It took three attempts for him to get Genie to let some sustenance pass through her lips. By then Vida was anxious, impatient and angry.

"You need to let me go," Genie finally said in a tired voice. She said it easily, as though she was simply asking him to fix something in the house that was broken.

He chose to ignore her and instead tried to force a spoonful of porridge into her mouth. It took too long a moment for her to open her mouth.

"I'm tired, Vida," she whispered after swallowing the porridge slowly, painfully.

He ignored the sorrow in her eyes as he shoved another spoonful into her mouth, all the while aware that he could have tried a little tenderness.

This time she gagged, bringing up the two spoonfuls she had just taken in.

He tried to force another spoonful into her mouth. This time she clamped it shut.

Tears—he could not tell if they were his or hers—fell onto his hands. He pressed his forehead against hers. "Please, Genie. You have to eat. The medication is too caustic—you can't take it without food. You know that," he said, opting to be gentle this time.

"I'm not taking the medication either."

He looked at her. She looked at him, determined.

"The war veterans have taken over the Beauford Farm and Estate," Genie said.

The neutrality in her voice did not let Vida know what this had to do with their current situation.

"You need to let me go."

And that was when he knew that this change had not unfolded over a mere five days. It was something she had planned. Deliberate. Determined. Decided. While sitting across from him at breakfast. While lying next to him. While running her fingers idly through his hair. At some point in all that normality she had decided to give up the fight. Carelessly. Callously. Cruelly.

Fear, desperation, anger and something dangerously akin to hatred coursed through his veins, boiled his blood. He shoved the spoon in her mouth.

She spat the porridge in his face.

"You want to die?"

"Yes. Yes, I want to die," she said calmly. It was the calmness that scared him the most. It was a resignation; evidence that she had already reconciled herself to the idea.

He walked away but did not get too far before crumpling to the ground. "How could you want to leave me?"

"I thought that love was a giving thing. Now I know that it is selfish."

"But we agreed that we would never speak of love."

"This was because I was so sure you would keep your promise."

"This is not what the promise held."

"You cannot save me, Vida," Genie said. "Not this time. This time you have to be brave."

But he had saved her. He had taken her to Mater Dei Hospital (she was too weak to put up much resistance) and watched as a nurse tried to find a viable vein for the intravenous drip, pricking needle after needle in both arms and only succeeding on the eleventh try. He saw the accusation in Genie's eyes with every prick of the needle and chose to ignore it.

A few days later, Dr. Mambo, looking almost happy, said that Genie's hospitalization had been a blessing in disguise because lesions had been found in her cervix just in time...before they turned cancerous. They would have to be monitored, of course. More medication would have to be administered, of course. More precautions would have to be adhered to, of course. But, all told, it had been a blessing in disguise.

Vida was grateful but did not feel the blessing.

A week later, Genie came back from the hospital healthy, and seemingly back to her old self. She carried on as though nothing had happened—as though she had not deliberately tried to leave him. As though she had not *wanted* to leave him. He could forgive her many things, but, at that moment, he could not forgive her initial willingness to leave him.

The years, mostly happy, went by and he grew to forgive... and forget. On the morning of his fifty-seventh birthday Vida woke up to feel Genie's warm breath against his skin. "Happy birthday, dear Vida," her lips whispered softly against his before kissing him lightly. "Happy birthday to you." What man on earth would not want to turn fifty-seven this way?

He opened his eyes then to find her smiling down at him. His right hand reached up to pull her face down towards his. She did not stop smiling when their lips met.

Later, her legs locked around his waist with a tenacity that let him know that in that moment he was the only thing that mattered to her. Her eyes fixed on his with a fiercely singular focus that was suddenly overwhelming. He found himself about to say something. There were only so many things a man's heart could contain. There were things that he had managed to find only with her...he could not deny that... beautiful things that he felt blessed with. Before he could stop the words, they were already traveling the space between them. He heard himself say "I love you." Then he watched as her eyes lost focus. She looked at him intently and intensely, but she no longer saw him. She had given herself over to the feeling. Her brow furrowed. Her mouth opened and one word breathlessly came out: "Vida." Then she let go of it all in wave after wave. And inevitably he crested one of those waves.

As Vida watched Genie walk towards him carrying his suitcase for his trip to Stockholm, he tried not to think too much of his unrequited "I love you." She placed the suitcase in the boot of the car and then fixed his collar, hugged him from behind and kissed his neck twice. "You remind me of rivers I swam in a long time ago. You are home to me," she whispered in his left ear, and then, through the pure cotton of his shirt, she kissed the jagged keloid on his shoulder that had been made by Goliath's broken Castle Lager bottle, all those years ago, before he became a saved man.

He did not understand the words. Was this her way of speaking to him of love?

When he turned to ask her what she meant, she kissed him so sincerely that once again he found himself transported to the field of tall, yellow, almost golden elephant grass, transformed into the man with the familiar tingle in his fingers.

BOOK TWO

PART I

—◆—

Epistemology

Genie

When Genie was among the sunflowers, it was like a remembering; a remembering of a self all but forgotten. There was nothing she enjoyed more than digging her toes into the moist reddish-brown soil first thing in the morning. She loved the prickle of her skin when her bare arms came into contact with the long, thin stalks of the sunflowers. She would turn her face towards the sun peeping through the sunflower petals and, eyes closed, listen to the hum and buzz of the busy bees above. She strongly suspected that she had once upon a time been a sunflower, for she too was thin and tall, reaching for the sky; she too had a brown face that was turned up towards the sun; she too loved the gentle sway of the breeze. The only difference between herself and the sunflowers was that they had yellow halos and hers was reddish-brown like the soil, but differences in life were allowed and to be expected.

Her childhood among the sunflowers dances and flashes in Genie's mind as she watches the bloodstain grow and morph on the white sheets. For a while the bloodstain had looked like a butterfly, a moth, some winged crimson creature. Now... well, now it looks like the map of a country...a country with rather fluid borders...a country she knows well.

She wishes more than anything that she had been able to save the mattress, but she fears the blood—her blood—has soaked right through the sheets and onto it. Vida will have to buy a new one. She feels a deep sense of regret because this has been his favorite mattress. They have been together for more than twenty years and have had three mattresses: the first proved too lumpy, the second too springy. It was this one, the third, that had been just right—firm with a little give. Once she started bleeding she should have shifted to the floor, saved the mattress, and saved Vida the trouble of having to buy a new one. But now she is too weak to do anything but lie here and wait. Alone. With nothing for company but Vida's absence.

It was Marcus who had taught her an important lesson about absence. Because of him she had discovered that an absence, like a presence, occupies space—it has proportions, parameters and a sense of permanence. Because of him she had realized that an absence is actually more steadfast than a presence: you cannot take another's presence with you wherever you go, but another's absence need never leave you. Because of him she had learned that an absence, like a presence, is something you could come to know intimately.

And suddenly, as if conjured by all this absence, there is a presence.

A boy, Sikhumbuzo, who sits a few rows in front of her in class, points an accusatory finger at her as he screams "You are dead! You are dead! You need to lie down on the ground. I have *killeded* you! I have *killeded* you! On the ground now!" His chest is puffed up with something that truly terrifies Genie. They must be playing either "RF vs. Terrs," "War," "Bazooka" or "Take Cover," because all these games involve having to make rat-a-tat-tat sounds while you point handmade wire AK-47s at each other, lob imaginary grenades and detonate equally imaginary landmines. The gleeful eagerness required to kill off all of your friends and be the last one standing is what defeats Genie in the end. She throws down her wire AK-47.

"You have *killed* me. I am dead," she says to Sikhumbuzo before walking away.

"You cannot walk away. You are dead! You are dead! You need to lie down on the ground. I have *killed* you. I have *killed* you. On the ground now. Those are the rules of the game. You cannot not follow the rules of the game. You are dead!" Sikhumbuzo shouts, looking both angry and hurt.

Next thing Genie knows she is standing on the carcass of an abandoned car, Brown Car, surrounded by a field of sunflowers. She has Penelope in the crook of her right arm and Specs in the crook of her left arm. Penelope and Specs join her in looking over the hazy blue hills in the distance. The sunflowers turn their heads towards the hazy blue hills as well and wait patiently with them. Together they watch as Genie's parents become a giant pair of silver wings that take to the skies and turn into a flash of light and color as they glint and gleam in the sunlight. The giant wings become smaller and smaller until finally they are a mere speck in the azure sky. And then, as if by magic, the tiny speck turns into nothingness and her parents vanish completely into the sky.

Genie is still in the safety of the sunflowers when she sees two army trucks drive up the dirt road and make their way towards the Beauford Farm and Estate compound. In the army trucks are *sojas* carrying very real AK-47s and wearing garish red berets. Soon after the *sojas'* arrival, she hears incessant screams, intermittent rat-a-tat-tats, incoherent voices shouting, incomprehensible voices wailing. She smells the smell of burning flesh...not mouthwatering, but nauseating... definitely not something edible...not an animal that you eat... a different kind of animal...a human being...someone. *Someone* is burning.

And then suddenly it is all over. No screams. No rat-a-tat-tats. No voices shouting. No voices wailing. But still the smell of burning human flesh.

She hears the army trucks come back down the dirt road.

One of the trucks stops next to the sunflower field. There is the shuffle of boots on the dirt road. Then the smell of burning grass. "Put it out," a voice booms. "What have sunflowers ever done to you?" The truck starts up again and the boots start their shuffle...stop...hesitate.

The sun has begun to set on the horizon, marking the end of the day. Genie knows that all the days that break henceforth will never be felt the same way.

She opens her eyes.

She looks around her. Has she been dreaming or just remembering? She does not know. She is not on the Beauford Farm and Estate. She is not among the sunflowers. She is in a room. A lovely room filled with whites, creams, golds and richly reddish-brown teak wood. Her room. The room she shares with Vida. Their room. On a bed. A lovely bed now stained red with her blood. Her bed. The bed she shares with Vida. Their bed.

Yet still the smell of burning human flesh lingers.

Her stomach heaves but nothing comes up. She has nothing left to give.

At least she, knowing that this moment was inevitable, had the foresight to take care of some things. She had Vida's only suit dry-cleaned. She remembers standing at the dry-cleaner's, holding Vida's jacket to her nose and breathing in his scent as the woman behind the counter looked at her with a raised eyebrow but did not say anything. She personally ironed his favorite white shirt and made sure to starch his collar. She had Stefanos buff Vida's shoes to a brilliant shine. She had Matilda assemble and lay out his accessories: a handkerchief, a tie, a pair of argyle socks and an Ivy cap.

Funny that during her final moments her thoughts and concerns should be so domestic.

After a lifetime of believing she was in flight, of believing that she was something spectacular in the sky, had she rather been a hybrid thing—something rooted but free to fly? Could such a hybrid thing even exist?

All she knows is that in this life she has reached for something and touched it. And that is enough. When, at the end, all that remains is a blood-soaked mattress that will have to be thrown out, a mattress with a bloodstain that has taken the shape of a country, perhaps what matters then is that it is enough...has been enough...was enough.

Matter. Interesting word, that. She allows herself to fall into it. Into its darkness.

She is back in the field of sunflowers. With Marcus, this time. Together they watch as the boot of a car pops open and out of it slowly unfolds an impossibly tall man. He is unlike any man they have ever seen before. He is taller than even the sunflowers, or so it seems. He is magnificent. It is when he looks directly at them, through the sunflower stalks, that Genie knows for sure that this magnificent tall man is her father, Golide Gumede. Her father, she has always known, would arrive like a hero in a story.

His eyes zero in on hers. And Genie struggles loose from Marcus' tenacious grip and runs out of the sunflower field towards her father. Her father gets down on his knees and reaches out a hand to touch her gently, tentatively, as though she truly were the most precious and beautiful thing in the world. In that moment she knows that her mother has been telling the truth all along. She, Genie, was hatched from a golden egg. She smiles at her father, revealing the gap between her two front teeth. Her father smiles too, revealing the gap between his two front teeth. An inheritance.

Hoisted on her father's shoulders, Genie can, for the first time, see above the heads of the sunflowers. She notices that the sunflowers' faces are no longer facing the sun but have turned, each and every one, towards her father and her as they make their way home. She sees her mother, Elizabeth Nyoni, running towards them with a rainbow of color trailing behind her, her blonde hair all but flying away, her arms outstretched in joy and welcome.

Genie knows without a doubt that the future has arrived.

The crunch of car tires on gravel, the squeaky swing of a gate opening, the dance of headlights on the bedroom wall pull Genie out of the darkness she had entered and into the darkness of the room.

She hears footsteps on the stairs.

Vida.

Finally.

Home.

Vida

Vida knows instantly that the house is dark because Genie is not in it. On a normal day the lights in the kitchen, in the living room, and in their bedroom would be on. Genie hates walking into an unlit room. The back door leading into the kitchen is not locked; Vida does not know whether to find this suspicious or not.

He turns on the kitchen light and immediately notices two glasses on the kitchen table. *Two* glasses. Both empty save for a desiccated wedge of lemon at the bottom of each. It is the desiccation of the lemon wedges that fills his heart with fear. Something is not right. Where is Genie? Where are Matilda and Stefanos? How long has everyone been gone? What exactly has happened here? Without being aware of what he is doing, he makes his way to the bedroom.

In the bedroom, Genie is sleeping peacefully in a bloom of her own blood.

The next thing that Vida becomes fully aware of is that he is standing in the cold corridors outside the Intensive Care Unit at the Mater Dei Hospital. Dr. Mambo is gently touching him on the shoulder, explaining to him that there is really nothing he can do and that it is best for him to go home. She is trying to be kind, he knows, but he cannot find the kindness in what she says.

"You standing here, looking like that, will not change things either way."

Looking like what? Vida looks down. That is when he notices

it. On his trembling hands. On his shirt. On his shoes. Blood. Genie's blood.

"Please, Vida. Go home. Take care of yourself."

Once home he cannot bring himself to sleep. He cannot bring himself to take off his clothes. He cannot bring himself to take a shower. He feels that washing Genie's blood off his body would be a resignation, a betrayal. He does not want to go upstairs and face the bloodstained bed. He does not want to go upstairs and face the absence of Genie. So he sits at the kitchen table and looks at the two glasses with the desiccated lemon wedges. Genie has obviously had company at some point while he was away. He feels that this matters, but does not know how it matters.

And where are Matilda and Stefanos? Why are they not here? When such a thing happened, why were they both not here? It all seems too coincidental to be a real coincidence.

He feels that there are dots to be connected and that if he connected the dots, he would know something really worth knowing. But he is tired. Mind and body. Tired.

In the early hours of the morning, when he is just about to fall asleep or has been asleep for a little while without realizing it, still thinking that he is thinking when in fact he has been dreaming, a memory from the day before presents itself. His only suit, newly dry cleaned, still in its protective plastic covering, and his favorite shirt, ironed with a crisp collar, just the way he likes it, both hanging from the coatrack with, beneath them, his favorite shoes polished to a brilliant shine; an ivy cap, a pair of argyle socks, a handkerchief and a tie laid out neatly on the footstool next to the coatrack. He had noticed the clothes as soon as he turned on the light. But more surprising than that had been Genie's suitcase at the foot of the bed...the bed on which Genie lay bleeding.

He pushes himself away from the kitchen table—bounds

up the stairs—rushes down the corridor—opens the door to their bedroom—makes a point of not looking at the bed with its bloodstain—and opens Genie's suitcase. And then the truth of his situation makes itself known. There, placed neatly among Genie's childhood clothes, are Penelope and Specs... and Blue's baby-blue silk slippers. Genie had prepared herself to leave him. And she had done her best to prepare him as well.

But none of this does anything to solve the mystery of the two glasses with desiccated lemon wedges in them. It is now clear to him that Genie had made sure that Matilda and Stefanos were not there when she entertained whoever it was. Who was this someone who had paid Genie a visit? Who was this someone for whom she had opened the door and fixed a drink that required a lemon wedge? Who was this someone for whom she had taken the time to cut a lemon into wedges? She had taken the time to collect his only suit from the dry-cleaners. She had taken the time to enter her old bedroom and pick up the three possessions she had entered this home with—her suitcase, her rag doll Penelope, and her teddy bear Specs. She had taken the time to put Blue's baby-blue silk slippers in her suitcase. She had taken the time to leave clues behind—clues that let Vida know, without a doubt, that just as easily as she had chosen to enter his life, she had chosen to leave it. That she had chosen this end for herself.

Feeling betrayed, Vida enters the shower fully clothed and lets the water wash the blood—Genie's blood—off his body and clothes. That is when he sees them: a pair of sunglasses on the ledge of the basin. They do not belong to him. They do not belong to Genie. Someone has entered not only their kitchen but their bathroom as well—and Genie has let whoever it was into their sanctum. He looks at the pair of sunglasses, unable to comprehend what they signify, until the water washing over his body turns ice-cold.

In an impotent act of revenge, he wears the clothes that Genie had so carefully prepared for him to wear to her funeral. He walks out of their bedroom, down the stairs, through the kitchen—where he makes a point of not looking at the two glasses on the kitchen table—out the back door, down the driveway, through the gate and onto the streets. He walks with no thought of where he is going. All that matters to him is that he is putting distance between himself and the desiccated lemon wedges, the packed suitcase and the bloodstained bed.

The sunglasses are safely tucked in his breast pocket.

Jesus

———•———

Genie watches Vida, fascinated as he blows perfect smoke rings out of his mouth. She captures one floating ring in her mouth before it disintegrates into nothingness. Then she starts giggling uncontrollably and infectiously. He cannot help but laugh. She sits and he lies on one of the kopjes in the backyard, both high on premium Tonga dagga. The night air is comfortably cool. They have come out to watch the stars—brilliant and seemingly close enough to touch in an ink-black sky—but all they have done is look at each other.

He reaches up and gently pulls her head down towards his. She smiles and leans forward to kiss him. They have never kissed before. Their lips touch lightly, tentatively, imperfectly.

Then Vida is filled with the knowledge that this moment is not real. He tries to hold on to the moment—a memory within a dream—for just a little while longer, but, cruelly, unforgivably, Genie's touch fades away. Thankfully, her scent is still there, warm vanilla, on his shirt collar.

Vida opens his eyes.

The sunlight—harsh even in winter—is blinding.

His eyes accustom themselves to his surroundings. Pavement—cold, grimy. Awning—sun-beaten, tattered. To-ing and fro-ing people. Helter-skelter traffic. Noise and noxious fumes. The heart of the city. Diseased now. But still beating its erratic beat.

How long has it been, three days since he took to the streets? Downings' Bakery closed down years ago, so he no longer has the security of the alleyway nor the comfort of freshly baked bread.

Something is fluttering on Vida's chest. He looks down to see a colorful bird. The bird looks at him quizzically. It flutters again, a little unsteadily. A broken wing on the mend.

"Aren't you a colorful one...pretty," he says. "And friendly too." He is overwhelmed by a need to touch the bird—to touch the colorful feathers—before it flies away. He tentatively lifts his right hand.

Just then someone shoves *The Chronicle* newspaper into his hand. "You made the headline," the person says, walking away before Vida can clearly make him out.

Frightened, the bird flies away. Vida feels robbed and angry.

He looks at the newspaper in his hands. In big bold letters the headline reads: "JESUS BACK ON STREETS." There is a picture of him—Vida—taking up half the page. Definitely not his finest hour, which, of course, is exactly why he made the headline. Mouth wide open and drooling. An open bottle—half empty—of something he no longer remembers drinking, dangling in his hand.

Despite the sensational headline and embarrassing picture, the reporter, one Bhekithemba Nyathi, does not have much to report. The story reads: "The man once known as 'The Messiah of the Streets' is back. Having first disgraced the streets with his presence in the 1980s, when he could be seen still faithfully wearing his RF military fatigues long after the liberation struggle had ended, the ex-soldier disappeared without a trace in the mid-1990s. He is now back, thankfully minus the military attire. The question on everyone's lips, of course, is: 'Why is Jesus back?' Some say he is one of those white farmers whose land has been rightfully reclaimed. Some say his illegal activities (we can only wonder what those are) have finally caught up with him. Some say he gambled away his immense wealth. If he has a sober moment, we would like to ask him some questions and get to the bottom of this."

Vida gets up. Finally he has something to do—something other than waiting. He swoons and steadies himself against the wall. He has one serious babalaas, but he is determined. He needs to set the record straight. Make things right again.

He has never been known as "The Messiah of the Streets." Ever.

He has never been a white farmer. Ever.

The only thing he ever gambled was his life. But everyone did that in the 1970s in one way or another.

This Bhekithemba Nyathi needs to be taught the facts.

He stops, suddenly uncertain. There was a bird that landed on his chest a few minutes ago, wasn't there? Or was he imagining things? He hopes not. He wants to take comfort in the knowledge that such a colorful bird exists and that it would feel safe enough with him to land on his chest.

"There was a bird...I had a bird...a colorful bird. Not so long ago," he finds himself asking—no, telling—a complete stranger. The stranger, a street vendor selling sad-looking tomatoes and onions on the corner, looks up at him and smiles. Her eyes, however, seem to look through him.

"I had a bird...a beautiful and colorful bird...didn't I?" Vida repeats, this time making sure to state it as a question.

"Are you talking to me?" the street vendor asks, an uncertain smile on her lips. "I'm afraid my eyes are not for beauty to see," she says.

It is then that Vida realizes that the woman is blind. "I'm sorry," he mumbles as he continues on his journey. He turns back and says to her: "There is no beauty to be seen. Not anymore." But with all the street noise he is sure that she does not hear him.

Vida had thought his disheveled appearance would create a problem; however, it turns out to be surprisingly easy to enter *The Chronicle's* premises and gain access to Bhekithemba Nyathi.

"I have never been a white farmer," Vida says, tossing the newspaper onto Bhekithemba Nyathi's desk. "I'm having a bloody sober moment. So here I am. Ask me why I'm back on the street," Vida says, pacing the small room. It is true that he is sober now. Walking the streets always has that effect on him—clears his head and helps him focus.

Surprisingly, and to his dismay, Vida finds himself struggling not to feel sorry for Bhekithemba Nyathi. He wants to feel angry. He needs to stay angry. Anger is an active emotion. It is much better than being reconciled. But this Bhekithemba Nyathi sitting in this minuscule, decrepit office is arousing his sympathy. How could he not, when everything around him is sadness. The chairs—there are only two—are so old that the cushioning has been completely eaten away by years of overuse. One of the legs of the desk is leveled by a brick. And wafting through the only window in the room is the acrid smell of sunbaked urine from the alleyway below.

Pathetic. If he had to work in this environment every day, he too would write with a poison pen.

"Jesus," Bhekithemba Nyathi says.

"The name is Vida."

"Vida de Villiers. I know. How may I help you?" Bhekithemba Nyathi asks, managing, somehow, to look professional.

"I have never been a white farmer. Never been white. Never been a farmer."

"You look white."

"Well, I'm not. I'm Coloured."

"I see."

"And I was never known as 'The Messiah of the Streets.'

They just called me Jesus."

"I know, but you have to admit that 'The Messiah of the Streets' has a nice ring to it."

"It very well may have, but they just called me Jesus."

"Would you like some tea?" Bhekithemba Nyathi asks, suddenly getting up. "Let me make us some tea. I have a good green tea. My wife sends it to me. She's in England. It will calm you, help you relax."

"I don't want to be calm. I don't want to relax. I want you to print the facts. Vida de Villiers is back on the street because Imogen Zula Nyoni is lying in a coma in Mater Dei Hospital, and he refuses, absolutely refuses, to go home without her."

Bhekithemba Nyathi sighs heavily. "Look, Vida, I know about Imogen. There is no way I can print that story—a man driven to the streets because his wife is lying in a coma in Mater Dei Hospital?"

"We are not married," Vida corrects.

"We live in a time of HIV and AIDS," Bhekithemba Nyathi continues. "Everyone knows someone in hospital who is fighting to survive. That fact alone—that we *all* know someone who is struggling to be alive—should be the headline every day, but it is not. It is our reality, the way we live now, our truth. So of course we cannot acknowledge it, let alone print it. We cannot print what matters, we never print the truth, but we still have to sell the paper somehow. So in the end, all we have is sensationalism. And that is what your story had to be. I am really sorry...truly."

"I can't go back to a home she's not in..." Vida says, realizing with dread that he is dangerously close to crying.

"I think I will go ahead and make us that cup of tea," Bhekithemba Nyathi says, leaving the office and making sure to close the door firmly behind him.

Vida understands that he has been given a chance to cry in

private. He appreciates it.

"Jesus wept," Vida says when Bhekithemba Nyathi returns after a while with a kettle of boiled water in his right hand and two mugs—one chipped, the other slightly cracked—in his left. "Maybe that can be your headline tomorrow," Vida says with a sad smile.

There are a few awards and certificates on Bhekithemba Nyathi's desk. Vida examines them. Apparently, once upon a time this Bhekithemba Nyathi was quite the accomplished journalist.

"Those are from another lifetime," Bhekithemba Nyathi says, handing Vida the slightly cracked mug. "The eighties and nineties. We had some room then—granted not much—but some room to do actual journalism." He puts a teabag in each mug and then pours the water. "Those were the days."

Vida sits down on the de-cushioned chair, suddenly feeling exhausted.

"I'm the one who broke the Golide Gumede story in the eighties," Bhekithemba Nyathi says, his chest slightly puffing up with pride, a faraway look in his eyes. "Met Imogen, and her mother, Elizabeth...Very interesting family, that one. You could tell just by looking that something was different there. It was like they were inhabiting a world of their own. And happy—very, very happy. And Imogen was a revelation... so bright...intelligent...sharp. I think *she* actually interviewed *me*. Shame what happened...damn shame. I sometimes think that if I hadn't written that story, then none of it would have happened....Well," he says, snapping back to the present, his shoulders sagging under the memory of it all.

"Saved my life, Golide Gumede did," Vida says. "Found me in the bush listening to Janis Joplin."

"You were listening to Janis Joplin in the bush?"

"I was seventeen years old and stupid—and very much

in love with Janis. I took her everywhere. He had his AK-47 pointed right here." Vida points at his forehead. "Could have blown my head off. But he didn't."

"And years later you married his daughter. I think that's something worth drinking to," Bhekithemba Nyathi says, taking a sip of his green tea.

"It certainly is," Vida says, also taking a sip from his mug and not bothering to correct Bhekithemba Nyathi this time. Choosing, instead, to take comfort in the fact that in someone's world he and Genie are married.

Galen House is populated with too many people, all ailing from something. The intake section is full. The corridors are full. Dr. Dingani Masuku's waiting area is full. The nurses look hurried, harried and hostile, the doctors seem absent-minded and aloof.

"Do you have an appointment?" the young nurse behind the desk asks without bothering to look up from the patient files she is working on. That is the other thing the waiting area is filled with, piles and piles of khaki and manila patient files.

"No."

The nurse twists her mouth. "Take a number. Take a chart. Fill out your name, medical history and what brings you here today. Try to be as brief as possible. Do you have medical insurance?"

"Yes."

The twist in the nurse's mouth loosens. "With which company?"

"I'm here to see Dr. Masuku."

"All these people are here to see Dr. Masuku. Some of them even have appointments."

"It's about his...daughter. Genie."

The nurse looks at him then. There is a flash of recognition.

"Oh. Jesus. Of course. I'm sorry. I thought…He's with a patient now. But if you go into the second examination room, he will be with you momentarily."

In the examination room, Vida has no choice but to sit on the green leather examination bed. The other chair, a rolling bar stool, is obviously the doctor's chair. The room smells antiseptic—too antiseptic, as though it is afraid to entertain even a single germ or the notion of dirt. Instead of reassuring Vida, the smell worries him.

"Good afternoon, Mrs. Sigauke," Dingani says, drawing open the white curtain as he reads from a chart. "The ticker still not ticking correctly, I see." Dingani finally looks up from the chart, with a smile that quickly dissipates. "Vida. You're not Mrs. Sigauke."

"I know I'm not."

"What are you doing here?"

"I came to inform you that Genie is in a coma. She's at Mater Dei Hospital. In ICU."

"I see," Dingani says. "I see." He sits down slowly. "I see." He looks defeated by something that he has been struggling with for a very long time.

Dingani reminds Vida of a lion he once saw at a zoo in Stockholm. The lion was alone, in the snow, so very far away from the savannah. Its coat looked mangy and moth-eaten. It was the most miserable creature that Vida had ever seen. When he looked at it, it looked away, almost as though it was ashamed. Vida understood that the lion had lost its pride and that was why it was capable of feeling shame. But he did not blame the lion. He blamed the people who had removed it from its natural habitat.

That is what Dingani, sitting there without his family, reminds Vida of: a lion without his pride.

"Why?" Dingani asks.

"Why what?"

"Why is she in a coma?"

Whatever sympathy Vida had for the prideless Dingani instantly disappears. The man is no lion, he is an ostrich.

"Why is she in a coma?" Dingani repeats.

"Why do you think?" Vida asks. He holds Dingani's gaze until Dingani looks away.

"I had heard something, of course, but one does not want to believe such a thing to be true."

Vida watches as whatever has been propping Dingani up gives way, leaving him hunched over and hollowed out.

"What did you do?" Dingani asks the question quietly, looking at the black-and-gray checkered linoleum floor of the examination room.

Vida does not know whether Dingani has directed the question at himself or to him. He decides to leave before he finds out. He jumps off the bed and makes his way to the door.

"This is your fault. Your fault." Dingani's voice is louder this time, but he is still looking at the floor, and so Vida still does not know whom Dingani is addressing.

"Marcus will be so devastated," Dingani says as Vida opens the door. "They are so very attached to each other, Marcus and Genie, so very attached....Probably best not to tell him... not yet."

Vida closes the door firmly behind him, without turning around.

Marcus

———

This is an ending. Marcus feels it in his bones. He can barely make out Genie through the dust. He sees her open her mouth to say something. The voice that comes out of her mouth is not hers but Karen Carpenter's. She is singing the opening lines to "Calling Occupants of Interplanetary Craft."

Marcus wakes up with a start.

Karen Carpenter continues singing. "Calling Occupants of Interplanetary Craft" is his ringtone; it means his phone is ringing. Marcus reaches for the phone on his nightstand and answers it.

On the other end is his mother's voice, breaking.

"I'm sorry, mum. We have a bad connection," Marcus says as he sits up in bed.

She speaks louder, more deliberately, but all he can make out clearly is the word "coma." It is 4:37 a.m. She lives in Belgium now; a new life for herself. He strongly suspects that there is another man in her life. If something has happened to him, this new man in her life, she should not have called.

"Who is in a coma, mum?"

This time the only word he can make out is "father."

"Is it dad? Has something happened to him? Is he in a coma?"

"Not—father—sister—"

Marcus' wife, Esme, makes a contented sound in her sleep and snuggles closer to him. The alarm clock on the bedside table switches from 4:37 to 4:38 a.m. He gets out of bed and goes to stand by the window.

"Has something happened to Krystle?"

"No, not Krystle. Genie. Genie is in a coma."

This time he hears her clearly enough, but finds himself apologizing again. "I'm sorry. I'm afraid I don't quite understand."

"Your father called me. Genie fell into a coma a few days ago. Of course Vida did not inform him as soon as it happened. Took his sweet time—"

"Genie is in a coma?" he interrupts, trying to sound calm, without succeeding.

"Now Marcus, I don't want you to worry. I'm sure she'll be fine, of course." His mother says this in a rushed way that is not at all convincing or reassuring.

"Of course," Marcus says, trying to sound convinced and reassured.

"You know how Genie is...resilient." He can tell from the quiver in his mother's voice that she is attempting to smile and not succeeding. "Your father and I have discussed it and have both decided that it is best that I go home. Your father is alone....And this is...Well, he shouldn't have to be alone at a time like this." Marcus knows his silence is making her nervous. His mother has never liked silence. "Now I don't want you making any rash decisions, Marcus. You do not have to go home. Your father and I will handle this."

"What exactly is it that needs to be handled?"

"Not—home—Genie—" His mother's voice is breaking up again.

"I'm sorry, mum. We have a bad connection," he apologizes before clicking off his phone. All he can hear now is the sound of his heart beating—rapidly.

Home.

His fantasy of home always begins with the smell of something warm, welcoming, inviting...vanilla...and woodsmoke. Then the image. The moonlight comes in through the window and falls onto the narrow bed. Genie's body is covered by a thin, threadbare blanket. Her back is turned to him. He knows that she is aware of his presence because her hand lifts up the blanket. She is not quite awake. She does not turn to face him. He climbs into the bed. The wire springs under the thin mattress creak—a comfortable sound. The saggy cushioning makes the bed sunken in the middle so that he naturally gravitates towards her. He interlocks his cold feet with her warm ones. She does not complain. He gathers her in his arms, pulls her to him. She says something delightfully domestic: "Did you remember to lock the chicken coop?" "Mm-hmm," he replies. He looks up at the mosquito net hanging above the bed. Vanilla and woodsmoke are trapped in the mosquito net, the mattress, the thin blanket, her well-worn nightdress, her hair, her skin. He breathes in deeply. Without even trying he falls fast asleep.

Home. A sanctuary. A safe haven. What would have been had his parents not come to take him away from the Beauford Farm and Estate.

The dawn is breaking. How long has he been standing here? The alarm clock by the bed reads 5:42 a.m. He looks around the room. The four-poster bed, the vanity, ancient and heavy (it has been in Esme's family for generations). The oak wardrobe. The oak wardrobe. There are two of them, identical —one for her and one for him. Both mostly function as decorative pieces since Marcus and Esme have and use a large walk-in closet. The ottoman—never used, but which looks useful next to the antique-looking but fully functional telephone, which is also rarely used these days. The travel-weary and weather-beaten set of suitcases in the corner that he had bought at an auction because they reminded him of something—a journey not taken perhaps—that made him nostalgic somehow.

He goes to the suitcases, opens one of them and retrieves the copy of the 1965 world atlas that Genie had sent him. He tries not to think about why he has chosen to place the world atlas in this suitcase as he flips to the page he has turned to time and time again: the page with the small reddish-brown handprint on it.

Marcus sees Esme move in the bed. He quickly puts the atlas back in the suitcase. Esme's hand reaches out, searching. Not finding him there, she wakes up panicked, instantly fully alert. Her eyes quickly scan the room. They find him. She relaxes. He smiles at her reassuringly. "It is a beautiful morning."

Esme gets out of bed. "Having trouble sleeping again?" she asks as she walks towards him.

"A little."

Her arms steal around him. He takes one of her hands and kisses it. This is an old gesture, one that they have both grown accustomed to.

"Was that a call you received earlier?"

"Yes."

"Is everything okay?"

"It was mum."

"Is she still apologizing?"

"Something like that."

"Have you forgiven her?"

"Something like that."

"Marcus?" Esme tries to turn him around. Tries to make him face her.

"All felled, felled, are all felled."

Who had he heard reciting that poem before? Genie? Chris?

"All felled, felled, are all felled." That is what had happened to the trees of his youth. His mother had all the jacaranda trees in their yard cut down. She had the trees felled and *then* left her husband and her home for Belgium a few months later. What had been the point?

Marcus disengages Esme's arms from around his waist, taking great care to make the gesture not seem like a rejection.

Thankfully, his phone rings. He waits for Esme to leave the room before answering.

"Dad?"

"Your mother told me she'd called you. I'd asked her not to. Didn't want to worry you. You haven't told Chris yet, have you?"

"No. Not yet."

"Best not to. You know how Chris is. And really there's nothing to worry about. Genie will be perfectly fine. You know how...resilient she is. She'll bounce back. She'll ..."

Something has crept into his father's voice that Marcus does not like. Fear.

At work, his father is always in control, always in charge. This man stumbling through words, blindly grasping at snatches of reassurance, is not his father. He loves his self-assured father. This man he does not like. This man he wants to hurt.

Marcus says to this man: "If anything happens to Genie, it will be your fault." The words surprise him. Immediately he wants to take them back.

But his father is not surprised by the words. He even seems to have been anticipating them. "You're right. Of course, you're right. It is my fault. It is all my fault."

The line goes dead.

A sudden silence.

A feeling of terrifying loneliness overwhelms Marcus. He quickly punches in Chris' number. The phone rings and keeps ringing. That's Chris for you. She is probably angry with him over some perceived injury that he isn't aware of having inflicted. "Hi. You've reached Krystle Masuku. Please state your business after the beep."

"Chris. Marcus here. Whatever is going on with you, you need to get in touch with the family. Genie is in a coma. I need to go home. I need to be with her."

Krystle

As Krystle nears her apartment complex, she fumbles for her keys that have, as usual, fallen to the bottom of her handbag. She ignores her ringing cellphone. Marcus. Third call from him. Not terribly good at taking a hint. The last time he had called her so obsessively, he had wanted to talk about the jacaranda trees that their mother had chopped down. "I want to be left alone," she says under her breath. And, almost as if having heard her, the phone stops ringing.

Just then she almost steps on something. A shiver runs through her. She is briefly excited by the sudden occurrence of the unexpected.

Something is lying on the ground. Dead. She begins to walk away but finds herself going back to check. A hatchling lies broken on the cement. The chest goes up...down...then up again. Breath. A beating heart. Life. She finally allows herself to exhale.

She looks at the hatchling and immediately decides that it is a "he," even though she has no way of knowing. He is very, very tiny. She looks up. Treetops, roofs, but not a nest in sight. Where could he possibly have fallen from? He must have fallen a great distance. It is remarkable that he is alive at all. She moves to help him and then stops herself. If she helps him will she really be doing more good than harm?

Chink-chink.

She turns to the sharp, metallic sound. Another bird. A full-grown California Towhee is hopping along nearby.

Ever-watchful. The mother. Krystle is suddenly filled with dread and uncertainty. Will the mother attack her if she moves him away from the footpath and places him in a safer place? Will the mother reject her baby if she, Krystle, touches him? She has heard that that happens, that mother birds reject babies that have been touched by human hands. But you cannot believe everything that you hear. Especially about mothers.

Aware of her presence and obviously frightened by her, the hatchling makes an attempt to get up and move away. He briefly struggles to stand, then gives up. He shuts his eyes and with great effort turns his head away from her, allowing whatever will happen next to happen. He probably thinks that she will harm him and it saddens her to know that he has reconciled himself to this fate. Life is cruel. What an unfortunate lesson to learn so young.

It is something she too has come to accept—being reconciled to her fate. Her life with all its disappointments, the most recent being a dissertation that remains unwritten after three years and a PhD that remains unearned after six years. She wonders if this is all there is to life, this being reconciled—which may or may not be better than the waiting. Waiting to fall in love, utterly and stupidly. Waiting to finally knit something (perhaps for someone) from the piles of yarn her grandmother has sent her over the years. Waiting to realize one of those magnificently unrealistic dreams she had as a child—becoming a world-renowned ballerina all the way from Africa; a five-foot four inch supermodel; a devoted wife of an equally devoted husband who is, quite naturally, an architect...

The hatchling is no bigger than her thumb. She can actually see the movements of his still-beating heart. He is dark. Dark gray with scattered tufts of downy feathers, like loose clumps of soft-gray cotton wool. One tuft rests on the top of his head—a Mohawk—giving his face a rebel-like quality. His tongue is sticking out. Do birds have tongues? Well, either way, she will have to remove him from harm's way. She rummages through her bag looking for something to lift him with. She finds a recently received postcard with a picture of the Victoria Falls on the front. The postcard is from her once-upon-a-time sister, Genie, who has scrawled on the back, in her elegantly undulating handwriting: "Remember, there will be the time of the swimming elephants." Krystle has no idea what that means. Genie has always been...cryptic, but she is grateful for the card nonetheless because she can put it to good use now. As gently as she can, but probably not gently enough, she lifts the hatchling off the ground.

Chink-chink.

She carefully, as carefully as she can, places him among some shrubbery where the sharp and ever-watchful mother can see him. She has not done much, but hopefully it is enough. His soft-gray tufts of downy feathers flutter and for the first time she realizes just how windy it is. Is that what precipitated his fall? His unforgiving environment?

Chink-chink.

Will the mother come to protect him? Will she stay with him or fly up to the nest? Can the mother carry her baby back to the nest? Is she strong enough? Krystle has so many questions. Why does she know so very little about birds?

She has done the best she can. She will have to leave it at that. She walks away quickly, not looking back, not wanting the feeling to overwhelm her, even though she knows such concern is already too late.

She has only just put down her handbag in her apartment, when she decides to go back and check on the hatchling. She finds him having moved off the postcard onto the cold, damp earth—perhaps of his own volition, perhaps propelled by the wind. The mother is nowhere in sight. Probably returned to the nest. Is it because Krystle touched him? Well, she cannot just leave him alone, can she? There is nothing else to be done. She will have to take him off the cold, damp earth, out of the wind and into her apartment.

She returns to her apartment and prepares a place for him. She has lived in the same apartment for six years and has never had a visitor—never invited anyone in, never taken the trouble to make someone feel welcome, feel at home. This is all alien to her. What would make him—he who is broken—feel safe? A warm place. She increases the room temperature. What else? A container that will not be constraining, that will actually allow him some freedom to move and breathe. She immediately finds a small fruit basket. Perfect. She lines it with soft tissue paper. He will need further protection in his new, unnatural environment. She finds a suitable cardboard box, but she needs to make it cozy. She places some of the balls of yarn that her grandmother sent her in the box. At last they have come in useful. She remembers the mother's sharp, metallic chirp and immediately thinks of the scatting Ella Fitzgerald as a substitute. She shuffles through her playlist until she finds the song "Mr. Paganini" and presses play.

Soon she is outside again, attempting to transport him, via the postcard, safely into the comfortable container. Her hands tremble, overwhelmed by a sense of urgency. To her dismay, the postcard has become entangled in the shrubbery. She attempts to lift him up. Was he this fragile and frail before?

This cannot be happening. He is falling again. He lands on the ground with the quietest thud. Her heart skips a beat. His does not. He opens his mouth and lets out a long, silent scream.

"I know, I know."

She carefully maneuvers the postcard out of the shrubbery and gently puts him in the container. He rests his head on the edge of the container. Eyes shut, beak firmly pressed together, stubborn-like. It occurs to her for the first time that he is a fighter, perhaps even a survivor, a rebel with a cause. She takes him into her home.

She goes to bed early and cries herself to sleep. The buzzing of her vibrating cellphone wakes her. Marcus. She does not answer it. She goes to check on the hatchling. Still alive. Thank God. Please don't die. Please don't die. Please don't die. This is not a prayer. This is a request. She does not do prayers, though she believes in God; she simply learned a long time ago that he does not answer hers.

She watches the dawn break in a blur. All she can hear is the sound of her own heart beating and her occasional sniffle. She checks on the hatchling. A blur. Blinks. Sees him clearly. Chest goes up...then down. Breath. Life. Thankfully, he is still there. She was right about him. He is a survivor. A rebel with a cause.

"I called earlier about a hatchling; a California towhee," Krystle says to the impossibly tall man wearing hospital scrubs and adjusting his glasses behind the desk on which she carefully places the box. The man automatically reaches for a notepad and a pen.

"Name?" He blinks at her and does not even attempt a smile.

"Mr. Paganini."

The man blinks again. "First name?"

"I didn't give him one."

The man frowns.

"Oh, you mean my name? Krystle Masuku."

The man's frown deepens.

"K R Y S T L E," she spells as he writes, "M A S U K U."

He briefly looks in the box, then picks it up carefully and

walks away with it.

"One hatchling, California towhee, for the incubator," the blinking, unsmiling man says, going through swinging double doors.

"Number?" A voice says from within.

"She named it. Mr. Paganini."

"She named it?"

Krystle does not know what to do. Is that it? Is that all there is to it? Should she have taken a picture? She should have taken a picture. Without a picture she might forget him. And she does not want to forget Mr. Paganini.

Her phone rings. Marcus, yet again. She ignores it.

The blinking man comes back through the swinging double doors. He readjusts his glasses. Then he comes to an abrupt stop in the middle of the room and frowns. He is obviously surprised to find her still standing there. "Was there something else?" he says, patting his pockets as though the something else might be found in them. "Did you want your box back...the postcard?"

"Box? Postcard? No. No, I...ummm. I'm sorry, I didn't get your name."

"Xander Dangerfield."

"You have the name of a superhero," Krystle says before she can stop herself.

He smiles a surprisingly dazzling and dashing smile. "Are you in need of rescuing?" he asks, this time not blinking. His eyes meet hers and he holds her gaze. "A damsel in distress?"

It is Krystle's turn to blink. Rapidly and repeatedly. Is he flirting with her? Does he think she is flirting with him? Is she flirting with him? "I'll...call to check on Mr. Paganini. Thank you Xander...Dangerfield," she says, happy she can find something, anything, to say as she blindly searches for the door, suddenly feeling trapped and very, very disoriented by a feeling that is not in the least reconciled.

Frantic to have something to do, she finds herself clicking on her cellphone. *You have nine new messages. First new message...*Thankfully, she is out the door.

"I need to go home. I need to be with her." Krystle listens to these sentences over and over again. "I need to go home. I need to be with her." The rest of the message she cannot take in. How can Genie—her once-upon-a-time sister full of love, life and laughter—be in a coma? "I need to go home. I need to be with her." Rewind. "I need to go home. I need to be with her." These last two sentences she understands perfectly. That is her brother, Marcus, casting himself, once again, in the role of hero.

If Marcus is once again the hero, that can only mean one thing. In this story—this story, which is not make-believe; this story, which is not child's play; this story, which is all too real, in which Genie ends up in a coma—Krystle is the bad guy. And there is no escaping that fact.

Esme

And just like that, all of a sudden, they are that thing again. A family.

A family that does not include her, Esme.

There is the grandmother, Eunice. The father, Dingani. The mother, Thandi. The son, Marcus. The daughter, Krystle. The adopted daughter, Genie. And that's it. The family unit. Complete. They have barely spoken to each other for almost three years, ever since that business with the jacaranda trees and Thandi leaving for Belgium. But now Genie has brought them together again.

They, the family, as a unit, have decided after many phone calls that they will all go home to be with Genie.

No one has bothered to ask her, Esme, if she would like to join them.

They have, rather conveniently, forgotten that she loves Genie too.

Years earlier, Esme had opened her eyes and been surprised to find herself sitting in the front passenger seat of a tiny car. An alien was talking to a DJ on the All Hit Radio Show. A woman's voice was laughing infectiously.

Esme was confused. Where exactly was she? Karen Carpenter's voice started singing "Calling Occupants of Interplanetary Craft."

This was all too disconcerting.

The last thing that Esme remembered was Krystle at the

airport saying, in her characteristically sarcastic way, "Welcome to Africa"...and the stifling and oppressive heat.

Now, next to her a young woman was driving, hunched over the steering wheel. She was...colorful. She wore a patch-work dress and a multi-colored scarf, but her colorfulness was more than that. Her hair was the color of flames and created an amber-brown Afro-halo over her head; she had dark, smooth skin with a glow and sheen to it; her mahogany neck was long, graceful, and supported her head at an impossibly acute angle. She had high cheekbones and almond-shaped eyes. She looked like something that an artist would draw—incongruous, features exaggerated, but somehow beautiful, perhaps more so because so very different, so very original, so unique.

"My, aren't you a picture?" Esme had said, looking at the woman.

The woman looked at Esme and smiled at her—a radiant smile. There was a gap between her two front teeth. "Goodness, where are my manners?" the woman suddenly said. "I'm Imogen Zula Nyoni. Almost everyone calls me Genie—friend or foe. You can call me Genie, too. I am..." An expectant silence filled the air. "What am I?" Genie asked Krystle and Marcus through the rear-view mirror.

"Our once-upon-a-time sister," Krystle replied.

"I like the sound of that. I am their once-upon-a-time sister," Genie said, smiling with satisfaction.

"Mum and dad adopted her," Marcus said, attempting to make things clearer.

"But it didn't quite take," Genie said, with her radiant smile.

"She left us to be with Jesus," Marcus said, with something hard at the edges of his voice.

"I see I'm still unforgiven," Genie looked at Marcus in the rear-view mirror, the expression on her face difficult to read.

"Oh. So you're a Christian?" Esme asked.

"A Christian? Oh good god, no! Definitely not. Christians are too hypocritical for me. I like to call a spade a spade—even if I'm the spade."

Although she had divulged quite a bit about herself, Esme felt that she still had not quite got hold of Genie, who, although present, colorful and bright, seemed oddly ephemeral. Genie seemed to be on the verge of disappearing just as easily as she had appeared.

"Don't bother trying to make sense of Genie. No one can make sense of Genie," Marcus said, sounding uncharacteristically angry.

Suddenly the car screeched to a halt and Genie jumped out.

"Are we good, do you think?" Krystle asked Marcus once Genie was out of the car.

"I think so," Marcus responded.

Esme was sure they were talking about Genie. But what about Genie? She could not help thinking there was something beautifully tragic about her. Something secret that had made Marcus never tell Esme about her.

Genie got back in the car, clutching a bouquet of red and yellow wildflowers.

"The flame lily. Our national flower. Welcome," Genie said, giving the flowers to Esme.

"Thank you," Esme said. "I'm sorry about your parents," she added, wanting to give Genie something in return and finding that she only had condolences to offer.

"What about them?"

"I thought that...since you were adopted..." Esme hesitated.

"Oh...My parents did not die. They flew away," Genie said, flashing her radiant gap-toothed smile again.

And Esme believed her. Believed that Genie's parents had

flown away. Believed that Genie herself could, at any moment, at that very moment even, let go of the steering wheel
and fly away. Simply fly out of the window towards the sky
and become a multi-colored ribbon in the sky, a rainbow, a
wondrous thing to behold.

Esme looked at the flowers. Flame lilies. They resembled
frozen flames and were shockingly beautiful. How could she
not love the shockingly beautiful creature that had given
them to her—Marcus' and Krystle's once-upon-a-time sister,
Genie?

Esme has been married to Marcus for twelve years. Has
been with him for fourteen years. His parents attended their
wedding. Were there for the birth of all three of their children.
They had even attended her graduation from college and her
graduation from law school.

But now, after many years of making her feel part of the
family, they have closed ranks, leaving her, Esme Masuku, out
in the cold. A mere in-law, an outsider.

It was their beauty that had seduced Esme and made her,
almost from the start, want to be a member of the Masuku
family. It was after she had married into the family that she
saw them for what they really were: fragile to the point of
being brittle. They were delicate and sensitive to the touch.
The Masukus were like a glass menagerie; beautiful to look
at, perfectly, meticulously, painstakingly put together, but always just a breath away from shattering. They needed to be
handled with care, and she has been careful.

Even now, as she places a black suit discreetly at the bottom of Marcus' suitcase—just in case—Esme is being careful.
She knows that the possibility of Genie's death is a reality that
the Masukus are yet to acknowledge, if not to themselves
then definitely to each other.

She lays out the pair of jeans she likes best on him, a

t-shirt made of good breathable cotton, perfect for travel, a pair of broken-in loafers ("skoeners," he calls them), underwear, socks and his favorite leather jacket.

So this is how her husband will leave her. These are the clothes he will be wearing and this is the suitcase he will be carrying when he walks out of her life.

Marcus, bless him, is blissfully unaware that this is their ending. But Esme knows that if Genie dies, then Marcus, her husband, this man forcing himself to whistle nonchalantly as he takes a shower, is never returning to her.

She knows this because she knows things that Marcus does not know about himself. He does not know that he moves away from her in the middle of the night while they are asleep; that he has asked her more than once while deep in the fog of sleep who she is; that when he wakes up with a start it is always after calling out "Genie." He goes in search of Genie every night. He does not know this about himself because in the morning all is well again. In the morning he is her loving husband. In the morning she tells him nothing of what has happened during the night. In the morning she moves beneath him, above him, beside him until all he knows is one name—Esme.

Esme enters the bathroom, undresses, steps into the shower and kisses Marcus, stopping him mid-whistle.

This is how she will let him go.

What was it Genie had once said to her? "My way of loving him was to let him go. Your way of loving him will be to keep him. It was not easy to let him go. I dare say it will not be easy to keep him, but I have every faith that you will, and you need to have that faith too."

But Esme has long understood that she has Marcus during the day only because he is with Genie in the night—in memories, in dreams, in fantasies, in nightmares. If Genie ceases to exist, then what is to say Marcus will come back from the only place he knows he can find her—the night?

Marcus & Krystle

Marcus is, of course, facing the wrong direction, cellphone to his ear. Krystle's cellphone vibrates in her hand, but she does not answer it.

"We travel not to reach a destination but to arrive with love, in love, to be with those we love." This is what is printed on the back of his t-shirt. Deep stuff. Not something she would readily associate with her brother.

She taps him on the shoulder. He swivels around. Facing her is not a forty-something-year-old man, but the boy with little legs, eager to grow, bounding up the stairs two at a time. So this is what Genie's coma has done to him: made him eleven again.

I am Six Million Dollar Man and you are...

"Li'l sis," he says, reading her face, trying to gauge something. "I was just calling you."

"I know."

"You didn't answer."

"I know." She removes something from her handbag. "Consider this my olive branch," she says, handing it to him. It is a cluster of jacaranda flowers. "First bloom."

She smiles. He smiles. They hug. The beginnings are always nice.

"Pretty deep t-shirt you've got there."

Marcus examines the front of his t-shirt as though noticing it for the first time. Red, orange, green and blue lines intersect and diverge haphazardly. Marcus frowns. "Yes. I suppose it is rather labyrinthine...deep." A flash of recognition. "Oh. It's the T. You know, the Massachusetts public transportation system."

"I know what the T is, thank you very much," Krystle says, going to stand behind him again. She reads: "We travel not to reach a destination but to arrive with love, in love, to be with those we love."

"Is that what it says on the back?"

"Yes. That's why the words are coming out of my mouth. It's called reading. You should try it some time."

"Rather appropriate for the occasion," he says, turning to face her.

"Rather on the nose. Poor Esme."

"Poor Esme?"

"She picked out your clothes, didn't she?"

"Yes."

"You know there is a word for relationships like yours."

"Loving. Symbiotic. Caring."

"Not healthy."

"That's two words."

"Unhealthy then. Co-dependent."

"What do you mean 'Poor Esme'?"

"I mean just that...Poor Esme."

"Chris!"

"She wants you to come back to her."

"But I haven't gone anywhere."

"Says the man waiting for a flight at the airport."

"Oh, come on. You know what I mean."

"Hopefully you'll get to know what Esme means. And soon," Krystle says, patting him on the shoulder.

Marcus

As the airplane descended upon the land of patchwork green, brown and yellow fields, Marcus looked out of the window and remembered a time when his entire life had been contained in one of those patches—the Beauford Farm and Estate. From up there, the country seemed so peaceful, so quiet, so tranquil. But it has not been any of those things, not since the liberation war, which has since given way to ethnic genocide, civil unrest, political disturbances, massive emigration—all within the span of thirty years: a generation.

Marcus and Krystle exit the baggage claim area and there they are: his mother, his father, his grandmother. His family. So very changed and yet so very much the same.

His mother sashays towards them, arms outstretched, looking every bit like an actress on stage. A lipstick smile on her lips. But her eyes are sad—so very sad that Marcus cannot look into them for fear of seeing something reflected there that he has yet to acknowledge. Her eyes are the only indication that the play she is in is a tragedy. She throws her arms around him, and he, not knowing what else to do, kisses the only imperfection on his mother's otherwise perfect face, the bite mark from the day he left the Beauford Farm and Estate.

Marcus shakes hands with his father. A strong, firm, manly handshake that belies the helplessness they both feel. Marcus takes comfort in their tacit pact to feel one way and act otherwise with each other. It is a silent reunion, as it should be. Marcus leans down to hug his grandmother, whose weak legs have confined her to a wheelchair. She pierces him with a paradoxically focused but vacant stare. Just as he disengages his arms from around her neck, she grabs hold of his hand and, suddenly lucid, whispers: "They are plotting to overthrow the government."

Marcus kneels down in front of his grandmother and pats her hand in a way that he hopes comforts and reassures her. Who are "they"? Marcus wonders. His grandmother's arthritic index finger seems to be pointing in the direction of his parents. "Who are you," his grandmother suddenly says to him, her face contorting in fear, her eyes brilliant with paranoia. "Who are you?" she screams. "You are one of them."

"Welcome home," Krystle says to Marcus, as they all quickly exit the airport terminal.

Krystle

You can never go back home. You can never make the same journey twice. The past is always another country. Clichéd as these aphorisms are, they are all true—tragically so, Krystle thinks. She never comes back to the same country, the same home. Something always develops while she is away. Things change abruptly. Case in point: the house she grew up in. What was once a grand double-story building with a yard full of jacarandas and flamboyants and a manicured and watered evergreen lawn is now a skeletal frame with a single flamboyant tree (thanks to her mother) and an unkempt yellow lawn (thanks to her father). It did not take decades for things to deteriorate—just a few years.

Her mother, a once stand-by-your-man wife, at some point had just stopped standing by her man. Her father, a once avid gardener, at some point had just given up being avid about anything. A development. An abrupt change. Sad. Tragic really.

"You know, the reason Marcus has not been speaking to you is because of the jacarandas," Krystle volunteers as the car comes to a stop at the top of their driveway. She finds herself, as she always does, agitating things. She cannot help herself. She feels that her family needs—no, deserves—to be agitated.

"Is that true, Marcus?" Thandi asks.

"It's more complicated than that," Marcus says, getting out of the car, not quite able to hide the sadness in his voice.

"But I made sure to save the flamboyant. The one you liked

playing in. The one with the tree house. You'll see why the jacarandas had to go once you enter the house," Thandi says, pulling Marcus towards the house.

"See!" she says once they are in the house, pointing at the huge cracks in the walls. "The roots were destroying the foundation of the house."

"There were always cracks," Krystle says, nonplussed.

"Were there?" Marcus asks, genuinely surprised.

"The cracks were not as big as they are now," Thandi says, defensively.

"If we had let the trees grow—"

"The point is there were always cracks," Krystle cuts in.

"No. The point is Marcus has to understand why we cut down the jacarandas. It was to save the house."

"It was a jacaranda tree," Marcus says, almost in a whisper.

"What?" Thandi asks.

"The tree house was in a jacaranda tree, not a flamboyant. So you can go ahead and cut the tree down if you want," Marcus says, running his left hand over one of the cracks. He turns and attempts to smile at his parents but cannot.

A development. A change. Sad. Tragic really.

"All felled, felled, are all felled. Of a fresh and following folded rank. Not spared, not one," Krystle recites Gerard Manley Hopkins' "Binsey Poplars" as she makes her way up the stairs, the rest of her family in tow.

Her grandmother's slow progress up the stairs is aided by both her father and Marcus, whom she has forgotten that she has forgotten.

"So it was you who recited the poem," Marcus says. "I couldn't remember if it was you or Genie."

"It was both of us. We had to recite it in Mrs. Finlay's Grade Five class. It was a rite of passage at our school. A successful recitation meant that you automatically got into Miss Forbes's

A-stream Grade Six class. Genie particularly likes the lines, "O if we but knew what we do. When we delve or hew—Hack and rack the growing green! Since country is so tender to touch, her being só slender."

"Since country is so tender," Dingani says, speaking for the first time since entering the house. Her father is another change. He looks like a shadow of his former self.

Krystle opens the door to her bedroom. The room has been frozen in time: the 1990s. Posters on the walls; popular fiction, magazines and comic books on the bookshelf; clothes in the wardrobe. This is the only thing that has not been allowed to change. Forced to remain the same, it has become uncanny, something at once familiar and unfamiliar. She knows why her room has been preserved: it serves as a monument to Genie's time with them, but it really is a monument to her absence.

When the Masukus learned that Genie had left them to live with Jesus, Krystle's grandmother, Eunice, had descended on the room like a fury. (Her grandmother. Another change. Once strong and formidable. Now senile and frail.) Her grandmother had got down on her knees and ripped from the floor the adhesive tape that she herself had put there when she found out that Genie was coming to live with them. The tape was supposed to divide the room in half, but it really gave Krystle the lion's share of the room. The Masukus, one and all, pretended not to notice. Genie had never complained.

Having ripped off the adhesive tape, her grandmother set to work stripping the bed, emptying the clothes chest, the laundry basket, the bookshelf on Genie's side of the room. She had the gardener and the maid carry the bed, the chest, the laundry basket and the bookshelf outside. All Genie's belongings were piled high in the middle of the yard. Eunice poured paraffin on top and struck a match, consuming Genie's existence in flames and sending it up in smoke. While doing all this, her grandmother spoke of Genie's betrayal after everything, *everything* they had done for her. To run off with a man twice her age—a vagabond at that—making the Masukus the joke of the town. After everything, *everything* they had done for her. Such betrayal could not be borne.

"Why are you crying?" her grandmother had asked Krystle before slapping her across the face. The first and last time she had struck her. "That girl has proved herself to be a disappointment. Never, ever cry for someone who has disappointed you. You hear me? Never, ever cry for the ungrateful," her grandmother said, taking Krystle's face in the palms of her hands before engulfing her in a hug. Krystle wished that, like her parents and Marcus, she had not been at home to witness Genie's erasure from their lives, that smoldering ash.

Krystle realizes that the rest of her family members have followed her into the bedroom. They look around. They wait, almost expectantly, for Genie to descend from the roof, materialize from the wallpaper, rise up from the floorboards. How old would she be, this Genie that they are waiting for? Ten years old, as when she first arrived? Eighteen years old, as she was when she left? Thirty-nine years old, as she is now, lying in a coma at Mater Dei Hospital?

Her father, her mother, her brother and her grandmother leave the room quietly. They—the lucky ones—can leave. She cannot. She has to live with the absence. She has to live with a Genie who is not there.

Krystle looks at the telltale line left behind by the adhesive tape. She gets down on her knees and traces the grimy demarcation with her index finger. Tracing the evidence that Genie's life with them had not been as easy as they all liked to remember. They had loved her in their own way, the only way they knew how...jealously...possessively...imperfectly.

Vida

There are tubes everywhere. There is a feeding tube in her nose. There is a breathing tube in her mouth. There is a tube attached via a syringe to a viable vein in her right hand. There is a catheter in her urethra. The bag that collects her urine has been chastely covered by a baby blue cozy cover: an attempt at respect and dignity that seems mockingly too little too late.

Genie's body is in distress. Vida feels it. He also feels the absence. He knows that Genie is not here. The Genie he knew, the Genie he experienced, is somewhere else. Perhaps she is working to come back to this body, this body that was once hers. Perhaps she is not. Her body looks bereft. He wants more than anything to touch it, to give it solace, comfort, life. But he has been ordered not to. In fact, his hands have been encased in surgical gloves and his mouth shielded with a surgical mask.

Dr. Mambo has told him in clinical terms what has happened to Genie. She has been kind enough to not fill him with false hope. She has been a friend enough to say that she will accept and support his decision whatever it may be.

It has been seven days.

Seven days since he returned from Stockholm. Seven days since he found the two glasses with the desiccated lemon wedges on the kitchen table. Seven days since he found Genie's childhood suitcase packed and placed at the foot of the bed. Seven days since he saw the sunglasses on the bathroom basin. Seven days since he left The House That

Jack Built. Seven days since Genie has been in a coma. For seven days he has tried to hold on to his anger. For seven days he has failed. He does not feel anger. He does not feel sadness. He does not feel sorrow. He just feels.

He looks at her body bereft, and he knows. He knows. It has been seven days since Genie left him. Wherever she is, she is not coming back...not to this body...not to this life...not to him.

Vida is defeated. He can accept any change except death. Death, like a jealous lover, consumes completely. Death will not allow him to intervene.

Looking at her body lying there, Vida understands with amazing grace that the body is a threshold, an entry point for something else entirely, something elusive and ephemeral, something precious and beautiful, something that can fly away without a moment's hesitation.

He knows what he must do next.

Dr. Mambo

Dr. Prisca Mambo does not think that in all her thirty years of practicing medicine she has come across anyone as defiant as Imogen Zula Nyoni.

"How long do I have?"

Those were the first words Imogen had said to her during their initial encounter. A schoolgirl in uniform with her hair reluctantly tamed by a blue, red and white scrunchy. She looked both younger and older than her sixteen years: younger probably because she was slightly built and older because there was an undeniable wisdom in her eyes, something more than just mere intelligence—a knowing that had already happened.

"How long do I have?"

Imogen had had to repeat the question. Since starting her practice in the 1980s, Dr. Mambo had told countless people that they were HIV-positive. It was never easy news to break, but she took some measure of comfort in the fact that the people she told were usually middle-aged and had lived their lives. She had never had to break the news to a teenage girl whose life was yet to begin. And Dr. Mambo had actually taken the coward's way out. Once she had received the results of the blood work from the general practitioner, she had decided to tell the girl's guardians the news, reasoning that they were better equipped to break it to the girl. So she was rather surprised when the girl made an appointment and came to it alone.

A name on a hospital chart is one thing, the bearer of that name sitting across from you is another. The number "16" next to the word "Age" on a hospital form is one thing, an actual sixteen-year-old girl sitting across from you is another.

"How long do I have?"

"As you may know, there is still no cure for HIV," Dr. Mambo said tentatively. "There is antiretroviral medication. ARVs. Expensive. Too expensive for us at this time...but hopefully in the future...in the near future...in the very near future... we will be able to make them affordable and accessible. We are making definite strides in that direction, so I am hopeful. Very, very hopeful. ARVs go a long way towards ameliorating the symptoms. So like I said, hopefully in the very near future you will have access to them."

"How long do I have?"

"With the ARVs, patients—people—have been known to live very long and productive lives."

"And without the ARVs?"

"Well there are many variables—"

"How long do I have?"

"On average, once the disease is no longer in its dormancy, patients—people—have lived for up to five years without the ARVs, but that is the average. Some patients—people—have lived for up to ten years...some even longer. A good, healthy diet and regular exercise can go a very long way towards mitigating the ravages of the illness."

"So realistically I have about another five years. So the best I can hope for is living long enough to turn twenty-one."

"I think you can afford to hope for more than that. You are young and healthy. And, like I said, the landscape is rapidly changing. I'm confident that you will have access to the ARVs."

Just then Jesus walked by the window, pushing his Scania pushcart.

Imogen surprised Dr. Mambo by smiling. "Don't worry, doctor. Five years is long enough for me to do something good with my life."

Dr. Mambo had witnessed many different responses from people after hearing that their lives would be curtailed by HIV/AIDS: women often cried; men often got angry; mothers often became frantic about the futures of their children; fathers often worried that they would not have time to provide enough financial security for their families; some patients (mostly men) got violent and threw things at her as they angrily inquired of her who had given them the disease. No one had ever smiled. This girl, Imogen, who had probably had the misfortune of receiving a blood transfusion that was contaminated, and who therefore had contracted the disease through no fault of her own, had, instead of anger, chosen to smile.

That was when Dr. Mambo had noticed it, the defiance in Imogen. It was in the way she held her head at a particular angle, the way she squared her shoulders, the way she looked you in the eye. She was determined to face and perhaps conquer whatever came her way. She had seen things, experienced things and understood things that could have broken her, but she had used them to grow even stronger instead.

And Imogen had made good on her word: she had done something good with her life. A few years after their first meeting, while shopping at Solomon's, Dr. Mambo had come across Imogen and Vida de Villiers standing in the spice aisle. Vida was reaching for a bottle of olive oil on the top shelf (olive oil is situated in the spice aisle at Solomon's) and Imogen was looking at him, watching him closely. She looked so... fulfilled. It was as though in that moment Vida was doing much more than simply reaching for a bottle of olive oil; it was as though he was giving her what her heart truly desired and that he had parted seas, moved entire mountains, slashed through fortresses and slain dragons just to give it to her. Vida put the bottle of olive oil into the shopping basket that Imogen was carrying and he looked at her with such contentment, it was as though she held every precious thing that heaven had bestowed on him in her arms.

It was that look that had let Dr. Mambo know that Imogen had done something good with her life: she had found someone to love and she had found someone to love her. Dr. Mambo took a lot of comfort in Imogen and Vida's love. Love was such a rare commodity. It took real courage to seek it, to hold on to it and to treasure it. Most people in her situation had long since given up being courageous. At a time when it would have been so much easier to allow one's self to give in to the barrenness of existence, love was the truest defiance.

Dr. Mambo so often saw Imogen and Vida together— driving in their impossibly tiny Austin Mini Cooper, walking the streets with their Scania pushcart that was always laden with scrap metal, shopping for groceries—that she started thinking of them as an inseparable unit: Imogen and Vida.

Dr. Mambo even thought of the HIV as *theirs*, not just Imogen's. And so it had been difficult to break the news to Vida. When he had brought Imogen to the hospital seven days ago, he had looked stricken, pale; could not speak, could only hold on to Imogen. It had taken two male nurses to pry her from his arms. And then he had stood there covered in Imogen's blood, waiting. It had been difficult to tell him that he need no longer wait. It had been difficult to see him walk away...alone.

Imogen has been her patient for more than twenty years now, and Dr. Mambo has seen evidence of her defiance repeatedly as she has struggled with pneumonia, tuberculosis and meningitis. This time, however, cervical cancer has given Imogen's defiance a different form: her defiance has presented itself as peaceful surrender.

Dr. Mambo opens the orange-and-brown curtains in the room, wondering, not for the first time, why anyone would have thought that orange and brown were appropriate colors for a hospital room. In her opinion, both colors are too morose and subdued to provide any real comfort and hope. A hospital room should make every attempt to be colorful, especially a hospital room with Imogen Zula Nyoni in it.

Rays of weak, wintry, early-morning sunlight streak through, providing the room with light, but not nearly enough. Hospital policy stipulates that no lights are to be turned on during the day except in the operating rooms. Dr. Mambo defiantly turns on the fluorescent light above the bed. It is the least she can do for the person lying on the bed.

But there is no person lying on the bed.

Dr. Mambo hastily picks up the patient chart and flips through it. She has provided strict orders that the patient should not be moved. She has not ordered any tests for the patient. No time of death has been entered. So there is no reason for Imogen Zula Nyoni not to be lying in her bed. Dr. Mambo flips through the chart again...and again. But still she cannot find the reason why the bed is empty.

To Dr. Mambo's relief, three nurses enter the room pushing a trolley piled with bed linens, hospital gowns, sponges, antiseptic soaps, gauzes, syringes of various sizes, a blood pressure pump, a thermometer, an array of disposable needles, scissors, cotton wool, and a blender with liquefied beige food in it. The nurses are evidently not happy to find a patient-free bed. "Where is the patient?" one of the nurses asks, mild accusation in her eyes.

Valentine

Valentine Tanaka knows who they are, of course. He knows everyone who visits The Tower. He has made it his business to know. He is after all the Chief Registrar of The Organization and as such he handles all the important moments in a person's life: birth, coming of age, marriage, parenthood, divorce and death.

They are the Masukus. Imogen had once searched for a word, a phrase, to describe them, and after a long pause had said: "They glitter."

To which he had replied: "All that glitters is not gold."

"Exactly," she had said.

Decidedly. He does not like the Masukus.

Collectively, they look superficial, like something out of a magazine, a high-end one at that, one that sells impossible dreams—beauty, success, happiness, self-fulfillment, wealth, all achieved with ease and a smile.

So when the daughter says, as her eyes scan his office and sweep over him, not even trying to whisper, "How Dickensian," and the father, mother and son snicker, all secure in the knowledge that the reference is beyond him, Valentine Tanaka, mere civil servant, has decided that he does not like any of them.

The father. A doctor. A surgeon. Processed by The Organization in 1987. Somehow manages to look both haggard and handsome—not an easy feat, that. His eyes never settle on anything for too long. He is unsettled. Hiding something. Or perhaps just used to hiding something. An old habit. Unbreakable even now when there is nothing to hide. But of course there is something to hide. There always is. He has never had the courage to tell his family his secret. So that even as they sit here looking perfect, there is something about the father that his family does not know—something that Valentine Tanaka does.

The mother. Once a housewife, then the owner of a flower shop. Lives overseas. In Belgium. Smells expensive. Head held high. A picture of beauty, elegance and respectability. This sheen, however, is merely veneer. There is an entire chapter of her life that fills her with shame. A chapter that Valentine knows of. Her misfortunes have been rather public, and, because of this, appearances matter to her.

The son. Part-owner of a dot-com company that did not go bust. Wealthy. Truly raking it in. Some guys have all the luck. Lives overseas. Married. Wife—lawyer. Three children. His legs crossed like a lady. Manicured. Probably pedicured as well. Hair barbered to perfection. A pretty boy. Not a man at all. A man...a real man does not take this much care of himself. A real man does not sit with his legs crossed. A real man does not allow himself to look so...shiny. His eyes, at least, are determined. Determination is a manly thing.

The daughter. Student. Born overseas. Raised here. Now lives overseas. Citizen there. Very little known about her. No records to speak of. Since she was born outside the country, The Organization did not record her birth. Since she left when she was seventeen, a year before she would have had to register for a national ID card, she does not have that either. She is the hardest to read. There is something broken there. She is held together by sheer force of will. Not as tall as the others. Eclipsed. But defiant. The black sheep. The rebel— perhaps even with a cause. She is the only one so far who has looked him in the eye.

"Yes. I suppose it is rather Dickensian," Valentine says finally, letting his eyes travel over his office at their leisure, enjoying taking center stage. The mountains of files balancing at impossible angles, the ancient filing cabinets, the bookshelves all spilling over with paper, and everything covered in layers of dust. Even the enormously old-fashioned but fully functional computer has a sprinkling of dust for good measure. "Too much paper and dust. The hallmarks of an ineffective and inefficient bureaucracy," he says, bringing his gaze back to them.

They stare at him blankly, suddenly feigning ignorance, pretending not to see—all of them. A family trait. Probably how they have always dealt with embarrassing and difficult situations.

He is determined to make them feel some humility, even if it is only a sliver.

"Or perhaps you meant that I'm the one who is Dickensian?" he says, thoroughly enjoying the moment when they all look at the floor simultaneously. Mission accomplished. Good job.

Lawrence Tafara—a colleague, not a friend, he does not have many friends—once said to him: "Ay, but Valentine, you're certifiably ugly." Lawrence Tafara had been drunk at the time. They both were. Heavy drinking was part of the job. He had given Lawrence Tafara a sound beating for that, even though he agreed with him. Certifiably ugly. That is what he is indeed. A crippled hunchback without the redeeming bell in the tower or the heart of gold to make him a tragic hero.

That was the thing that shocked people most about him—his lack of a heart of gold. When they came into his office to be processed, they could never reconcile the way he looked with what he did, or, rather, with the impossibly exacting way in which he did his job—asking for documents, evidence, proof. Failure to produce the required documents was never met with sympathy when a person encountered Valentine Tanaka, Chief Registrar:

Father's birth certificate?

But my father was born in 1908. Blacks were not issued—

Father's national ID card?

Well, the thing is, my father went to work in the mines in South Africa in 1938—

Evidence that he belonged to a particular kraal?

His family lived in Silobela, but his entire village was resettled in the 1950s.

At which point Valentine would draw a neat and straight diagonal line with his garish red pen through the application form.

How can I be expected to write a death certificate without any evidence of the man's existence? Come back with proof. A document, any document that proves that the man lying in the Mpilo Hospital mortuary really is your father. Come back with proof and I will be more than happy to issue you a death certificate.

We have here his cause of death form from the hospital. Signed by his doctor.

Evidence of death is not evidence of life. Come back with evidence of your father's life. Fill out another application. And you shall have your death certificate.

We cannot bury him without the death certificate.

Then don't waste your time talking to me. Go find the necessary proof of life.

Will we be required to pay the application fee again?

Yes. Of course. The fee pays for my time, which, today, you have wasted.

Yes. His lack of a heart of gold shocked people because they liked to think that if they pitied people like him and treated them nicely, they would be treated nicely in turn. The truth of the matter was that most disabled people were treated cruelly and harshly. He certainly had been. Even so, people really believed that they were nice to people like him and were therefore shocked to find him doing a job that required no pity at all, that required him to be cruel and harsh. Those who thought deeply about things probably concluded that he had chosen his profession because of the way he looked—that living with his certifiably ugly exterior had created a certifiably ugly heart and a need to exact revenge on his fellow man for his misfortune. But that was not the case at all. He did the job he did because it was a job that needed doing. He did the job he did because he was particularly good at it. As a student he had always strived to have the words "Good job!" scribbled in the teacher's red ink in the margins of his exercise book. Those two words had meant more to him than the perfect score or the gold star. "Good job"—a powerful phrase that let you understand the character of a person.

His job had absolutely nothing to do with the heart. Imogen had understood that.

It is the quizzical look on the son's face that alerts him to the fact that something is wrong. He has been silent for too long.

He has taken center stage only to make a fool of himself; the smirk on the daughter's face confirms it.

"How may I help you?" he asks, aware that his voice is too loud and brash—always the mark of someone who is, at heart, unsure of himself, not at ease.

"We are here to obtain form DS 8044 z."

"Why?"

"Because we need it."

"You wouldn't be here if you didn't need it. Why do you need it? For what purpose?"

"We need to declare our daughter missing."

"Are you sure your daughter is missing?"

"Yes, we are sure."

"How sure are you?"

"We are very sure."

"Well, you can only be very sure if your daughter has been missing for more than seventy-two hours. Has your daughter been missing for more than seventy-two hours?"

"Well...no."

"Then how do you know that she is missing?"

"We know because she is no longer in the hospital bed she was lying in."

"Well, perhaps, she got better and went home."

"She was in a coma."

"Are you sure the hospital did not simply misplace her? Happens more often than they are willing to admit."

"Yes, we are sure. We know exactly who took her."

"You do? Who took her?"

"The man she...cohabits with."

"The man she cohabits with? If she lives with him, and is with him, then technically—"

"She is not with him. He has taken her to another facility, probably a hospice, so that we will not be able to find her."

"Do you have any proof that this man took her?"

"He was the last person to visit her in hospital."

"That is not proof."

"We don't need proof. We know him. This is just the sort of thing he would do."

"Since you have no proof that this man took your daughter, your request is not going to be without problems."

The Masukus exchange a knowing look.

"How much?" the mother asks nonchalantly.

"How much what?" Valentine asks.

"Oh, come on. You know what we mean," the son says.

Valentine dislikes the overfamiliarity of the "Oh, come on."

Familiarity breeds friendship.

And friendship is a dangerous thing. Friendship compromises you always.

Bureaucracy and bribery go hand in hand nowadays, he knows this. It was not always the case. There was a time when bureaucracy went hand in hand with doing a job well simply because it was your job to do well. All Valentine wants is to do a good job.

"Form DS 8044 z is free. Money is not an issue here."

"I'm willing to pay anything...anything," the son says, uncrossing his legs, leaning forward in his chair, looking Valentine Tanaka in the eye.

"I'm sure you are. But I do not want your money."

They scoff. *All* of them.

"Of course you don't," the daughter says. She has the audacity to roll her eyes.

"You people amaze me. You really do." He is proud of the calm in his voice. "What is it? A feeling of self-importance? A sense of entitlement? Is that what makes you think everything—everyone—has a price tag? Everything is yours for the taking? Everyone can be bought? Whatever it is, you are in error if you think The Organization will bend to your will—do your bidding."

"Oh, come on. We just want form DS 8044 z," the son says, sounding conciliatory now, charming.

Valentine bangs an open palm on top of his desk, enjoying the fact that this makes them all start.

"No. I will not 'come on.' Do not tell me to 'come on.' You and I are not friends. You cannot tell me to 'come on.' This is very, very serious business here. You are attempting to bribe a member of The Organization. Have you any idea, any idea whatsoever, what could happen to you?"

The Masukus all look at the floor. Good job.

Valentine goes to stand by the only window in the office. It is grimy, but he looks out anyway. Jesus is not on what has become his usual corner since his return. Probably out roaming the streets. Valentine likes having Jesus where he can see him.

Hands in pockets, he plays with his jangling keys and repeats the question. "Have you any idea, any idea whatsoever, what could happen to you? Bribing a member of The Organization is punishable by imprisonment with hard labor. Did you know this?" He is not waiting for an answer. He counts to himself—one...two...three. The phone on his desk rings shrilly, startling the family. He walks over and answers it with no sense of urgency. "Speaking? Already? That was quick. What did you do? Really?" He chuckles. "Works every time. I'll be right there." He leaves the office without excusing himself.

He will be gone for exactly twenty-seven minutes. Just enough time for them to start suspecting that he will not be coming back. Sometimes he returns to his office to find it empty—sometimes not. You learn a lot about people by gauging how patient they are.

"I'm going out," he says to the clerk at the front desk.

"Making them sweat?" The clerk smiles knowingly.

"Trust me, *they* deserve it."

"Don't they all?"

"These ones more than most."

The front door creaks open and then bangs shut. The sunlight is blinding. Even though he knows that he will not find them there, he searches for his sunglasses in his breast pocket. "Hello old friend," he says as he squints the city into focus. The city is chaotic with too much life. The wide and once serene colonial streets are now choked with postcolonial hustle and bustle. He tries to hear the jingle of his keys through the noise of the city. With much concentration, he finally does.

He steps onto the pavement and allows himself to be

carried along by the throng until he finds himself at the National Art Gallery, where he expertly disengages himself.

He reluctantly nods his good afternoon to the security guard and receptionist. He tries to pass both of them quickly, but the receptionist is already saying her now all-too-familiar, "She hasn't gone anywhere sir. She's still up there waiting for you." To which he nods again and attempts a smile before bounding up the stairs, two at a time, aware that he must be cutting a very comical figure.

And there she is. As always. A flash of light. A dance of color. Suspended in the air.

"The Firebird."

There are some artsy types—students most probably—examining the latest exhibition. Thankfully they pay no attention to him. He listens to the jingle-jangle of his keys and takes comfort in it. He walks around "The Firebird." It never ceases to amaze. From every angle, "The Firebird" is something beautiful to behold.

Someone clears her throat behind him.

Valentine looks to find a dear white old lady looking at him, a sympathetic smile on her lips and a hint of disapproval in her eyes. It is only then that he realizes that his hand has left the jingle-jangle of his keys and is reaching out to touch "The Firebird."

"She's a thing of beauty, isn't she?" the dear white old lady says, moving closer to him, wanting to converse, making him feel trapped.

"Yes," he mumbles before hastily retreating and rushing out of the gallery, bounding down the stairs and almost forgetting to nod goodbye to the receptionist and security guard.

He rushes out of the gallery and into the blinding sunlight. He recently misplaced his sunglasses. No matter how many times he retraces his steps in his mind, he cannot remember where he left them. He really needs to buy a new pair. That is how he should use the extra thirteen minutes he now finds himself with—buying a pair of sunglasses.

He should wear them when he goes back to talk to the Masukus. Make his eyes something not for beauty to see. That should put the fear of God in them.

He mentally locates the nearest store that sells sunglasses and starts to make his way there. His progress is stopped by the sight of the son, Marcus Masuku, entering the gallery, hands in pockets, a man at his leisure. The Masukus gave up waiting for him after ten minutes? He expected them to last at least fifteen minutes...maybe even twenty.

He cannot believe he actually overestimated them.

He follows the son into the gallery. At a distance of course.

The son shakes hands with the security guard. "We thought you had forgotten us," the security guard says.

"Never. This is home," the son says as he heads over to the receptionist, who giggles at something he whispers to her.

He is a charmer, this one. A man of the people. No, not a man of the people—rather someone who needs to be liked by everyone. "Oh, come on," he had said to him—overly familiar, trying to charm.

He waits for the son to go up the stairs before following him.

He finds the son talking to the dear old white lady.

"She's a thing of beauty, isn't she?"

"She most definitely is."

"So what do you think she is? A bird?"

"Yes. A fine, rare bird."

"That's what I think as well. But Mike, that's my husband, he thinks she's a woman suspended in the air. What sense does that make? I say to him, "It's called 'The Firebird,' for heaven's sake."

The son reaches out to touch one of the dancing colors.

"Tsk-tsk," says the dear old white lady. "I don't think you should do that."

"Oh, it's all right," the son says, putting a hand on the dear old white lady's shoulder as though they are old friends. "I own this particular piece. I am Marcus Masuku." He points at the plaque and reads: "'The Firebird', by Vida de Villiers. Purchased by Marcus Masuku on November 7, 2007."

The dear old white lady believes him instantly, of course. A man like Marcus Masuku, with beauty, ease and charm, would never lie.

But that is all beside the point. How could he, Valentine Tanaka, have missed such a detail? His job is all about detail. And he is good at his job.

"I would take her with me," the son is saying, "but she is so popular that the gallery has asked me to keep her here."

"I think this is Vida de Villiers's best work," the dear old white lady says. "Do you know that he is back on the street?"

"Is he?"

"Such a pity. So much talent. He is my favorite artist. His Street Dwellers series made me weep. I was so proud...but it also filled one with sadness, you know. This series was much happier. More optimistic. 'The Theory of Flight: In Three Movements'—something romantic about it...The dear old white lady puts her arm around Marcus and they continue to talk like old friends. She reaches out and touches the flash of light. "I've always wanted to do that," she says with a naughty giggle. She touches the dance of color. "Oh. You should have been here a few minutes ago. There was a man. He wanted to touch her and I stopped him. Such a pity. He was a cripple. A sorry looking fellow. Just wanted to touch something beautiful, I suppose. I shouldn't have stopped him."

Valentine Tanaka cannot stay to hear any more.

Will the son figure out that he is the "cripple" that the dear old white lady is talking about? No, of course not. The son does not associate him, Valentine Tanaka, with galleries and fine art. The son thinks that he is at The Organization doing something harsh and cruel—perhaps even grisly—to someone, somewhere in The Tower. People always imagine the worst of him. But he is not the man the Masukus imagine him to be.

It was Valentine Tanaka's first case as a member of The Organization. A girl—about fifteen years old, wearing a school uniform—suspected of shoplifting at Meikles Department Store, accessories section.

It had become an epidemic—girls from private schools stealing knick-knacks in different sections of Haddon & Sly or Meikles stores. A compact disc pilfered here, a piece of candy pocketed there, a golden necklace secreted over there. The girls were masters of sleight of hand; they worked in groups, and, worse still, were suspected of having formed cartels. They needed to be stopped. They had been shielded by their uniforms for too long, as no one had ever suspected that these privileged children would have any reason to steal. But the stores had finally wised up and asked The Organization to help them deal with something that was obviously more complicated than petty theft. The Organization did not want to punish the privileged girls or destroy their brilliant futures, which is what would have happened if the stores had got the police involved; they wanted to understand why they were doing what they were doing.

Partly because the Meikles Department Store was right around the corner from The Tower, and partly because it was a simple case of shoplifting, Valentine Tanaka felt disappointed that this was to be his first case. It was going to be too easy.

He had wanted his first case to really showcase his abilities; to impress his superiors; to show that in spite of appearances he had it in him to get any job done...and not just done, but done well, done right. In short, to show that he could do a good job.

The girl was easy enough to spot. She had been standing in the accessories section for over an hour. She kept looking at the people around her. Valentine Tanaka and his partner did not actually see her take anything, but it was obvious what she was up to. She had the audacity to start a conversation with the security guard before exiting the store. As soon as she left the store, they grabbed her and walked her over to The Tower. Had he been more experienced, the fact that the girl did not struggle would have been a sign.

He sat behind a two-way mirror and, speaking through the intercom, told the girl on the other side of it to strip naked. The girl complied.

The female officer accompanying the girl collected the girl's clothes and left the room. It was only then, when she was naked and, he believed, vulnerable, that he asked for her name.

"Imogen Zula Nyoni," she replied, her voice strong, no hint of a quiver. She did not shiver even though he knew the room was cold. She did not cross her arms or try to cover her breasts or privates as he thought she would. She simply let her arms hang down by her sides.

Nor was she disconcerted by the disembodied voice that seemed to come from nowhere.

The female officer entered the room and shook her head.

"Where did you put them, Imogen?"

"Where did I put what?"

"The accessories."

"What accessories?"

"You expect us to believe that you spent an hour just looking at those..."

"Alice bands and scrunchies," the female officer whispered in his ear.

"You spent all that time looking at Alice bands and scrunchies without taking any?"

"Oh that? I didn't find any that I liked."

The nonchalance of "Oh that" struck him.

"It took you an hour to realize that you did not like any?"

"The colors were not what I was looking for. I was looking for an interesting blue. They didn't have it."

"An interesting blue?" he repeated, intrigued in spite of himself.

He looked at the girl, Imogen Zula Nyoni, really looked at her for the first time. He was not comfortable looking at a naked person, especially a girl. But now that he was looking at her—really looking at her—she did not seem naked at all.

His superior officer cleared his throat, reminding him that he too was being observed. Valentine Tanaka then nodded to the female officer.

"I don't think it is necessary. She didn't take anything," the female officer said.

He gave her a commanding look. She put on the rubber gloves in resignation and left the observation room.

He watched Imogen closely as the female officer entered the room.

She showed no signs of apprehension or fear. Even as the female officer snapped the rubber gloves for effect. No apprehension. No fear.

"Please bend over and place your hands on the ground."

Imogen did as she was told.

"Feet apart."

Again she did as she was told.

The female officer hesitated.

"Okay. That will be all. You may stand," he said, stopping the female officer from inserting her rubber-gloved fingers into every available orifice.

The female officer hurriedly, and, he believed, gratefully, left the room.

Imogen straightened up and actually—this he had a hard time believing—brought her left hand to rest on her left hip. Who stands akimbo like that during an interrogation, Valentine Tanaka wondered.

Apparently Imogen Zula Nyoni did.

The female officer returned Imogen's clothes and satchel. Imogen put on her clothes carefully. This time he noticed that her panties and bra were brightly colored and mismatched, purple and shocking pink respectively, not the run-of-the-mill black, white or beige. "I was looking for an interesting blue," she had said. Now he believed her.

Done dressing, satchel in hand, she now stood waiting.

"You may leave," he said.

That was not what she had been waiting for. Probably waiting for an apology. But The Organization did not do apologies.

Imogen looked directly into the two-way mirror for the first time and walked up to it. He expected her to spit on it—a brave few had been known to do that.

Instead she said: "You cannot break me. You see, I know for certain that my parents were capable of flight." And with that she left the room.

Intact.

Her parents. Capable of flight. He entered her name into the computer.

Her information came up. Mother: Elizabeth Nyoni. Father: Golide Gumede. Golide Gumede? Of course. Suddenly Imogen Zula Nyoni made perfect sense to Valentine Tanaka.

Now, the father, the mother and the daughter are sitting exactly where he left them—not talking to each other. They are all looking at their portable electronic devices. Without him in the room, they do not need to present a united front. There is a tension between them. Tension is good. He can use it to his advantage.

He is still determined not to like them, picture-perfect though they are.

His cellphone rings. A smartphone. Not the latest model. Not top dollar. But one that he is rather proud of.

"Hello?" he says. It is his wife wanting to know what he would like for dinner—beef or chicken. It does not matter which he chooses because he knows she has already defrosted the Kariba bream. So it will be fish for supper. She seems to take pleasure in disappointing him in little ways...or perhaps it is her way of surprising him every day. His wife is the one person that he cannot easily read. Which is the reason that he married her.

The daughter actually snickers when she sees his phone.

He sees how he must look to them. They think he is showing off. They think that he has answered the phone on purpose to show them that he owns such a phone. That he has been out all this time orchestrating a situation in which his cellphone will ring in front of them.

It would never occur to them that he bought the phone because he liked it. Liked the way it looked. Liked the way it felt in his hands. Liked the many things it could do. He had treated himself, bought himself something nice and beautiful for a change. But somehow these people think that his purchase of a phone has nothing to do with him, how he feels and what he needs—and everything to do with them. They see it as his way of desperately trying to acquire something that they naturally have—status.

A certifiably ugly man with a beautiful smartphone is a pathetic sight in their eyes.

"It looks like one of you is missing." He smirks at his own joke as he sits down at his desk.

"My son went out. Needed to stretch his legs," the mother offers, obviously not amused.

"Oh. I see," he says, before pressing the start button on the old computer, which whirrs to life. "I have spoken to my supervisor. Your case is difficult, but not impossible. To start the process I need your daughter's particulars. What is her name?"

"Imogen Zula Nyoni."

"I-M-O," the daughter starts to spell for him.

"I know how to spell, thank you."

I-M-O-G-E-N N-Y-O-N-I he types with two fingers on the keyboard...slowly...laboriously.

"It is such a unique name. Most people misspell it," the daughter explains.

"I-M-O-G-E-N, right?"

"Right."

"And you are Mr. and Mrs. who Nyoni?"

"We are Dr. and Mrs. Masuku. Dingani and Thandi."

"Is Nyoni her married name?"

"No."

"Eh. I'm sure you realize that there is a problem here. Masuku. Nyoni. Parents and daughter having different last names. How can I be sure—"

"She was adopted," the daughter says, cutting him off.

"What year was the adoption?"

"Honestly, is all this necessary?" the mother says, exasperated.

"Madam. I'm sure you appreciate the need for the most exact details in a case such as this. Year of adoption? Wait.

Our records show that Imogen Zula Nyoni was born on the third of September in 1978 and died on the twenty-second of December in 1987. Aged nine."

"This is utterly ridiculous. We adopted Genie in 1988," the mother says, getting up in a flash and making her way to the computer.

He stops her progress with a raised hand. "I'm sorry, madam. I cannot let you look at the computer screen. That is The Organization's policy. But I can print out a copy." He pushes a button and an old dot matrix printer wheezes to life.

"You have got to be kidding me," the daughter says, almost laughing.

It takes an eternity for the printing to stop. He carefully tears off the printout, which reads: "Imogen Zula Nyoni. Slain December 22, 1987. Death reported by Minenhle Tikiti—Relation: Aunt."

He hands them the printout. They all take turns to read it.

"Eh. I'm sure you can appreciate that it is not possible for me, or for anyone else in The Organization for that matter, to issue you form DS 8044 z."

"We have the adoption papers. We could bring them," the father says.

"The person you say is missing, this Imogen Zula Nyoni, is apparently already dead and has been for over thirty years. I'm afraid this is now a bigger issue. An investigation is necessary. The state might have to intervene...become involved."

The Masukus have been shocked into silence.

"If this person, this Minenhle Tikiti, who reported Imogen Zula Nyoni dead, can bring us the death certificate, we might be able to get to the heart of the matter."

Just then the door opens. The son enters.

"Marcus. Marcus. This man says that Genie has been dead for decades. Dead, Marcus!" the mother screams, rather too theatrically for Valentine's liking, taking all of them by surprise.

Gone is their composure.

Gone is their certainty.

Gone is their self-assuredness.

Good job.

The son sinks into his chair. Defeated. "I should never have let go of her hand..."

"It also says here that you reported that Imogen Zula Nyoni had been kidnapped by a Jestina Nxumalo in 1988. This too will have to be investigated."

"You can't be serious," the mother scoffs.

"I'm afraid there is no other way to take a kidnapping but seriously."

"Jestina did not kidnap Genie. It was the eighties," the mother says matter-of-factly.

"I'm sorry, what does the fact that it was the eighties have to do with anything?"

"You know what was happening in the eighties. People... disappeared," the mother says, brave but hesitant.

"People cannot and do not disappear," Valentine says.

"Well, they did in the eighties."

"People have bodies and bodies do not disappear."

"Well, Genie lived in a place where several people disappeared. We believed that Genie had also disappeared. But she had managed to escape with Jestina."

"First you said Imogen disappeared because it was the eighties, now she disappeared because she lived in a particular place."

"It was both the time and the place that made disappearances possible."

"This is...this is..." the daughter says.

"I believe the word you are looking for is *Dickensian*," Valentine offers.

"Why and how would you investigate the kidnapping of a person in 1988 whom you say died in 1987?" the daughter asks.

"And if she died in 1987, how were we able to adopt her in 1988?" the mother added.

"That is yet another complication. I will need to see your original DS 1D3 showing that you did indeed adopt the person you thought was Imogen Zula Nyoni. I will also need a certified copy of your DS 1D3 for our records."

"I can't believe this. Mr...." the son says.

"Tanaka. Valentine Tanaka."

"Mr. Tanaka, do you have any idea how difficult a time this is for us?"

"Imogen Zula Nyoni was officially reported dead in 1987. Officially reported kidnapped in 1988. And now you want to report that same person missing. Surely you can see how this presents The Organization with a problem."

Marcus

"Please tell me they have found her," Minenhle says opening the door, with a hopeful smile on her face. Upon seeing Marcus and Thandi, hope leaves Minenhle's face, but the smile does not. It remains frozen in a grotesque mockery of what it should be. "Thandi. Marcus. Please do come in," she finally says, opening the door wider and, almost reluctantly, letting them in.

Marcus has never seen his mother look uneasy. She is definitely uneasy now. She shifts in her chair, fidgets with the cushion, tries to sit back, and sits back up again. "The reason we are here is because in 1987 you reported Genie dead." His mother's words come out sounding like an accusation.

Marcus feels that there is a lamentable lack of ceremony in the way his mother has handled the situation. He says nothing, but he feels that, at a time like this, what is needed most is the civilization and care of ceremony.

Many different emotions sweep over Minenhle's face. She reins them in before she says: "I don't see the connection between 1987 and now."

"Well, we would like to file form DS 8044 z. We need to report her missing. We need to know where Vida moved her to."

"Vida? You think he moved her someplace?" Minenhle asks.

"We believe that he has secretly put Genie in a hospice so that she can die naturally," Marcus explains. "Of course, we cannot allow that to happen. We would like you to go to The Organization with Genie's death certificate as proof that she did not die in 1987."

Just then they hear the front door open.

"The crows are back at City Hall," Mordechai's sing-song voice says from the hallway.

"Good. It's where they belong. Where had they gone to? Crows don't migrate, do they?" Minenhle says to the living-room door, anticipating Mordechai's entry. "And they wouldn't come back in the winter, would they?"

"No," Mordechai says, still not having entered the room. "At least I don't think so. We really need to start learning more about birds."

"We have company. The Masukus. Thandi and Marcus," Minenhle says, warning Mordechai in advance.

Mordechai enters the room. "We've just been out for our evening constitutional," he says by way of explanation to Marcus and Thandi. In his right hand is a very colorful bird, eating from his palm.

There is something in the leisurely way Minenhle leans her head back and looks up at Mordechai as he makes his way towards her that Marcus likes.

"I think she wants to make friends with the crows," Mordechai says as the bird gingerly hops from his palm onto Minenhle's.

"I like crows, but I think being friends with them is a little too much. You can't fully trust crows. They are scavengers," Minenhle says to the bird. "You know what crows are called collectively? A murder. A murder of crows. I strongly suggest you think twice about associating with them. I don't think the association will end well for you."

"I didn't know you had a bird," Marcus says.

"Some days ago she flew into the window. Broke her wing.

I've been looking after her. We didn't think she would make it, but here we are."

Mordechai places some birdseed into Marcus' palm. The bird hops from Minenhle's palm onto Marcus', where it cocks its head and looks at him curiously.

"A bird in the hand is worth two in the bush, hey?" Minenhle says with a smile.

"Krystle had a run-in with a bird recently. Although I don't think hers came to such a happy ending."

"Happy endings are so very rare," Minenhle says, tenderly stroking the bird's colorful feathers.

"Which makes this a very rare bird indeed," Mordechai says in that voice of his that sounds like it's the beginning of a song.

A song about a bird.

The bird in the palm of Marcus' hand flutters and begins to twitter. Suddenly something occurs to Marcus. "I think... I think there was a bird like this on the Beauford Farm and Estate."

"Was there? I don't remember such a bird," his mother says dismissively.

"Yes, I think there was such a bird," Marcus says.

Mordechai sits on the armrest of Minenhle's chair between her and the Masukus, as though protecting her. "Police still have no news," he says to Minenhle. "She is definitely not in any of the mortuaries. So we can take comfort in that."

"Of course she is not in a mortuary. She is in a hospice. We just need to find which one Vida has put her in," his mother says.

"The Masukus would like for me to go to The Tower and tell them that Genie did not die in 1987."

"What does 1987 have to do with now?"

"A lot, apparently."

Mordechai and Minenhle exchange a look before he says, "Okay. We'll help you."

"'Okay. We'll help you?'" His mother's unease has given way to anger. "'Okay. We'll help you?'" she repeats as she hurries down the stairs at neck-breaking speed. "You should have let me handle it, Marcus. "'Okay. We'll help you?'" Helping *us*? They are helping Genie. She *needs* to be found. They should be doing this for Genie. I know you think they are nice people because she's Genie's aunt and Genie had an...attachment to them. *Has* an attachment to them. But those two are definitely not nice people. Without even looking for her niece, Minenhle declared her dead. Couldn't wait to wash her hands of her. And now, now they are already talking about mortuaries!" his mother screams above the clickety-clack of her high heels on the stairs.

"Well, at least they've agreed to help us."

"Help us? Helping us would have been answering your poor father's phone calls all this time. Instead of *making* us come here. But of course, *they* don't talk to *us*. And all because of flowers."

"Flowers?"

"The flower shop. The one I bought. Remember that Minenhle used to be a florist there—worked there for years? Well, she claims she wanted to buy it, too. That I knew that. And that that is why I bought it. To spite her."

"And did you?"

"Did I what?"

"Know she wanted to buy it?"

"She couldn't afford it. They lived in this dilapidated apartment complex, in that four-room apartment, for over thirty years, for heaven's sake. Everything in those four rooms is old—even the magazines. I hate to say it, but they are poor."

"So you knew that she wanted to buy it?" Marcus says, stopping in his tracks.

"No. No. No. You're not allowed to feel sympathy for those two at all. At all. They claim that your father and I stole Genie. Bribed the judge. But can you imagine Genie growing up in those four rooms?" his mother says, grabbing hold of his hand and leading him down the stairs.

Marcus is thinking of Genie growing up in those four rooms with Minenhle and Mordechai and their simplicity, comfort and domestic routine. Without him. The idea makes him feel lonely enough to cry.

Valentine

This is definitely no way to treat a lady, Valentine thinks as he looks at Minenhle Tikiti sitting across from him.

The gentleman outside, the one waiting for her—he definitely knows how to treat a lady. Valentine had watched them as they had waited in the crowded courtyard. They shared everything—their banana, their orange, their piece of cake, their newspaper, their bottle of water. Together they were patient. Content with simply waiting.

She had leaned heavily on the gentleman's arm as they entered the courtyard. He had removed his suit jacket to cushion the spot on the ground on which she had chosen to sit. They had not held each other after that. They had simply and comfortably sat close and shared everything.

In all things, the gentleman had been gentle, even in letting her go through the door alone. He had simply opened the rather heavy door for her and held it as she passed through, quietly accepting her decision to go through whatever came next on her own.

That is how you treat a lady, Valentine had thought, as though you have all the time in the world right in the palm of your hand.

People believed that because of his job he did not understand the beauty of gentleness—of patience—of calm. But Valentine has long known that in order to do a job well you need to take time to be patient, to be calm, to have clear objectives, to know exactly what it is that you want to achieve, to have a clear course of action. Whatever job you do, you do it with finesse and precision.

Most people did not understand or know this. Like whoever had done this to Minenhle Tikiti—sister of Golide Gumede; aunt of Imogen Zula Nyoni; florist, living with, but not married to, Mordechai Gatiro; interrogated by The Organization in 1978. Her interrogator had butchered her face, burnt her body, crushed her spine—without finesse or precision. Her interrogator, the infamous C10, had not understood what he was doing and why. He had simply received a directive and carried it out. Had he understood why he was doing what he was doing, he would not have simply hacked. at her. He would have understood that he was trying to get at something precious in her, and that he therefore needed to be careful, or that precious thing would be lost to him forever.

"And how may I be of assistance to you this morning?" Valentine asks.

"I am here to report an un-death."

"An un-death?"

"Yes," Minenhle says, handing him an original death certificate.

"Who is un-dead?"

"My niece. Imogen Zula Nyoni. In 1987 I reported her dead. She was not dead."

"So you lied?"

"No. At the time I thought that she was dead. But it turned out she was only missing."

"When did you find her?"

"I did not. Someone else did. In 1988."

"And you're only reporting this now. Why?"

"Because she has gone missing from Mater Dei Hospital and a form DS 8044 z is needed and apparently the only way you will issue it is if I declare her un-dead."

Those Masukus! That is not at all what he had said to them. Not at all. They had ordered this woman to come here and did not even think to offer her a ride.

"I've reported Imogen Zula Nyoni un-dead. I've done my part. Now please go ahead and do as you see fit," Minenhle says, getting up with difficulty. "However, this is something I must say: Vida de Villiers is not behind Imogen's disappearance. I know the Masukus want him, no, *need* him to be. I know that is what your investigation will find because, of course, money has exchanged hands and the Masukus will get their way, as they always do. But I want you to know that someone out there knows the truth. Vida is not responsible for Imogen's disappearance."

"I can assure you that no money has exchanged hands," Valentine says.

"It is too intimate, this interference, this role the state chooses to play in our lives," Minenhle says, looking him in the eye. "Too intimate."

"I can assure you that no money has exchanged hands," Valentine says again, even though he knows that she heard him the first time. He feels that he has to say this, otherwise he will say what he really wants to say: "Yes, I agree with you. It is too intimate, this interference, this role the state chooses to play in our lives."

At first Valentine had not seen any resemblance, except of course for that gap between the front teeth, but looking at Minenhle now he sees something familiar—something that is not physical. Something else entirely. Something unbroken. He realizes that Minenhle is in possession of a most precious thing. So he was right: her interrogator was never able to get at her most precious thing. He broke her physically, but left her intact.

You cannot break me. You see, I know for certain that my

parents were capable of flight. It is Imogen's voice he hears as he watches Minenhle pull at the heavy door, which creaks open and then bangs shut, as she walks into the blinding sunlight.

Again, Valentine finds himself watching Minenhle and her gentleman in the courtyard. She is leaning heavily on the gentleman's arm as they slowly leave. He cannot see from this distance whether or not they say anything to each other. They probably do not need to. The gentleman holds up an umbrella, shielding her damaged face from the sun.

Now, that is definitely how you treat a lady—with gentleness, patience and calm.

Minenhle holds up her left hand and cups it. A very colorful bird flies down from a tree and settles in the palm of her hand.

Just like that.

The bird hops onto her shoulder and perches there easy as you please.

He is surprisingly sad when they finally turn the corner and carry on with their journey out of his sight. He hopes to cross paths with them again—Minenhle and her gentle man, her Mordechai.

Valentine

"Who is it?" a voice inquires. He cannot tell if it belongs to the mother or the daughter.

"Valentine Tanaka," he says, straining his head out of the car window as he tries to get as close to the intercom box as he can.

No response.

"From The Organization, Registrar's Office," he adds.

There is no response, but the electric gate slowly rolls open. He drives through. Before him is the longest and windiest driveway he has ever seen. At the end of it is the grandest house he has ever seen. Majestic.

He has always appreciated the great colonial architecture of the City of Kings. The buildings had obviously been conceived and built by people who had clear objectives, knew exactly what it was that they wanted to achieve and precisely how to best execute their vision; people who understood the importance of finesse, precision and patience; people who had the time and took the time to do a good job. The post-colonial monstrosities being built today by the nouveau riche just do not compare to the great colonial architecture. They are grand without having a sense of unifying aesthetics, built by people who live in a volatile time that makes them feel too uncertain and unsettled to do a good job.

A series of sprinklers are busy trying to resuscitate the dried-up yard. Valentine finds it rather odd that in such a big yard there should only be one tree: a flaming flamboyant. He feels there is a story to be told there.

"You should have seen this place in the eighties," Lawrence Tafara says from the passenger seat. "I was just a sergeant then. We came here almost every weekend. Noise complaints from the neighbors. Man, did these folks know how to throw a party."

Valentine struggles a little to negotiate the curves and the increasingly uphill gradient of the driveway.

"It was hard, you know, not to feel envy back then when you saw people living like this," Lawrence continues. "They seemed to have it all figured out, to have picked the right chain of events to follow. There I was—I had worked for the BSAP, I had fought on the side of the RF, and what did I have to show for it? Two rooms in the townships that I called a house. These people, on the other hand, had not formed any allegiances, had not actively fought for our freedom. They had simply gone overseas at the right time and chosen the perfect moment to return as "been-tos." Somehow they spoke the language of the new country, understood its customs and mores. They got the highest-paying jobs, they fearlessly moved to the suburbs, they sent their children to the Group A schools—all without batting an eyelash. It was really hard not to envy them. They had come out on the right side of history with seemingly such little effort on their part."

Valentine is proud of himself. He has successfully negotiated his way up the driveway and has safely parked the car. He moves to get out. He sees Lawrence hesitate. "Intimidated?" he asks, amused.

"We could have done this via phone," Lawrence says, getting out of the car.

"Under the circumstances I think they deserve at least a home visit."

"You know what your problem is, Valentine?"

"That I'm certifiably ugly?"

"No. Your problem is that you have a heart of gold."

A heart of gold. Him? Valentine stops in his tracks. He is suddenly uncertain. He finds his right hand in his pocket seeking the comforting jingle-jangle of his keys.

It is Lawrence who ends up having to ring the doorbell.

The daughter opens the door. She looks at both of them suspiciously. Probably just her way of looking at people who visit the house. She makes no move to let them in.

"May we come in?" Valentine asks.

She opens the door wider and walks away, leaving them to follow behind.

Valentine must admit that it is a little intimidating being stared at so intently and intensely by five pairs of eyes—father, mother, son, daughter and grandmother. Here, in their home, their beauty looks menacing. It is difficult to look elsewhere when ten eyes are on you. Is that why all eyes are on him, so that he does not look elsewhere in the house...or at them too closely? What are they afraid that he will see?

Poor Lawrence is having a difficult time of it. The teacup and saucer rattle uncontrollably in his shaky hands. Tea spills onto the saucer, where it soaks the two custard creams perched precariously there, and onto the floor, where it stains the Masukus' Persian rug. Valentine has given Lawrence a few pointed looks, hoping he will take the hint and place the teacup and saucer back on the coffee table, but Lawrence only has eyes for the family sitting beatifically, in a semicircle, opposite him. For his part, Valentine Tanaka takes refuge in the faraway, unfocused and vacant stare of the grandmother. It is to her that he says:

"We are now in receipt of Imogen Zula Nyoni's death certificate. We received it from Minenhle Tikiti."

The silence relaxes.

"Some days ago, however, a woman's body was reported found on the Beauford Farm and Estate."

The silence becomes anxious again.

He watches as the Masukus look at each other quizzically, then look back at him, waiting for him to explain.

"Those who found the body claim that it is Imogen."

"It is not Genie's body," the son says.

"Given Imogen's connection to the Beauford Farm and Estate, The Organization will go and investigate."

"It is not Genie's body," the daughter says.

"If anything comes up, Lawrence Tafara here will be sure to get in touch with you. If you have further questions, you can get in touch with him." He looks pointedly at Lawrence Tafara, who looks blankly at him for a moment before remembering to remove his business card from his breast pocket and hand it over to the Masukus. It is the mother who takes the card.

"Lawrence here is Chief Superintendent over at Hillside Police Station. Brookside is under his jurisdiction."

"Yes, I am Chief Superintendent over at Hillside Police Station. Brookside is under my jurisdiction. You might remember me from the eighties. I came here a lot—noise complaints. I was a sergeant then," Lawrence manages to rattle before he is cut off.

"It is not Genie's body," the mother says.

"I am going to go to the Beauford Farm and Estate to personally investigate further. Trust me. I am on your side. I will get to the bottom of this."

"I wonder where that investigation will lead," the mother says, giving the father a knowing look.

It is not lost on Valentine that the father has not said anything since they arrived nor has he negated the possibility that it is Imogen's body at the Beauford Farm and Estate.

"I'm sorry. I don't understand, Mr...." the son says.

"Tanaka. Valentine Tanaka."

"Does this mean that you will not issue us with form DS 8044 z?"

Valentine is about to respond when something catches his eye. He watches in horror as the grandmother's mouth knots itself into an ugly grimace before unhinging itself. The left side of her face seems to disintegrate. "They are plotting to overthrow the government," she says out of the right side of her mouth, looking him straight in the eye. "They are plotting to overthrow the government."

Thankfully, her sudden outburst absorbs the family's full attention. They hover over her, embarrassed. "The beginning stages of dementia. Plus the after-effects of a massive stroke," the father explains apologetically. "We don't do politics," he adds for good measure.

Valentine gratefully gets up. "We'll leave you to it, then," he says, rushing towards the door, not even waiting for Lawrence. Lawrence has no choice but to follow him, a tea-soaked custard cream in hand. The last thing Valentine Tanaka hears before he shuts the front door behind him is the grandmother screaming "You are one of them!"

Marcus

Marcus should not have picked up the phone, he realizes too late. The fact that it was the landline that had rung and not any of their cellphones should have alerted him that the caller was not a close family friend. Family friends called cellphones.

The Masukus had all been sitting at the yellow Formica table in the kitchen, eating a rather elaborate breakfast of porridge, toast, bacon, eggs, grapefruit and coffee that his mother had risen uncharacteristically early to prepare. They were all still reeling from the news that Valentine Tanaka had delivered, all silently hoping that it was not Genie's body that had been found. Not knowing how else to behave, they had all opted for benign bonhomie. Even Krystle was making an effort, a great effort, Marcus suspected, to be pleasant. She was making a joke that the rest of them laughed at a little too heartily, about her inability, after six years of graduate school, to complete her dissertation. The fact that she called it the "phantom project" made Marcus strongly suspect that it had yet to be written. Whenever he asked her about it, she used words like "epistemological," "taxonomic," and "dialectic," words that did nothing to convince him that the dissertation actually existed.

Esme said that she understood Krystle's dissertation perfectly (even though she too had yet to see any pages) and had told him: "It's about the history of your country, how it was never able to become a nation because the state focused belonging too singularly on the land. In colonial times belonging was attached to being a settler and in postcolonial times belonging is attached to being autochthonous. This means that throughout your country's history there has always been some group or other that has not been allowed to share in a sense of belonging." He thought, although he never said as much, that Esme had got the wrong end of the stick, because the topic seemed too...political for Krystle.

"Sometimes I feel like a beached whale trying to push this gigantic all-consuming thing out into the world. Other times I feel like Jonah inside the whale wondering where the hell I am and desperate to find a way out," Krystle said, her smile letting them know that they should smile or laugh at this too—even though her feeling so anxious and overwhelmed was probably something they needed to be concerned about.

"Did you know that the tongue of a blue whale weighs the equivalent of an elephant?" his father had said, always reaching for facts in moments of uncertainty.

And then no one said anything. One second. Two seconds. Three seconds. The silence became threatening.

Then the phone rang. Mercifully. Without thinking, Marcus, who was sitting closest to it, reached over and answered it.

"Hello?"

He was greeted by a shriek so loud he had to pull his ear away from the phone.

This shriek lets him know that he should not have picked up the phone.

He stands up. Walks the little distance away from the table to the window and turns his back on his family. "Hello?" he repeats, this time in a whisper, as though not wanting the rest of the family to hear. But of course they can hear everything coming through the receiver, however faint.

"Is that you, Marcus?" a voice asks, suddenly sober.

"Yes. It's me," he whispers.

Then the person on the other end starts sobbing. Unadulterated sounds. From somewhere deep within. Loud, guttural, wet sounds of sorrow, of shock, of disbelief, of despair, of utter pain.

Marcus wants to think that the outburst is rather too theatrical, and, therefore, not heartfelt—something rehearsed even, a performance. But there is something palpable in the performance that tells him that it is real, that this is not a performance but the expression of deeply felt pain, the communication of the incomprehension of utter loss. He almost envies this person her ability to arrive so easily at this point—to accept the possibility of a certain kind of truth, a truth he knows he has to fight with every fiber of his being. She so easily touches the corners, and thereby defines the parameters, of something he is yet to acknowledge.

Marcus wants more than anything to hang up the phone. How dare this person —whoever she is—trespass so casually and so callously into their happy home? "Who is this?" He is glad to hear that there is a hard edge to his voice.

"Oh. I'm sorry," the voice says automatically, used to apologizing. "It is Jestina Nxumalo. MaNxumalo. Remember me from your childhood? From Beauford?"

"I remember," Marcus says, instantly feeling guilty for hating her for calling.

"I'm calling from Australia. It's where I live now," she says, her words made choppy by the heavy heaving that is keeping her sobs at bay.

"Oh. I see," Marcus says, knowing that, were this another conversation, he would have interpreted her mention of Australia as her way of letting him know that, despite her late start in life, she too has made it; that, in spite of his fortunes and her misfortunes in life, they were now equals of a sort in the grander scheme of things. In other words, he would have thought the kind of ungenerous thought he afterwards always felt guilty for having entertained. But on this occasion he thinks, rather generously, that Jestina mentioned Australia only as a means of locating herself for him in the vast geography of their diasporic world.

"I got a call from a man calling himself Valentine Tanaka. He says Genie's body has been found at Beauford. Is this true, Marcus?"

"He told us a body has been found. Yes."

"This man calling himself Valentine Tanaka says that Genie was HIV-positive."

"He had no business telling you that. That is private."

"So it's true?"

He absolutely refuses to respond to such a question.

"Marcus?"

He valiantly hesitates before he says, as he exhales, "Yes."

"Oh my God. What did they do to Genie?" Jestina asks, with anguish in her voice. "What did they do to Genie?"

"Who are *they*?" Marcus asks.

"This cannot be how it ends for Genie."

"Who are *they*?" Marcus repeats.

"I'm coming home. This man calling himself Valentine Tanaka wants me to come home, go to Beauford, and I shall. Things need to be made right."

"Who are *they*?" Marcus asks, hearing the quiver in his voice.

"They have never answered for anything. They have to answer for this. We will make them answer for this, Marcus. You hear me?" Jestina's voice is suddenly sober again. "We will make them answer for this."

The ominous and amorphous "they." Who are "they"?

"You hear me?" she repeats with an authority in her voice that he remembers well from their days on the Beauford Farm and Estate. "We will make them answer for this."

"Yes," he says, once again the obedient child of yesteryear.

"Their eyes are not for beauty to see." Jestina's voice holds both sympathy and scorn. "I pity them. They know not what they have. They cannot recognize the gifts that have been bestowed on them. Genie and I spoke of this often."

There is a crackling sound and then the line goes dead.

Marcus hangs up the phone slowly, reluctantly. He has no choice but to face his family. Stalling, he looks at his right hand and is genuinely surprised to see it clutching a pen— a red pen—poised over a long-forgotten and yellowed message pad that lies next to the phone on the windowsill, having apparently written, as evidenced by his red-inked chicken scratch: who are they?

A sudden fear seizes him, pounds his heart and prickles his armpits. He turns to face his family. None of them will look him in the eye—not even the often confrontational Krystle. They all look down at their plates. The food has gone cold by now, but they keep on eating politely, stoically, as though they are martyrs for continuing to shove spoonfuls of sustenance into their mouths.

"That was MaNxumalo."

"You mean Jestina? My parents' maid?" his mother says. It sounds more like a correction than a question.

"Yes," Marcus says, sitting down. "She says that she's coming home. Valentine Tanaka has asked her to."

His mother and his father share a look.

"I could hear her screaming through the phone," his mother says. "Rather presumptuous of her. She was always theatrical—overly dramatic. Rather comical, actually. But what right does she have? *We* are Genie's family and you don't see *us* making a production of it. We could, you know. We could make a production of it. But we're not, because that would be to lose the plot entirely. Entirely."

Marcus, still clutching the notepad and pen, puts a piece of dry toast in his mouth and chews mechanically.

"I don't trust her. Never have. How did she survive in 1987? My parents died. How did she survive?"

"She says that 'they' have to answer for this. I am not really sure who 'they' are," Marcus says delicately, steering them back to the here and now.

Suddenly there is a rustling and rattling at the kitchen door. The Masukus turn simultaneously towards the door, all of them—frightened. Something wants to gain entry. It rattles like a benevolent wind, but they know exactly what it is. They see it seep in through the slight opening under the door. They see the thing that they have tried to keep at bay enter effortlessly, almost like vapor. And like vapor it immediately settles, here, there and everywhere. It changes the color of everything it touches—darkens everything so that the entire house seems shrouded in mourning. Like a sickness it attacks them all.

His mother goes to fix herself a glass of Mazoe Orange Crush with vodka, heads to the den and looks into the distance as though it holds a future in which she is not particularly interested. His father sits looking intently at the palms of his hands, reading his lifelines as though trying to pinpoint the exact moment it had all started to go wrong.

Marcus looks down at his own hands, which are still clutching the notepad and red pen.

Who are "they"?

Krystle takes the notepad from him and reads what he wrote. "We all know who 'they' are. We cannot pretend otherwise any more," she says. "Genie cannot be dead. Not when there is so much still unforgiven."

Marcus sees the moment for what it is: the beginning of

something that will either bring his family together, make them stronger, or take advantage of their weakness and vulnerability and tear them asunder. He hopes it will bring them together, even as he realizes for the first time that they are all of them—*all* of them—fragile. But, in all honesty, what does he have left to him besides hope? He tells himself, although he is not altogether convinced, that hope is much better than being reconciled.

He knows that his father is in need of some reassurance, but he does not know what is appropriate to say in a situation such as this, so he puts his hand on his father's shoulder and gives it a gentle squeeze.

The eyes that look at Marcus lack conviction even though a small smile touches his father's lips. It is the smile of the already defeated.

Marcus returns his weak smile and gets up to leave.

"It all began here, didn't it? At this very table," his father says, running his hands over the smooth surface of the yellow Formica table.

"What did?"

"The end...Our end with Genie."

Marcus sits back down.

Marcus sees himself as a boy of seventeen falling in love under a jacaranda tree as he listens to a story about elephants swimming in the Zambezi River. He sees himself kissing the girl he loves—Genie, his childhood friend. He sees her say, "Our eyes are not for beauty to see," as his grandmother drags her away. He sees himself follow them into the house— confused. He sees his mother and father sitting at the yellow Formica table, eyes downcast. He sees himself reach out and hold Genie's hand, intent on pulling her away. He sees his screaming grandmother shake Genie. "You can't have him. Tell them, Dingani. Tell them! You cannot pretend not to see what has happened here any longer. It is time for the truth. They need to know the truth before it is too late." He looks at his father. "Genie is HIV-positive," his grandmother says. He sees the look of bewilderment enter Genie's eyes. He sees those eyes look at him—pleading with him to somehow prove that this is all untrue. He sees himself—he tries to stop his seventeen year-old self, but he cannot—he sees himself let go of Genie's hand. He sees himself raise his hand and wipe his mouth... the mouth that only moments before had happily kissed Genie's. He chooses to think that the look of disgust on his face has been exaggerated by time, sharpened so that the twist of the knife goes deeper. He sees a look enter Genie's eyes. It is a look he remembers well. He can still hear Genie's mother, Elizabeth, saying to eight-year-old Genie, "Let him go. You have to let him go." He can still see the look that enters eight-year-old Genie's eyes. It is the look of letting him go.

"But before that we were happy here, weren't we?" his father says now, his hands beginning to tremble as they continue running over the table's surface.

"Yes. Of course."

"That's why I will never get rid of this table. I know it is no longer the fashion...plastic and all...yellow at that...but we were really happy here. Once. Before."

Not knowing what else to do, Marcus lightly touches one of his father's trembling hands.

"You do love me, don't you?" his father asks.

"Of course."

"You haven't always."

"I always have."

"The way you looked at me that first day in the sunflower field when we came to get you—like I was nothing. No, not nothing—like I was an embarrassment...like I was lacking something...something important...vital."

"It was the shock of it, that's all."

"You were right about me, of course. You were right to think that there was something lacking within me. First impressions, hey?"

"Dad—"

"I hope you'll still love me after."

"After what?"

"After the reckoning," his father says. "We all have things to answer for."

Marcus nods. Yes, they all have things to answer for.

"There is no escaping it any more," his father says. "What happened on the Beauford Farm and Estate in 1987. I was responsible."

Dingani

Whenever Dingani thought about what happened in 1987 (and he thought about it often), he was convinced that it was directly linked to what had happened in 1965. There was no doubt in his mind that if his father, Mbongeni Masuku, had not been imprisoned for his "politics" in 1965, he, Dingani Masuku, would not have become directly involved in the deaths of all those people on the Beauford Farm and Estate in 1987.

Mbongeni Masuku had been your typical mid-twentieth-century husband and father: somewhat detached from his wife and child, infrequently—and therefore more terrifyingly—physically abusive, and an occasional drunk. In terms of appearances, he was like most men in their middle-class township: respectable, Christian and educated.

There was nothing particularly outstanding about him.

Once in awhile he would invite some of his teacher friends over and they would talk about the current state of affairs in their country. Talk often led to very loud debate and very loud debate inevitably led to inebriated shouting matches that often became physical and sometimes violent.

But even this was not extraordinary—educated colonized men had to vent their frustrations in some way. There was really no harm done. They always went back to work and carried on being the "good boys"—the exemplars of how the colonial system was good for the Africans, of how the civilizing mission had been successful, of how the white man's burden had been lightened and of how soon...but not quite yet... the Africans would be ready to rule themselves.

The life of Mbongeni Masuku's wife was, however, atypical. Eunice Masuku worked as a housemaid even though her husband had the highly respectable job of headmaster. Most middle-class wives were teachers, nurses or housewives: the vast majority were housewives. It was a mystery to most why Eunice Masuku worked at all.

However, there were things about the Masukus that their neighbors could not have known by simply looking at the beautiful couple living in their semi-detached, four-roomed house with its well-tended garden and their Volkswagen parked under their eucalyptus tree. They could not have known that, in addition to being a detached husband and father who was infrequently physically abusive and an occasional drunk, Mbongeni Masuku was also a sadist who emotionally and mentally abused his wife. They could not have known that he refused to help his wife apply to nursing or teaching school; knowing full well that a husband's approval and signature were required for both, he refused to sign her application forms. They could not have known that he intentionally left his wife with no "respectable" option for employment. They could not have known that he refused to provide for his family with his salary. They could not have known that Mbongeni Masuku did all this because he strongly suspected that the child his wife presented as his son, Dingani, was not his child. They could not have known that, in addition to being an atypical middle-class wife who worked as a housemaid, Eunice Masuku (with all her trappings of middle-class respectability) had worked as a prostitute in a shebeen in South Africa, which was where she and Mbongeni had met. They could not have known that she was living a very different existence from the one Mbongeni Masuku had promised her when he, a recent graduate of Fort Hare University, had spoken to her so eloquently in the Queen's English, which made her go weak at the knees. They could not have known that as she walked down the street, her head held high as her well-worn shoes gradually became caked in dust, she was, at that very moment, plotting her revenge. They could not have known that she had waited thirty-six months to exact that revenge—waited until her husband finished paying for the yellow Formica table and its four matching chairs that had become the pride of their kitchen. They could not have known that Mbongeni Masuku did not allow his wife and son to sit at the yellow Formica table. They could not have known that Eunice Masuku and Dingani Masuku ate every meal on the cold concrete floor of the kitchen.

Or perhaps they knew all this and much more. You can never be sure with neighbors and onlookers as to what they know just by looking at you, and what they do not.

Dingani, at nine years old, had no idea that his family was not quite like all the others. So on the morning he watched his mother stand by the living-room door and wave, almost regally, as his father drove away, with the sweetest smile on her lips, he had no idea that that was the last day that he would see his father.

He watched as his mother stood by the door, no longer waving, no longer smiling, but listening to the sounds of the Volkswagen gradually grow fainter. Once she was satisfied that the car was a safe distance away, she closed the door and turned to him.

"Go wash your face and put on your blue suit," she said, suddenly frantic and agitated. "And brush your teeth and comb your hair." She started unbuttoning her plain, baby-pink housemaid's uniform. She stepped out of it. Underneath she was wearing a beautiful dress with large blue-violet flowers.

Until that very moment he had no idea that his mother had such a pretty dress. He stood transfixed, watching her. She seemed to be transforming before his very eyes. She walked towards him, leaving her housemaid's uniform on the floor—a careless gesture that was completely unlike her.

"Don't just stand there. You need to be quick about it," she said, breaking the spell. "Wash, brush, comb."

"Are we going somewhere?" he asked as she grabbed his hand and led him to the bathroom.

"Today is the day our lives change," she said, scrubbing his face with Lifebuoy soap and, for the first time, not seeming to care that the soap got in his eyes. "After today we will definitely be going places. The sky is the limit for us."

They walked out of the house and kept on walking for what felt like hours, his hand held firmly in his mother's white-gloved hand. Dingani watched the blue-violet flowers dance on his mother's body. He became thirsty and still they walked on. His legs grew tired and still they walked on. His eyes became heavy and still they walked on. His mother never slowed down her pace—not even when he slowed down as they approached Lobengula Street. He did not know much about the city, but he knew that Africans were not allowed, by law, to cross Lobengula Street (unless they worked in the city or the suburbs), or to walk on the pavements. He had often heard his father speak of this to his teacher friends as an "injustice."

His mother dragged him along. "It's all right. This is how I go to work every day," she said over her shoulder.

There was a lot to comprehend in the colonial city—the tall buildings, the careening cars, the multitudes of people. It was awe-inspiring: Dingani's eyes had no choice but to betray the blue-violet flowers on his mother's dress to observe all that was around him. His awe did not decrease when they left the chaos of the city and started walking down the more subdued avenues lined with the jacarandas, flamboyants and acacias of the suburbs. Dingani was grateful for the shade the beautiful trees provided. All was quiet here. The only thing that disturbed the peace was the bark of an overly protective dog. All was green. All was big. Big yards containing big bungalow-style houses.

Dingani did not have to be told that this was where the good life was. It was so tranquil and peaceful...so very different from where he lived, where everywhere was dust and everything was noise, where people lived cheek by jowl, practically on top of each other.

Before that day, Dingani had never aspired to anything. He now had an aspiration—to live here, in the suburbs, some day.

They finally arrived at their destination. His mother rang the cowbell attached to the gate, and the gardener was suddenly in front of them in his faded blue overalls and black cap, slightly askew. "Hell—"

His greeting died halfway out of his mouth. He frowned. Hesitated.

"Open the gate, Philemon," his mother said, with authority in her voice.

Philemon seemed to have formed the appropriate response, but then he looked at Dingani, weighed up a few things and decided not to say anything.

"Open the gate, Philemon," his mother repeated.

Philemon looked her up and down and then sucked his teeth and spat. "Are you not knowing that today is a workday? Why are you dressing as if you are for church?"

"Open the gate, Philemon," his mother repeated, her tone letting him know that he was trying her patience.

"Is that not being Madam's dress?" Philemon asked, both fear and malevolence flashing in his eyes.

"Madam gave it to me."

"Madam will not be liking this," Philemon said. "Madam will not be liking this at all."

"Who is at the gate, Philemon?" a voice from within the yard said, making Philemon start.

"It is being Eunice at the gate, Madam."

"Well, don't just stand there like the fool you are—let her in. She is already ten minutes late as it is. Honestly, every day is a new day for you people, isn't it?"

"Yes, madam," Philemon said, as he quickly opened the gate. "Every day is being a new day for us, madam," he said, his tone switching uncertainly from jocular to serious, trying to gauge Madam's mood.

She went back into the house.

"Is Mr. Coetzee here?" Dingani's mother asked Philemon as she entered the yard.

"Heh?"

"I asked if Mr. Coetzee is here."

"Eh. What are you wanting him for?"

"That is my business, not yours."

Philemon made a sound of sheer contempt and disgust in the back of his throat. "If you were my wife—"

"If you were my husband, I would have killed myself a long time ago."

Philemon laughed mirthlessly. "Pride. Too much. That is being your problem, Eunice. Pride."

"Spineless. Too much. That is being your problem, Philemon. Spineless."

And that was the end of that conversation.

They walked up a winding driveway that had cars parked along it—more cars surely than one man could know what to do with, Dingani thought—then past the veranda as they made their way towards the back of the house where the kitchen door, also known as the servants' entrance, was located.

"Eunice, is that you?" a voice said, as his mother's white-gloved hand was opening the top half of the kitchen door. "Just in time. You can help me with this—" the voice said, and then suddenly stopped. "What on God's green earth are you wearing?"

"A dress, madam."

"I can bloody well see it's a dress. It is a dress I gave you. How on earth do you intend to work in that dress?"

"I do not intend to work."

"I beg your pardon?"

"I am not here to work, madam."

"I cannot believe this...Then why, pray tell, are you here?"

"To see Mr. Emil Coetzee."

The voice within did not respond.

"I know he is here, madam. I heard you speaking on the phone to Mrs. Simpson about his coming here today."

"Well. I never!" Fear made the voice shrill. "The sheer effrontery. Always listening, always sneaking around, always snooping. One cannot have privacy in one's home with you lot."

"Dear? Why all the commotion?" a male voice said, in a poor attempt at a whisper. "I told you I need peace and quiet today. We are discussing some matters of great national importance,"

"I know, dear, but Eunice here wants to see Emil Coetzee."

Silence.

Then the male voice asked, "And how does Eunice happen to know that Emil Coetzee is here?"

"Well...Well...Who knows with servants? They are re-sourceful. They have their ways, don't they?"

"I wouldn't know—"

"I heard Madam talking to Mrs. Simpson on the phone," his mother said, not attempting to whisper.

"I will thank you very much to not take part in a conversation that you are not a part of," the woman's voice said, with venom.

"And I will thank you very much, Agnes dear, not to discuss matters of national importance with Mrs. Simpson. You know how important this meeting is to me. You know the strings I had to pull to get it to take place here. If your loose lips cost me my promotion..." The male voice within trailed off ominously.

"Is everything all right in there?" another male voice said from within.

"Yes, yes. Of course, Emil. Just some domestic trouble."

"He means trouble with our domestic," the woman's voice corrected, sweetly.

Dingani heard his mother clear her throat before saying, "Mr. Coetzee, I would like to speak with you, sir."

There was a long silence.

Dingani watched a bead of sweat form and then travel down his mother's neck before disappearing into a blue-violet flower on her dress.

"Mr. Coetzee is a very, very important and busy man," the woman's voice finally said.

"I know Mr. Coetzee is a very important man. That is why I need to speak to him."

"And how do you know that he is an important man?" the woman's voice asked, fear making her voice loud and shrill again.

"Because I read the newspaper, madam."

Another silence which threatened to be long was cut short by Dingani's mother when she said, "I know you are in charge of Domestic Affairs, Mr. Coetzee. I believe you will find what I have to say very important."

"What is this about?" the man, Emil Coetzee, said, finally coming to stand by the door. He was larger than life, filling the entire doorway with his presence. His barrel chest seemed to be filled with too much air. But the most impressive thing about him was the glasses he wore: dark, round discs that did not allow you to see his eyes and automatically made you more curious about him.

"It is about my husband," Dingani's mother said.

Emil Coetzee chuckled, but the corners of his eyes did not crease in mirth. "I don't handle those kind of 'domestic affairs,'" he said, but did not move away from the door. "So what's the story here? You found your husband putting it good to some strumpet?"

Dingani saw his mother raise her chin a little and pull down the skirt of her dress. Her eyes never left the dark discs on Emil Coetzee's face. Dingani looked back at Emil Coetzee in time to see his head incline ever so imperceptibly. Emil Coetzee had looked at the top of his mother's bosom. Dingani was sure of it.

"My husband and his friends...They are plotting to overthrow the government. They should be charged with treason."

This time Emil Coetzee laughed—a real, rumbling and tumbling laugh.

"My husband is Mbongeni Masuku," Dingani's mother continued, undeterred. "And every fortnight he meets with the following men ..."

As his mother recited a list of names, Emil Coetzee's laughter slowly died.

"They are plotting, you say?"

"Yes, they are plotting to fight for independence. I have

heard them."

"Why tell me this?"

His mother did not respond to the question directly, instead she reached into her purse and pulled out a carefully folded piece of newspaper that she just as carefully unfolded and showed to Emil Coetzee.

Dingani made out the word "Reward" on the paper.

"Hell hath no fury," Emil Coetzee said.

And in that moment it was evident even to Dingani that his mother had won whatever was worth winning in this case.

"My son wants to be a doctor some day," his mother said. This was news to Dingani. "I am here to make sure he becomes one."

Emil Coetzee's black discs looked at Dingani's mother for a long time.

"I'll see what can be done," Emil Coetzee said, as he turned to walk away, closing the top part of the kitchen door behind him.

Dingani heard his mother take a deep, calming breath. It was shaky.

She looked at him for the first time since they had arrived. "Your father disappointed me," was all she said by way of explanation, before taking his hand again and leading them away from the back door of the kitchen (the only entrance she and Philemon were allowed to use), away from the veranda, away from the cars that were too many for one man (one of which belonged to Emil Coetzee), away from Philemon watering the roses in the garden.

"So. Are you getting to speak to Emil Coetzee?" Philemon asked in a mocking tone while opening the gate.

"Yes," Dingani's mother said, as she walked away from her life of domestic service. Triumphantly.

His father never made it home from school. The Organization of Domestic Affairs picked him up and processed him. After a short trial in which he was found guilty of being an African nationalist, he was sent to prison to serve a life sentence for treason. Mbongeni Masuku died in prison a few years later and was buried by the state in an unmarked grave. His wife and son never visited him.

For her part, his mother, as soon as she returned from her talk with Emil Coetzee, took her maid's uniform and placed it in her small front yard, poured paraffin on it and set it on fire in front of her neighbors. She then went to Mpilo Hospital and, after explaining that her husband had been imprisoned and she had no other means of supporting herself and her son, filled out an application for the nursing school.

On that day Dingani had felt a foreign emotion—fear of his mother. He determined resolutely to never disappoint her.

When they sat at the yellow Formica table for the first time later that night, his mother ran her hand over the surface of the table. "The year 1965," she said. "This is the year that we became truly respectable. This is the year that we became somebody." She took a thoughtful sip of her tea and nodded resolutely. "Politics is not for us. Politics is too...messy...and spades are never really spades."

It was only years later that Dingani was struck by how fearless his mother's act had been. What had made her so certain that Emil Coetzee would do as she asked? What had made her so certain that her husband would never come back again? What had made her so certain that her neighbors, knowing what she had done, would carry on with their lives and let her carry on with hers as though they had no such knowledge?

She had been so sure of herself, so sure she would succeed, so sure that she had done the right thing, that Dingani could not help but feel that such certainty meant that she had been right in doing what she did.

Determined to never disappoint his mother, Dingani excelled in everything he did: school, sports, music. And his mother kept her promise, she built a respectable life for them. She became a State Registered Nurse; she put Dingani in the best school that an African child could attend; she erased all traces of Mbongeni Masuku from their lives—all save his yellow Formica table with four matching chairs.

Through her hard work they became somebody.

His mother made life so comfortable and respectable that for the next nine years all Dingani had had to worry about was the name of his band. They were called the Wanderers. But were they rather Wonderers? Were they seekers or were they thinkers? He and his bandmates Xolani and Jameson were forever trying to decide and were never quite satisfied. It became something of an existential crisis, with Xolani opting for the Wanderers and Jameson opting for the Wonderers. There was a real danger of the band splitting up if the issue was not resolved.

It was up to Dingani, who had come up with the name originally, to confirm the name of their band. The name had just come to him one day, but it had simply been an idea—something in his imagination that had manifested itself as sound and not image. He did not know if what he had thought of for a name was Wonderers or Wanderers. Not wishing to disappoint either, he came up with a compromise: The Wandering Wonderers. The band was happily known as The Wandering Wonderers until Jameson asked why they could not be known as The Wondering Wanderers and another debate ensued. When the band went to play at Stanley Hall in 1974, some of their posters read "The Wandering

Wonderers," while others read "The Wondering Wanderers," others "The Wanderers," and others "The Wonderers." One poster even read "Dingani, Xolani and Jameson. Stanley Hall. December 31, 1974. New Year Bash! Be there!" Whatever their name, the truth was that Dingani's band was a very good band. Choosing not to be seduced by the politically conscious soul and reggae music of the era, the band paid tribute to 1950s and 1960s pop music and this they did so well that, despite their identity crisis, they were hugely popular.

And that is how it came to pass that on December 31, 1974, at Stanley Hall, Dingani, while strumming his guitar and wailing "Don't let me down" into the microphone, fell in love with a girl who had a pink carnation in her hair.

The pink skirt of her dress had fluttered just so as she swayed to the music, catching his attention. Her eyes were closed. Her hands were in the air. "Don't let me down." She was a very pretty girl, but to his surprise that was not what had attracted him to her. Instead it was that she obviously felt things so very deeply and was so self-possessed that she could allow herself to completely lose herself in a sea of people. "Don't let me down." He instantly loved the freeness of her spirit.

"So which is it?" she asked when the band stopped playing and he finally mustered up the courage to approach her. "The Wandering Wonderers, The Wondering Wanderers, The Wonderers or The Wanderers?"

"Which do you think it should be?"

"I think you already know the answer to that."

And Dingani suddenly knew the name of his band with a certainty and assuredness that he had never possessed until that very moment.

The girl's name was Thandi Hadebe.

In the course of their relationship, Thandi was once a runner-up, twice a first princess and then crowned queen of several beauty contests. Eventually, she acquired the much-coveted spot on the cover of *Parade* magazine. However, as she posed for the photographer by looking into the distance as though it held a future in which she was not particularly interested, she realized that she had not had her period for three months. This discovery was most unfortunate, because not only was her career as a model taking off but Dingani had just received a scholarship to study medicine in the United States of America. America!

Thandi knew the baby could not be America-bound because it would be in the way of two young people trying to realize impossible dreams. And so she decided that she would have the baby and that her parents would raise it.

Dingani married Thandi with his mother's full approval. His mother liked Thandi for being a young woman who knew how to take care of disappointments. If her son could come home a doctor with a medical degree and bring with him a wife with a bachelor's degree, they would automatically enter the highest levels of African society—perhaps even European society. They would be respectable. They would be envied.

They would be somebodies.

Dingani became a doctor. Thandi did not pursue a bachelor's degree, and a modeling career did not pursue her. She did, however, get a job dressing mannequins in the windows of a high-end department store and made a ridiculous amount of money doing so. Their lives were good. Their lives were very, very good. In fact, their lives were so good that they never needed to go back home to a country that was newly independent. The only thing that presented itself as a problem in their lives was the child Thandi had left at the Beauford Farm and Estate.

They were still trying to decide what to do about the child when they started hearing stories from back home about the disappearances taking place in the region where their child lived. After much deliberation, they felt they had no choice but to go and save him.

It would be unfair to suspect that Dingani and Thandi had given any consideration to the fact that they could realize the kind of life that they desired—the tranquil, evergreen and peaceful life that Dingani had glimpsed on the day he and his mother had met Emil Coetzee—much more quickly in the country that was newly independent than in the United States of America. Even though the letters Dingani received from his mother mostly contained news of the Europeans' exodus and the high-paying jobs and the vast suburban homes they were leaving in their wake, there is absolutely no evidence to suggest that these letters had any bearing on Dingani and Thandi's decision to return home.

Besides, what matters most is that they did return and that they did save their son—Marcus Malcolm Martin Masuku.

Dingani and Thandi did indeed enter the highest echelons of society, as Eunice had predicted. Dingani was even able to purchase Emil Coetzee's mansion...for a song, he always liked to add. Although it was one of the grandest homes in the country, Emil Coetzee's house had proved difficult to sell because Emil Coetzee had committed suicide in it on the eve of the country's independence. This fact had not deterred Dingani. He felt that it was only proper that he should live in the house of the man who had played such a pivotal role in shaping his future. His mother moved into the house as well, bringing with her the yellow Formica table with its four matching chairs.

Dingani and Thandi entered the most respectable social circles; they sent their children to the best schools, they belonged to the most exclusive clubs and they vacationed at all the high-end resorts.

Having finally arrived where his mother had wanted him to be, Dingani should have been happy, and he would have been, were it not for politics. His childhood friends, Jameson and Xolani, had not been as fortunate as to attend university in the United States of America; they had instead gone to the only university the state had to offer and, while there, they had become politicized, radicalized. They might not have had any political affiliations and leanings before independence, but they definitely did after independence and they held on to them tenaciously.

Whenever Dingani thought about politics, he saw the blue-violet flowers on his mother's dress, and felt an overwhelming fear come over him. He remained steadfastly apolitical. But whereas Jameson and Xolani had not minded how apolitical Dingani had been before independence, they definitely minded now. They wondered what kind of man he was if he did not have political views of any kind. What did he stand for? What did he hope for? What made his life anything more than just an empty shell? He would have liked to disagree with them, but when he saw Jameson and Xolani argue into the early hours of the morning with passion (a passion that he had witnessed in his own father—a passion he had never felt himself—a passion he suspected was fundamental to being a man) he began to think that perhaps he needed some politics in his life.

But where to find politics? He was already a man over thirty, with responsibilities, and politics was something that seemed to germinate when one had just entered adulthood and was finding one's self and one's place in the world. Then, one evening, as he and Jameson and Xolani sat on his veranda having sundowners and discussing whether or not everyone who had taken part in the civil war should be considered a revolutionary, Dingani said casually, without much thought:

"Now you see, a man like Golide Gumede is the kind of man that this country really needs. The man is building an airplane from scratch. Believes he can do it, too. He is innovative. Radical. Fearless. If this country had even just one hundred such men and women, then this thing we call independence would hold more promise. I think you both make the mistake of thinking that revolutions have to involve masses of people. Real revolutions happen on farms, in workshops, in garages and in basements, usually in the middle of nowhere, propelled simply by the need to realize a dream."

Xolani and Jameson looked at him but did not say anything. Dingani thought that perhaps he had said something wrong, but this was something he thought he felt passionate about. "A man like Golide Gumede has the kind of vision that leads not to thousands of people dying senselessly on the battlefield, but to thousands having their lives actually change for the better. Visionaries, and not politicians, are the real revolutionaries," Dingani said, very satisfied with himself and not quite caring, for the first time, what his friends thought.

"How do you know what Golide Gumede is or is not doing?" Xolani asked, his voice neutral.

"Because I saw him in the process of building the airplane."

Another silence followed, but this time the look in their eyes held something that Dingani wasn't able to read.

"You know Golide Gumede?" Jameson asked, sounding awestruck.

And that was when Dingani realized his friends were looking at him with respect. His chest puffed out a little bit. "Of course I know Golide. He practically raised my Marcus when I was in the States," he said, exaggerating for simplicity's sake.

"And…and…you saw this airplane he is building?"

"Of course I did. I already said I did."

"And…and…do you know what he intends to do with this airplane?"

"Fly it, I suppose."

"Are you sure this is Golide Gumede, civil-war hero, we are talking about?"

"Yes."

"What does he look like? The man was so elusive. They were never able to capture him—physically or photographically."

"I have always imagined him as big, boxy and bald," said Xolani.

"He is none of those things," Dingani said, his voice swelling with authority. "He is tall, almost impossibly tall, lanky, and an albino."

Xolani's drink actually shot out of his mouth, spraying Dingani's moccasins. "An albino?"

"Yes."

"And you are absolutely sure the man you are speaking of is Golide Gumede?"

"Yes," Dingani said, sounding somewhat irritated, "I am absolutely sure."

There was another long silence.

"Perhaps some day you can take us to meet Golide Gumede. Both the man and the airplane will be a sight to see."

"Perhaps," was all Dingani said in response, as he allowed himself to feel his importance.

When The Organization came to pick Dingani up at his private practice the next day and took him to The Tower to process him, all he wondered about was which one of his friends was a spy for The Organization—Xolani the lawyer or Jameson the advertising executive? He did not know. At times it seemed to him that, based on the questions he had asked, Jameson must have been the spy, and then at other times it seemed to him that, based on the questions he had asked, it must have been Xolani.

He had a lot of time to think before a man he would later learn was The Man Himself entered the room and asked him one question: Why is Golide Gumede building an airplane? At first Dingani said that he did not know, which was the truth. But after the question had been asked several more times in the same measured voice by The Man Himself, Dingani suddenly remembered Thandi's laughter as she sat in front of their dressing mirror, applying a sweet-smelling lotion to her hands and wearing a red satin nightdress: "Can you believe he really thinks he can fly Elizabeth all the way to Nashville in that thing?"

"He wants to take his wife to Nashville, Tennessee," Dingani said, relieved. "His wife has dreams of being a country-and-western singer," he added, to make the story more convincing.

The Man Himself was not convinced by this and asked the question again, "Why is Golide Gumede building an airplane?" The Man Himself did not seem to be in a hurry. He did not seem angry. He seemed as if he had the kind of patience to sit there for days and continue asking the one question.

"Why is Golide Gumede building an airplane?"

But Dingani had no such patience. "Because he is planning to overthrow the government," Dingani said. For years afterwards, he all but convinced himself that he had said those words because he had fully expected The Man Himself to laugh at the ludicrousness of the notion, the way Emil Coetzee had laughed when Dingani's mother had said the same thing about his father in 1965. But The Man Himself did not laugh. He simply looked at Dingani and allowed the expected silence to fall between them, after which he said: "You have not disappointed me." Then he got up and left the room, leaving the door open behind him, giving Dingani his freedom.

For weeks nothing happened and Dingani told himself that his conversation with The Man Himself had not amounted to anything, but then news came from the Beauford Farm and Estate, informing him that Thandi's parents, along with many of the compound's residents, had been killed.

When he did everything in his power to adopt Imogen Zula Nyoni, he refused to think too deeply about why he needed to have her belong to him. He was almost successful in convincing himself that there was no direct connection between his conversation with The Man Himself and what happened on the Beauford Farm and Estate. But then one day he received a check for an exorbitant amount in the mail. It was from The Man Himself, and it was made out to Dingani Masuku in respect of services rendered. He looked at the check for a long time, not believing what he saw: the blue-violet flowers of his mother's dress. They were all over the check, and they were spreading onto his hands, onto the desk, onto the walls, onto the ceiling—intent on covering every surface. He hid the check in his desk but the blue-violet flowers still covered every surface.

Similar checks arrived on the twenty-second of every month, and every month Dingani religiously hid them and reconciled himself to the omnipresence of the blue-violet flowers. Then one day he received a call from The Man Himself telling him that it would be advisable to deposit the checks. From that day on, on the twenty-third of every month, Dingani deposited the checks in a trust fund for Genie. He chose to look at this as a kind of victory, but he had to admit that it was a victory that left the bitter taste of ash in his mouth. It was also a victory that was short-lived. As the economy began to falter and the

Masukus' lifestyle became more difficult to maintain, Dingani found himself having to put the monthly checks to other uses and even, eventually, having to squander the ash-tasting trust fund in Genie's name.

The Survivors

———•———

Beatrice Beit-Beauford knows that she can no longer trust her mind—too often now, it fails or deceives her—but she is sure, almost, that this place that she is looking at is the place of her birth, her home, the Beauford Farm and Estate. But it cannot be. Beauford Farm and Estate is lush and verdant, something is always growing or being harvested. Beauford Farm and Estate is always busy with people and livestock. This great, great expanse of dust fields and mud huts cannot be Beauford Farm and Estate, therefore her mind must be playing tricks on her...again. And yet, those blue hills, hazy and distant, look so familiar...and the skeletal house they are driving towards now could be the house she grew up in...if it were stately. But it is not.

Kuki had told her that they were going to Beauford Farm and Estate, so why is she taking her somewhere else?

"When will we get to Beauford?" Beatrice asks Kuki, who is leaning over her steering wheel and squinting at the dust, trying to see the road ahead.

Kuki looks away from the road and smiles at her sympathetically, which is the only way that Kuki smiles at her now. Kuki squeezes her hand briefly before returning her focus to the obscured road ahead. Whatever her faults may be, you cannot ask for a truer friend than Kuki, Beatrice thinks, and just then a field of sunflowers bursts into view.

"Home!" Beatrice beamingly exclaims. "Beauford."

Valentine is well aware that the situation in which he currently finds himself is far from ideal. When he had imagined this moment, he had seen himself driving up to the Beauford Farm and Estate with a few people—Vida de Villiers, Jestina Nxumalo and perhaps a member of the Masuku clan, probably (but not preferably) the son. But now here he is, at the head of what can only be called a convoy—the Masukus in their entirety, of course, had to come, Kuki Carmichael and Beatrice Beit-Beauford had to come, even Bhekithemba Nyathi had to come, but he at least generously gave a ride to Minenhle Tikiti and Mordechai Gatiro, who also had to come. A procession of four cars...a cavalcade...a column.

Valentine hopes that he has parked his car in the right place. In front of him is a skeletal house, a crumbling edifice that is held together by ivy and the memory of its former grandeur. There is absolutely no sign of life. He and his passengers—Vida and Jestina—alight one by one and stand in the barren dustiness, at a loss as to what to do next. They watch the other cars park.

That was one bumpy and dusty road, Valentine thinks as he looks back at the long, thin stretch of patchily tarred road that has been eaten away by years of neglect.

Almost imperceptibly, a torn lace curtain moves behind one of the windows. Proof of life. A few moments later the front door yawns open and a man comes out. Even though he is small in stature and still standing in the distance, Valentine can tell that the man has an axe to grind. He is probably also carrying some kind of weapon in the hand he has behind his back.

"I will handle this," Valentine says to the others, sotto voce.

"Private property!" the man shouts, not breaking his stride.

"I don't doubt it for a minute," Valentine says. "Is this the Beauford Farm and Estate?"

"Fair and square," the man says, finally coming to a stop a few meters away from Valentine.

"Is that what you're calling the place now? Fair and Square?"

"We are here, fair and square. We buy property from Miss Beatrice. We don't land-grab."

"Oh. I see. So this is the Beauford Farm and Estate?"

"Private property. You are trespassing. Go now!"

"Sir. We mean you no trouble—"

"Then why you bring white man?"

"White man?" Valentine asks. He looks at his fellow travelers—of course, Vida. "Oh him? That's not a white man. That's—"

"Jesus?" the man asks, excitedly moving forward. "Jesus! It is you."

Vida frowns at the man.

"It is you. It really is you," the man says, reaching out both hands to Vida. He realizes that he has a gun in one of his hands. He hesitates, looks at Valentine and then at Vida before placing the gun in his waistband. "You don't remember me, do you?" the little man says, disappointment plain in his voice. Valentine immediately notices that he has done away with his broken English.

"Goliath?" Vida asks.

The brightest smile beams shockingly on the little man's face. "You do remember me! I thought you would not recognize me because I've grown," Goliath says, proudly playing with a scattering of beard on his chin.

"You have not grown much," Vida says.

Goliath laughs long and heartily at this. "Such are the challenges of life," he says as he brings his laughter to a close.

"So you're living here now?" Vida asks.

"Yes," Goliath says. "I found that city life no longer suited.

Genie is the reason why we came to settle here," Goliath explains. "She talked of this place, about the sunflowers. She made it seem so...enchanted. I had to see it for myself. I had seen sunflower seeds, you understand? Grayish, black, ugly things they are. But she made the flower so beautiful in my imagination, I had to come here and see it. And I did. Years ago. Came. Saw. Loved the place. She was right. It is a beautiful flower. I promised myself that when the time came for The Survivors to settle, we would settle here. But when we arrived, we found that war veterans had already settled here. You can see the results." Goliath gestures towards the mud huts standing starkly in the barren fields. "We are not part of *that* resettlement scheme. We bought this patch of land fair and square." He rubs his thumb and forefinger together. "Money. Remember how tourists loved taking our picture with our Street Dweller statue? Foreign currency. Black market. We started as small fish...then grew...eventually becoming too big for the pond. The people trading on the streets nowadays are absolutely ruthless, unprincipled and undisciplined. They are an undesirable element. They are too hungry to care. Not at all like us. A different animal altogether. Remember how we used to conduct ourselves with dignity? We had a code of ethics. But now the streets have gone to the dogs. So we decided it was time to settle. Bought the land, direct purchase from Beatrice Beit-Beauford herself. Fair and square."

Just then Beatrice and Kuki alight from Kuki's car, as do the Masukus and Bhekithemba, Minenhle and Mordechai from their respective cars.

"Ah...Miss Beatrice...Here she is...You can ask her about the squareness and fairness of it," Goliath says, looking slightly confused by Beatrice Beit-Beauford's visit, but standing his ground all the same.

The vacant look in Beatrice's eyes and the benign smile

on her lips let everyone know that there is no point in asking her anything.

The front door opens hesitantly and cautiously. Men and women come forward, slowly but with determination. "The other Survivors," Goliath says, proudly motioning towards the motley crew. "You won't believe who I've got here," Goliath says to The Survivors. "Jesus," he says, responding to his own question. "Remember Jesus?"

"How could we forget Jesus?" one of the women says as a baby hungrily suckles at her breast. Vida recognizes her as the girl he once tried to save from prostituting herself to the Indian businessman.

"That's the wife and child," Goliath says, trying not to sound proud.

He looks past Vida, expectantly. "Speaking of wives, where is Genie?"

"We were told that she was here," Valentine says.

"Here? She is definitely not here."

"We were told that a body was found here," Vida says.

"A body? That was Genie?" Goliath points towards the war veterans' mud huts. "There was much ado a few days ago. They are always harvesting bones. Human remains. That is why they will not let us plough the fields. But a few days ago they claimed they had found a fresh body in the sunflower field. We didn't believe them. And now you say this body belongs to Genie?"

"We'll have to see it for ourselves to determine that," Valentine says as he makes his way towards the mud huts.

"You'll need us to ease your passage," Goliath says, rushing to the head of the group. "They don't take kindly to strangers. Although there is no love lost between us, we at least have become familiar to them."

On their circuitous route to the mud huts, Goliath leads

them past a series of dilapidated and debilitated yellowy-gray concrete houses with stained and corrugated asbestos roofs. Over the years the compound houses have come to lean on each other and that is the only reason that they are still standing now.

"Where are all the people who used to live here?" Jestina asks.

"When we came here there were no people," Goliath's wife says.

"How can a place have no people?"

"Chased away by the war veterans, most probably," Goliath says.

"I think it is HIV...AIDS. Once it enters a small place such as this..." Goliath's wife says as she lets her voice trail off. "You should see the number of bones and bodies the war veterans have dug up."

So it is just as Jestina has long suspected: on that nightmarish day, the *sojas* with the red berets brought more with them than just their hatred and AK-47s. She has never told anyone what had happened to her and what had happened to Mrs. Hadebe, what Mr. Hadebe was forced to watch... What had happened before she was ordered to put the rat poison in the Hadebes' tea and forced to watch them drink it. Instead of speaking the unspeakable, she had chosen instead to cloak herself in shame. As they gang-raped, shot and pillaged their way through the compound, they had also, probably unbeknownst to themselves, found another way to decimate the compound. It did not have to be all of them who carried the disease. Just one—the result would have been the same.

And now to find out that Genie too...But no. This is a thought that Jestina cannot reconcile herself to. Genie had only been nine years old at the time. The *sojas* could not have...but what if they had...and Genie had chosen to remain silent...to the grave.

Tattered and torn. Tall and proud. War veterans. Carrying battle-weary AK-47s.

"Are you here about the body?" the war veterans ask.

"Yes," Valentine replies.

The war veterans lead the way. Past the mud huts. Over the barren fields. Through the sunflower field. The sunflower field grows of its own volition, has its own rhyme and reason.

Finally they arrive at a cold-storage unit. They heave open its heavy door and reveal stacks and stacks of neatly arranged skeletons. The dumbfounded awe that then fills the room is akin to reverence.

"They are so neatly arranged," Valentine says. "So tidy."

"We were very careful," the war veterans say.

"They seem to be almost cataloged."

"Yes, they are," the war veterans say neutrally. "There are the bones from the war. There the bones from what happened after the war. The bones from HIV and AIDS."

"How did you differentiate the bones?" Valentine asks, clearly fascinated.

"Coins. In the seventies and eighties almost everyone died with change in their pockets. Not so in the nineties."

"This is a job well done," Valentine says.

The war veterans allow themselves to feel the pride of the compliment.

"It is all we have done since we arrived. Excavate. That is why the fields still lie fallow. But we thought it was the best way to handle so many bones. With care."

"Yes, of course," Valentine says. "With care."

"The body is this way," the war veterans say as they lead the way into the deeper and darker recesses of the cold-storage room.

A streak of sunlight shining through a high, dust-covered window falls across the body of Imogen Zula Nyoni lying on a metal slab.

Quieted. Unbreachable. At peace.

A truth inescapable.

"We knew who she was as soon as we saw her," the war veterans say.

"We would know the daughter of Golide Gumede anywhere. We do not know how she got to the sunflower field. We just woke up in the morning and there she was...She must have been alive. At least for some time because her feet were burrowed into the soil."

"We should take comfort in the fact that she chose her own ending," Jestina says.

A profound silence settles the room.

"No," Kuki says firmly, breaking the silence. "No," Kuki repeats, backing away from Genie's body. "No." She has no idea what she is denying or refusing. "She was my friend." Why choose to lie at a moment like this, Kuki wonders. She was never friends with Genie. Beatrice is the one who was friends with Genie, and Kuki never quite understood their friendship. "She is my friend," Kuki hears herself repeat. Why does she, Kuki Carmichael, née Sedgwick, and once upon a time Coetzee, need to have people believe that she and Genie were friends?

As dusk descends upon the Beauford Farm and Estate, the visitors prepare to leave, with Genie's body, which has been gently wrapped in a mosquito net and placed at the back of Valentine's jeep.

Marcus looks over the compound again, trying to imagine the life he would have had if his parents had not come to take him away. He cannot. Had his parents not come to take him away, he would not have had much of a life.

Home.

Where has it been all this time?

Marcus thinks of the world atlas that Genie sent him, the one that is safely secreted in a suitcase in the home he has made with Esme. He sees the page that is besmirched by a handprint that is reddish-brown: blood. The handprint is small—that of a child. That of a girl child.

Genie.

It is in that moment that Marcus realizes that he has been holding on to something that Genie let go of a long time ago.

A boy shyly walks up to Marcus and hands him a photograph. "I found it in the ceiling," the boy says, not quite sure what to do with the silence around him.

"We used to talk about how we would hide in the ceiling with the things and the people we loved best, if strangers we didn't trust came to visit," Marcus says, his voice breaking as he looks at the photograph.

A young Marcus and a young Genie are smiling at him from the interior of Brown Car. Both of them are missing their two front teeth. They look unbelievably happy. Marcus smiles at them through the years, but his smile is uncertain because he does not remember having the picture taken.

Jestina Nxumalo takes the photograph from Marcus. "We will always remember what happened here," she says, as she remembers Genie climbing into the ceiling to retrieve her suitcase the day they both left the Beauford Farm and Estate. "But we can never truly know what happened here."

Genie

Genie chooses this particular moment, with the survivors as her witnesses, to fly away on a giant pair of silver wings... and leave her heart behind to calcify into the most precious and beautiful something that the world has ever seen.

As the survivors watch her ascend she experiences love as the release of a promise long held.

And then the clouds...

Valentine

Valentine watches as The Man Himself struggles to tie the knot of his bow tie. Slightly embarrassed to see The Man Himself fail for the third time, Valentine lets his eyes wander around the opulent and stately room. It is a room that evidently understands that it houses a very powerful man; its deep emerald greens and ruby mahoganies are awe inspiring.

But it is also a room that is staid, with the stale scent of decades-old smoke on everything. The only thing that has changed, really, is that instead of Emil Coetzee occupying the room, The Man Himself does. And the only original thing that The Man Himself has contributed in his entire thirty-something years of occupying this room is not even truly original: he changed the name of this particular branch of the state from The Organization of Domestic Affairs to The Organization (which is what most people had always referred to it as anyway). Soon after he took office, he watched with satisfaction as all the stationery was changed to reflect his contribution. And then he sat back, relaxed, and did exactly the same things that Emil Coetzee had done in that room.

"Don't tell anyone this, but I usually get the clip-on ones. Saves one all this fuss," The Man Himself says, bringing Valentine's attention back to him.

"But today is a very special occasion. I thought I should 'go all out,' as they say. A funeral. Just the sort of thing that makes people think that one cares deeply about things,"

The Man Himself says, his eyes never once leaving Valentine's. He finally manages to knot his bow tie.

"Yes, sir," Valentine says. He is very uncomfortable. He has never liked wearing suits, and this one fits him a little too snugly. He has the desperate urge to shift in his seat, readjust his jacket and loosen his collar, but he does not do any of these things because they would be a sure sign to The Man Himself that he is uncomfortable.

The Man Himself comes to sit at the edge of the desk, next to Valentine. In his hands he carries two cigars. He offers one to Valentine.

"I don't smoke, sir. Thank you."

"You don't have to smoke to smoke a cigar. You smoke a cigar to make a statement."

"Thank you all the same, sir."

"You smoke as a form of congratulations," The Man Himself says as he puts the cigar in Valentine's front pocket and pats it in place. "And congratulations are in order, aren't they?"

"Are they, sir?"

"Of course they are," The Man Himself says, lighting his cigar. "You pulled it off, Valentine."

"Pulled it off, sir?"

"Come, come, Valentine. I am head of Domestic Affairs. I'm the Chief Intelligence Officer. I know."

"You know, sir? Know what?"

"That Imogen put you up to all of this."

"Up to all of what, sir?"

"Must say, I didn't expect it of you...You are such a good... foot soldier. So invested in doing your job well. So what was it? You loved her, I suppose."

Valentine decides not to respond to that.

"Hit it on the head, have I? Of course you loved her, why else would you do it?" The Man Himself scoffs. "Complete waste of time your being in love with Imogen. She was completely devoted to that De Villiers chap. So what good did it do you? You'll likely lose your job—perhaps even lose worse over this...Which, of course, is why I've let you get this far. So that you understand the nothingness of what you've done. You know, to the rest of the nation you're just a group of crazy people intent on burying an empty box. That is all they see. The emptiness of a gesture. Was it worth it?"

"Yes, sir."

The Man Himself is taken aback by Valentine's response, but recovers quickly. "And all because of love?"

"Love of a kind, I suppose. But not the kind you imagine."

Love. Was there another word to express what Valentine felt the day he read the story of Golide Gumede in the newspaper? There was a man building an airplane and suddenly all things were possible. Valentine's family laughed at the idea that an African, an albino at that, thought that he could build a plane. Valentine did not laugh. Valentine loved the idea that flight was possible for someone like him. Valentine believed.

"You really thought a woman like that could love a man like you? What really saddens me, Valentine, is how absolutely unoriginal you are."

"Why did *you* do it, sir?"

"Do what?" The Man Himself asks, frowning. He is aware that there has been a shift in the power dynamics of the conversation, and aware, more terrifyingly, that he does not know when the shift occurred.

"Was it because he was capable of flight?"

The Man Himself laughs mirthlessly. "I see I did not teach you well. It does not matter why. It never matters why. You do it because you can. I did it because I could. Power. That is what it gives you. That ability."

Valentine smiles. The Man Himself's laughter dies abrupt-ly. He is done playing games. "I did it because a man like me does not let a man like Golide Gumede build an airplane. I did it because power is a very delicate thing."

"Thank you for telling me why, sir. Now, I'll tell you why I helped her. Because she was someone who had lived a life that mattered. They all had."

The Man Himself's frown deepens; he is evidently waiting for Valentine to explain further.

"That is all there is to it. It really is that simple. Her life mat-tered. She was never just a statistic. She was always more than just a tragic life. She was a precious and beautiful something. She deserved to choose her own ending."

Valentine reaches in his pocket and retrieves a precious and beautiful something and holds it between his thumb and forefinger. "Eighteen. We counted. Genie made eighteen. This is what happens to the hearts of those who believed and followed Golide Gumede. Seventeen died on the twenty-second of December in 1987. Seventeen of these were found on the Beauford Farm and Estate in a disused well. Genie made eighteen...and yet you have one more of these... a nineteenth. I suspect that you actually have two. I don't expect you to tell me the truth, but I'll ask anyway, what did you do to Golide Gumede and Elizabeth Nyoni?"

"What does it matter, since you know I will not tell you the truth?"

Valentine stands up and smiles. "Beauford Farm and Estate belongs to The Survivors. They will decide what to do with the precious and beautiful somethings."

The Man Himself throws his hands up in resignation. "I don't understand you, Valentine. I don't understand you. You too would stand to benefit if we took over the land. I don't understand you at all."

"It is all right, sir. *I* understand *you*, perfectly," Valentine says. He walks away, making sure to close the door firmly behind him, leaving The Man Himself in the stately, staid and stale room. The seat of power.

The Real Revolutionaries

The denizens of the city go about surviving their day-to-day lives: street vendors sell and hawk their wares; cars careen at neck-breaking speeds, not because they have anywhere particular to get to in a hurry, but because they were built that way, the cars stop only to buy calling cards, newspapers, vegetables and fruits—all of dubious worth; pedestrians walk with purpose even though they know that all they will find at their journey's end is disappointment.

The hearse moves to the side of the road to let a wedding convoy pass by. The wedding convoy zigzags on both sides of the street, dancing with danger and cheating death, horns blowing loudly. With the wedding convoy safely in the distance, the hearse resumes its journey.

"When I started this business in the sixties, I was lucky if I worked on one body per week," the undertaker says from the funereal confines of the hearse. "We had three trades back then: the white trade, the Coloured trade, the African trade. You were supposed to take care of your own kind, so I was only allowed to do the Coloured trade. If I got to do three funerals in a week, then that was a very good week. I could actually do it all on my own. Went to pick up the body at the mortuary. Brought it here to prepare it. Held the viewing. My brothers put together a contraption for me that lifted the body from the gurney to the slab and from the slab to the dressing bed and from the dressing bed to the coffin. So I really could do it all alone. Needed help putting the coffin in the hearse, but family members usually preferred to do that themselves. Took the body to the cemetery. The chaps from the City Council had the grave already dug. Family members helped lower the coffin into the earth and I always helped shovel the soil onto the coffin. I watched as crying family members walked away. I watched as the chaps from the City Council left with shovels resting on their shoulders. I was always the last one to leave. Paying my last respects to a body that I had come to know intimately.

"During the war things heated up and I found myself doing anywhere between seven and ten bodies a week. There were too many people dying for the trades to really matter. The whites still primarily took care of their own folks, but occasionally would handle a wealthy African. The Africans still dealt exclusively with their own kind because there was no shortage of black bodies during the war. As a Coloured man I was permitted to work on Africans and indigent whites as well.

"I will admit that things got a bit hairy, but I could still do things on my own. I just no longer had the time to help with the burial. I was often the first one to leave. But I always stayed until the coffin had been lowered into the earth.

"In the mid-eighties I had to take on an assistant because all of a sudden I was doing twenty to thirty funerals per week. I stopped going to the cemetery altogether. I left all that to the assistant. I thought I was overwhelmed then, but now Mendelsohn's Funeral Home and Parlor is like a factory. I have twenty employees.

"All thanks to HIV and AIDS. The city has gone to pot. The country has gone to pot. Factories closed. Tourism done. Eighty percent unemployment. No money in pockets. No money in bank accounts. Yet I am rolling in it. Death is the only lucrative business. I have not touched a dead body in over ten years, but I have money sticking to my fingers because of dead bodies. I never thought I would say this, but there is such a thing as too much death. And I say this as an undertaker.

"All this death cannot be healthy for us as a community... a city...a country. It cannot be healthy...."

The undertaker gestures towards something on the pavement. "You don't see that every day. Time was people used to stop when a hearse passed by. Remember that? Cars would stop. Bicycles would stop. Pedestrians would stop. Men would take off their hats. Place them over their hearts. Pay their last respects. Nobody does that any more. I suppose they are all too busy burying their own dead...No. You definitely don't see that any more. Once upon a time that is how it was done. With respect."

Vida looks in the direction that the undertaker's nod has indicated. There, across the street, amid all the hustle and bustle and to-ing and fro-ing of the streets, stands a man. A vagabond, to most. He has removed his hat from his head and placed it over his heart. A newspaper is carefully folded and placed under his arm. Vida knows that both the easy and cryptic crossword puzzles of that newspaper have been filled out neatly and correctly.

"Stop the car," Vida says.

"I'm leading the procession—there is too much traffic."

"Please stop the car. I know that man."

Vida exits the hearse and runs across the street, well aware that the man may not remember him. "David," Vida says.

The man carefully unfolds the newspaper under his arm. The headline reads: "IMOGEN ZULA NYONI FLIES AWAY."

"I am sorry for your loss," David says.

These are the only words Vida remembers David ever having uttered.

It is David who walks him back to the hearse. It is David who sits with him next to the coffin on top of which sits an effusive bouquet of flowers meticulously arranged by Minenhle. Genie's suitcase is in the coffin. In it, among her childhood clothes, are Penelope and Specs and Blue's baby-blue slippers. With David beside him, Vida opens the coffin and retrieves the suitcase. There is courage in letting Genie go. There is courage, too, in not letting Genie go entirely.

They have done it, Marcus thinks as he watches the soil slowly cover the coffin, shovelful by shovelful. They have finally let Genie go. Marcus wonders, and not for the first time, if Genie ever belonged to them.

Belonging—is it an emotion? Is it a way of being? Is it an action one takes? He had felt that he belonged to Genie all these years, but now he is not sure if it was something he felt, something he was or something he did.

He looks at his family. His father, his mother, his sister and his grandmother. Krystle's head is resting on their mother's shoulder, her eyes closed. All of them look bereft and exhausted. It is the look they have had ever since Dingani told them what he did in 1987. They are all silent. The silence has become a familiar companion.

He sees, rather than feels, a hand in his. He looks at the owner of that hand. His wife. Esme.

This is his family. Fragile. This is where he belongs.

Marcus finds himself leading the procession out of the cemetery, but he does not feel like heading home. Home. The house with the cracked walls. The yard with the felled jacaranda trees. The family with no Genie.

He looks at his family and is gripped by a sudden sense of urgency.

There is a place that he must see. There is a place that his family must see. He feels that they have to see it now more than ever. Instinctively he knows that seeing this place could be the very thing to strengthen them.

He changes course.

To his surprise the rest of the funeral procession follows him: Minenhle Tikiti, Mordechai Gatiro, Jestina Nxumalo, Valentine Tanaka, Bhekithemba Nyathi, Kuki Carmichael, Beatrice Beit-Beauford, Dr. Prisca Mambo, The Survivors, The War Veterans, Stefanos and Matilda, David the puzzle-solver, Mr. Mendelsohn the undertaker and Vida de Villiers.

By the time the procession arrives at the Victoria Falls and stands at the banks of the mighty Zambezi River, a new dawn is breaking. They all stand there watching the sun do what it has always done—rise from the east, full of promise.

A man, a very tall man with glasses, wearing a cap and a loose shirt that declares him to be a very rare thing nowadays—a tourist—stands a respectable distance from the motley group. He is aware that they are waiting for something to happen, perhaps some traditional African ritual that he will luckily be able to capture on the expensive-looking camera that dangles hopefully on his chest. The man blinks once. Twice. Thrice.

"Krystle?" the man says, hesitantly, obviously not wanting to disturb their peace.

Krystle turns around and blinks at him.

"Krystle Masuku," the man says more assuredly.

"Xander Dangerfield?" Krystle asks incredulously.

"You remember," Xander says, obviously pleased.

"What are you doing here?" Krystle asks, still incredulous.

"I thought I should see it for myself."

"See what?"

Xander is about to answer, then he puts up a finger.

"Wait," his finger says. He starts patting his pockets. "Aha!" he says triumphantly, as he retrieves something from his back pocket. It is a postcard of the Victoria Falls. On the back, in Genie's handwriting, are the words, "Remember, there will be the time of the swimming elephants."

"How? How could she have known?" Krystle asks, her hands trembling.

Xander blinks at her.

"Oh. Never mind how she knew. She knew, and you are here now," Krystle says leading him to the people waiting on the banks.

And that is when they appear with their formidable grace. Majestic. A herd of elephants, raising dust beautifully in the early morning savannah sunlight. The bull at the head of the herd raises his trunk and trumpets terrifically. All the elephants come to a gradual standstill on one side of the Victoria Falls. And then the elephant dives in close to where the waters plunge over the edge. Every breath is held in unison. The ancient river and the mighty animal in perfect harmony.... A rite of passage made sacred by its sheer audacity. There is a wonder to it all....The possibility of the seemingly impossible.... And there's this feeling that you get...a knowing...You become aware of your place in the world....You understand that in the grander scheme of things you are but a speck...a tiny speck... and that that is enough....There is freedom...beauty even, in that kind of knowledge....It is the kind of knowledge that finally quiets you. It is the kind of knowledge that allows you to fly. You have to experience it for yourself.

Overhead an airplane flies; its silver wings flash in the golden sky.

—•—

Acknowledgements

First, a great many thanks to the extraordinary Jenefer Shute, whose immaculate and insightful reader's notes showed me what was possible. Thank you for seeing my vision so clearly when even I had difficulty articulating it. Thank you for believing in that vision and advocating for it. I can never thank you enough for making the editing process such an enjoyable partnership.

To the wonderful people at Penguin Random House South Africa, there is so much to thank you for. Fourie Botha and Beth Lindop, thank you so much for believing in this novel, for encouraging me at every step, for involving me in other creative aspects, and for always being understanding. Gretchen van der Byl, thank you for the amazingly beautiful cover that tells the story.

A special thanks to Jessica L. Powers and Vaidehi Chitre for, through our writers' group, providing me with a creative outlet when I needed it most. Thank you for all the feedback and support that helped *The Theory of Flight* take shape. Thank you for all the conversations, laughter and red velvet cake. Keren Weizberg and Donni Wang, thank you for being another set of eyes when I needed clarity.

To Catalyst Press—Jessica Powers and Ashwanta Jackson—thank you so much for your time and talent in the creation of the North American edition and for making the process collaborative. To Karen Vermeulen, thank you for giving *The Theory of Flight* yet another gorgeous cover that tells the story;

the novel has been twice blessed in this regard.

My creative journey has definitely been marked by intellectual forces: Maria Koundoura at Emerson College; Ruth Bradley and Jonathan Butler at Ohio University; Sean Hanretta, Saikat Majumdar, Andrea Lunsford and Kathleen Coll at Stanford University; and Rhonda Frederick at Boston College. Thank you all so much for challenging and encouraging me along the way.

To my friends over the years, thank you for believing me when I said I was going to be a writer someday. Paula Waters, thank you just for being. Kendra Tappin and Dominika Dittwald, thank you for long conversations in parked cars. Yvonne Edmonds and Tara Thirtyacre, thank you for your support at pivotal moments. Arnold Tshuma, thank you for the many years of much-needed laughter. Wandile Mabanga, thank you for believing even when I doubted. Joy Mountford, Hillary Smith, Devora Weinapple and Patricia Frumkin—thank you for the sisterhood when I needed it most.

And last, but definitely not least, thank you for the most precious gift of all: family.

To my first family—Njabulo, Ntokozo, Nicholas, Thembekile and Sibongile—thank you for welcoming me to the fold. More importantly, thank you for allowing me to spend hours in sunflower and maize fields with my imagination.

A great many thanks to my grandparents, Sibabi Charles Ndhlovu and Kearabiloe Mokoena-Ndlovu, for providing me with a worldview that put the men in the red berets in their place. Gogo, thank you for doing many marvelous things, the most fantastic of which was weaving absorbing and engaging stories seemingly out of thin air and creating wondrous worlds in front of my very eyes. Khulu, thank you for throwing me in the air, cheering me on when I was second to last, answering my never-ending stream of questions with a smile and, most importantly, teaching me how to treat people who leave scars on the body.

Most of all, I am incredibly grateful to my mother, Sarah Nokuthula Ndhlovu, for being brave enough not only to bring me into the world, but also to allow me to be. Thank you for saving your walls by buying me a giant scrapbook. Thank you for being an African parent who let her daughter major in Creative Writing. Thank you for always being proud of my achievements and accomplishments, no matter how small. Thank you always for being the epitome of formidable grace.

———

OTHER CATALYST BOOKS
BY AFRICAN WOMEN

We Kiss Them with Rain

The terrible thing that steals 14-year-old Mvelo's song leads to startling revelations and unexpected opportunities. Life wasn't always this hard for 14-year-old Mvelo. There were good times living with her mother and her mother's boyfriend. Now her mother is dying of AIDS and what happened to Mvelo is the elephant in the room, despite its growing presence in their small shack. In this Shakespeare-style comedy, the things that seem to be are only a façade and the things that are revealed hand Mvelo a golden opportunity to change her fate. *We Kiss Them With Rain* explores both humor and tragedy in this modern-day fairy tale set in a squatter camp outside of Durban, South Africa.

The author, Futhi Ntshingila grew up in Pietermaritzburg, South Africa. Now she lives and works in Pretoria. She is a former journalist and holds Masters Degree in Peace Studies and Conflict Resolution. She loves telling stories about the marginalized corners of society, which includes women and children in South Africa and particularly those who live in the squatter camps. In her two novels published in South Africa, she features strong women who empower themselves despite circumstances that seek to disempower them. *We Kiss Them With Rain* is her debut into the North American market.

- *Selected as a USBBY 2019 Outstanding International Book*
- *2019 Skipping Stones Award honoree, Multi-cultural and International Books*

Bom Boy

Abandoned by his birth mother, losing his adoptive mother to cancer, and failing to connect with his distant adoptive father, Leke—a troubled young man living in Cape Town—has developed some odd and possibly destructive habits: he stalks strangers, steals small objects, and visits doctors and healers in search of friendship. Through a series of letters written to him from prison by his Nigerian father, a man he has never met, Leke learns about the family curse—a curse which his father had unsuccessfully tried to remove. Leke's search to break the curse leads him to strange places.

The author, Yewande Omotoso is an architect, with a masters in creative writing from the University of Cape Town. Her debut novel *Bomboy* (2011 Modjaji Books), won the South African Literary Award First Time Author Prize and was shortlisted for the Etisalat Prize for Literature. She was a 2015 Miles Morland Scholar. Yewande's second novel *The Woman Next Door* (Chatto and Windus) was published in May 2016.

Love Interrupted

Sisters, friends, aunts, mothers, daughters, grandmothers, mothers-in-law

In her debut collection of short fiction, Reneilwe Malatji invites us into the intimate lives of South African women—their whispered conversations, their love lives, their triumphs and heartbreaks. This diverse chorus of female voices recounts misadventures with love, family, and community in powerful stories woven together with anger, politics, and wit. Malatji crafts an engaging collection full of rich, memorable characters who navigate work, love, patriarchy, and racism with thoughtfulness, strength, and humor.

The author, Reneilwe Malatji was born in South Africa in 1968. She grew up in Turfloop township, in the northern part of South Africa, during the era of apartheid. Her father was an academic and her mother was a school teacher. Malatji trained as a teacher and worked as a subject specialist and advisor to provincial education departments. She recently completed a post-graduate diploma in Journalism and an MA in Creative Writing at Rhodes University. She works as a lecturer at the University of Limpopo in South Africa and has an adult son. *Love interrupted* is her first book.

Unmaking Grace

Family secrets run deep for Grace, a young girl growing up in Cape Town during the 1980s. Her family secrets spill over into adulthood, and threaten to ruin the respectable life she has built for herself. When an old childhood friend emerges after disappearing a decade earlier during a clash with apartheid riot police in the Cape Flats, where South Africa's coloured community makes its home, Grace's memories of her childhood come rushing back, and she is confronted, once again, with the loss that has shaped her. She has to face up to the truth or continue to live a lie—but the choice is not straightforward. *Unmaking Grace* is an intimate portrayal of violence, both personal and political, and its legacy on one person's life. It meditates on the long shadow cast by personal trauma, showing the inter-generational imprint of violence and loss on people's lives.

Born in Cape Town, South Africa, Barbara Boswell is an educator and literary activist. She is an alumna of the Women's Studies Program at the University of Maryland, College Park, where she lived for several years, and has taught at universities in both the USA and South Africa. Barbara is an Associate Professor of English at the University of Cape Town, where she teaches Black women's diasporic literature, African feminist literary theory, and gender and sexuality.